Tales i the SUPERNATURAL ROCKERY

Jon Ardeman

The Supernatural Rockery is the copyright © of Jon Ardeman
2015

All rights reserved
All the characters in this book, other than those historical figures clearly in the public domain, are fictitious and any resemblance to actual persons, living or dead, is purely coincidental.

Cover layout: Julie Evans www.julieevansillustration.com

Illustration: *'A marine iguana emerges from the rocks and dreams of the tides of yesteryear.'* ©*Jon Ardeman*

Foreword

You walk past a neighbour's house and are surprised to see that she has built a new rockery in the front garden. You are intrigued by its sudden appearance. What caught your interest? Is it the sparse alpine plants, or the haphazard arrangement of large rocks that jut from the freshly turned soil? It must have been heavy work for one person. Come to think of it: what ever happened to that wastrel, cheating husband of hers?

This rockery, a chaotic jumble of tales, is not a textbook of rocks and mineral characteristics, nor is it a guide to the 'New Age' properties of certain gems or crystals. The collection is constructed of thirteen different stones, bizarre fictions. The stories are of people caught between a rock and a strange place: the interface of the natural and supernatural worlds. They are tales of mystery and imagination, some with mayhem or even murder. Yes, minerals are always in there: either boldly displayed as a solid foundation, or almost hidden away, partially concealed in the undergrowth.

A garden rockery with its mimicry of topography is best viewed in three dimensions; front to back, top to bottom, side to side and so likewise, there is no order to these stories; the seductive diamond may lie upon a bed of common slate, an amber bead may attract you closer than the magnetism of ancient ironstone; soft chalk may prove to be as deadly as the lust for gold. Let your eyes wander where they will.

Jon Ardeman

"Mummy, do you know why we have alive things and dead things?"
"No; why is that, Tilly?"
"Because if things were alive underground they'd all be screaming."

    Tilly Butler   age 6 ¼

Tales from the Supernatural Rockery

Contents

A ROCKERY:	*Illustration*
GOLD ORE:	*Restless Mbuzo*
BRIMSTONE:	*The Pilgrims' Regress*
GREENSAND:	*Slipped Away*
ROCK:	*A Very Big Rock*
DIAMONDS:	*A Girl's Best Friend*
OCHRE:	*Past Tense*
AMBER:	*La Résine d'Être*
SLATE:	*Metamorphosis*
EARTH:	*Tenant Trouble*
IRONSTONE:	*The Crossing*
EMERALD:	*Hidden Imperfections*
CHALK:	*Like Chalk and Cheats*
QUARTZ:	*The Mote in God's Navel*

ACKNOWLEDGEMENTS

The Supernatural Rockery – an illustration

GOLD ORE

Restless Mbuzo

Gold: they say it gets into your blood, but with some people it runs so much deeper; it gets into their very soul. I know, because one of them used to work for me. I was a section mine manager in those days, on a well-known gold mine not so far from Johannesburg.

I have to admit that Piet (his name has been changed) was a tireless worker. The way he worked his underground gangs you would think that it was his own gold they were mining. With his high production bonuses, it might as well have been; Piet's pay packet regularly exceeded my own. He used to work as an electrician, but the pay and the bonuses for the miners were too good to ignore. He still had plenty of private electrical jobs that he worked on in the afternoons. You would find him in his garage, fixing fridges and vacuum cleaners, for a cash fee, of course. Perhaps I sound a little jealous, but if there is a line between industriousness and greed, Piet crossed over it years ago.

The Xhosas who worked on his gang nicknamed him "Duduma" which means, "Thunder" in their tongue and in the Fanagalo *lingua franca* of the mines. It was an apt description. Anyone not working at a pace to ensure Duduma a big bonus was in serious trouble. He would appear on the horizon, his voice roaring out above the noise, his big hands knocking hard hats flying and boots connecting with some unlucky backside. Then he would charge off to find the next gang, still bellowing, but disappearing as quickly as a summer thunderstorm. Surprisingly, there were few official complaints about Piet. I suppose everyone benefited from the gang bonuses, with Piet taking the lion's share, of course. It's a lot different nowadays; what with all these management and team motivational courses with a less arbitrary discipline system. There's no place for a "Duduma" on a modern mine. A contented work force is a cherished thing into today's industry.

However, on that day as I went underground to visit Piet's work area, such thoughts were still years in the future. We had had arrived at the miner's box when there was shouting and cap lamp beams flashing down the underground haulage. One of the black workers came running towards us.

'Nkosi! There has been a bad accident. Man really bad, come quick, Nkosi!'

The Mine Captain and I hurried after him, running awkwardly along the uneven surface of the track. As always the air was hot and sticky and I was out of breath by the time we climbed into the narrow stope where the gold ore is actually mined. We saw the injured Boss Boy (they are called team leaders now) lying near the winch. He lay on his side, blood oozing from a ghastly wound where his arm had once been. He was badly cut on his chest and other arm. He lay there muttering in between raspy breaths.

Piet was also there, attempting some rudimentary first aid; but it was hopeless. The trauma of the injury had staunched the flow of blood so it wasn't pumping out of the horrendous wound as you might have imagined; but merely dripped out onto the clean white bandages.

Drip. Drip. Drip.

Unlike the boss boy who just lay there muttering, I would have been thrashing around in agony; but the end result would have been the same. He died before the paramedic arrived.

'What the hell happened here?' I yelled at Piet.

'Meneer, we were just pulling the stuff with the scraper when the winch driver saw the boss boy's light in the stope.' He indicated the driver who operated the scraper winch. He was still trembling from the shock. I couldn't get anything coherent from him.

'How could he have got injured like this?'

'I don't know Meneer. Maybe he took a chance crossing the gully while the scraper was moving.'

Piet pointed at the area in which the scraper scooped up the broken gold ore and was pulled down the gully by the cable winch.

'Shit! Where's his other arm?'

I was out of breath, hot, and for the first time in my life; I was feeling very claustrophobic. I didn't want to go and search for a mangled arm wrapped around a scraper blade. Piet and I trudged up along the gully while the others strapped the body onto the stretcher. We followed a blood trail along the edge of the stope. It appeared that he had dragged himself, head long, over the sharp-edged quartz rock that had lacerated him like broken bottle glass.

Piet found what was left of the solitary limb. He pointed along the gully: 'He must have been knocked over by the scraper. It must have run over him, severing his arm. Then he somehow crawled back into the stope down to where we saw him.'

'What? Dragged himself three hundred feet over this stuff, with only one arm? And nobody saw him? Or even heard him? Why didn't he pull the wire to signal the driver to stop the winch or call for help?'

It didn't make sense. I lay down on the edge of the stope and the safety wire was still within easy reach. I pulled the cord and could hear the whistle sound clearly.

Piet shook his head and wiped the sweat from his neck.

I'd had enough. I marked the nearest wooden support stick with miner's chalk to indicate the location of the accident. A surveyor would need to come down underground and draw up a plan of the accident site. I headed back down the gully. I instructed Piet to carry the severed arm.

The day before the official enquiry, the winch driver was killed in the same stope by a freak accident. There were no witnesses but it seemed, for some reason known only to the winch operator, he had taken the safety screen from the winch. Then, with the winch still running, he'd been caught up on the scraper cable and slowly pulled into the winch drum. It had a 75 horsepower motor that was easily capable of pulling over a ton of broken rock. It didn't stop because flesh and bone got in the way. His body was lashed to the rotating drum by a dozen turns of the cable before the drum was prevented from turning any further. I won't go into the sickening details; but this time, no one bothered to call the paramedic.

In the meantime, I had yet to prepare for the first fatality enquiry. It was there that I saw the team leader's full name for the first time. I've always found African names interesting. There's usually a biblical Christian name, Luke, and a family name and sometimes almost a nickname that can refer to his character, or appearance. I didn't recognise the word, so I asked Solomon, my senior team leader, what it meant.

'Nkosi, it means that this man cannot stay still; he is a man who cannot rest.'

'Restless,' I thought, 'Restless Mbuzo.'

I can't remember the African word now, but the name of Restless Mbuzo, I will surely remember forever.

After the two tragedies, several strange incidents occurred on the mine section. It was Piet who first reported them to me. He came into my manager's office and paced around in an agitated manner.

'Meneer, those machine boys won't go and drill the face. They refuse to go back into the stope. I've tried everything.'

I knew Piet's old fashioned management methods and shuddered to think how many sore heads and bruised bums added up to "everything". If the drill operators wouldn't go there, then the blast holes wouldn't be drilled and the crew's production schedule would fall behind. Both Piet and his underground team would lose their valuable bonuses. I thought cynically at the time that was what was really upsetting him.

I went down into the mine to the underground section where the trouble was brewing. I questioned the drill operators in Fanagalo, but even though I had spoken it for all my years on the mines, the drillers' answers didn't make any sense to me. Solomon translated for me in their home language. They were saying there was a *tokoloshe*, or bad spirit, haunting the mine. They had all heard it moving slowly over the loose rocks in the dark.

Scrape. Scrape. Scrape.

For once I agreed with Piet. 'Bullshit!' I said. But they insisted, miming the action of someone crawling along and making a scraping sound with each movement. It was clear that something had scared them; their wide-eyed expressions showed they weren't faking their feelings of fear.

'It's a load of superstitious crap! There's nothing in there,' I said in annoyance. I turned my back on them and strode off to the stope with the mine captain, Solomon and of course, Piet.

The mined stope was completely silent, no drilling, no compressed air hissing away through leaky hoses. The air was hot and still. It seemed unnaturally quiet for a mine. Claustrophobia swept over me again.

'Let's check the rock face first. It could be that the timber support is taking pressure and creaking a bit.'

We had climbed up to about half way when a gust of cold air rushed into us. I shivered as the sweat-drenched overall clung to my skin. Without warning, a small pile of finely broken rock tumbled down into the gully, as if someone had missed a foothold and sent the stones rolling down. I shone my cap lamp around and there, directly above the place was the chalk mark that I had made a couple of weeks earlier. Before I lost my nerve completely, I headed up to the face. It looked like ordinary gold reef with grey quartz and that sparkle of pyrite or "fool's gold" that so often means that the real gold is present. The wooden supports looked good and solid. Everything looked normal enough but still, something felt very wrong. I strained to hear any noise, but our own breathing was the only thing to break the eerie silence.

I knew the gold reef was in a high-grade 'pay shoot' area, so I instructed the mine captain to call for the ore to be sampled. The assay laboratory later reported the samples turned out to be only 'trace' values, meaning the rock contained virtually no gold. I suspect that the sampling team never actually went into that particular area at all. They probably picked up rocks from a section of off-reef development somewhere else. No one asked for it to be re-sampled. The stope was closed down and sealed to prevent people from entering the area. In view of the rumours, it seemed an unnecessary precaution. A subdued Piet moved onto the next mining contract.

Solomon spoke to me about the old stope a few weeks later; 'Nkosi, the men are afraid. They say the spirit is still there. They say the rock weeps blood.'

'Solomon,' I told him, 'this is the modern world.' I pointed to the telephone on my desk: 'I can talk to my cousin in America with that! These aren't the days for spirits to go walking – they belong to the old times and stories around a fire. I'm sure poor Restless Mbuzo has found his rest.'

Nevertheless; because some of the mine workers had now refused to even to walk past the area, we visited the wretched place again. We stopped in front of the sealed area and listened. The sound was faint, but unmistakable.

Scrape. Scrape. Scrape.

'For God's sake! What's the problem? It's only bits of broken rock falling down into the gully,' I told the work crew. 'It's been dislodged by blasting, or minor seismic tremors. You've been working here long enough to know it happens all the time in these old areas.'

Dark reddish water trickled from a small drain hole in the seal.

Drip. Drip. Drip.

'It's just rust,' I pronounced. 'It's come from the old iron pipes left behind in the workings. There's absolutely nothing unusual here; see? No spirits or demons,' I forced a smile.

'Yes, Nkosi,' Solomon replied in that way of his that sounded more like; "No, I don't think so, Nkosi."

Back in the office, I was informed that Piet had decided to seek professional help for his drinking problem. He'd been having hallucinations and violent trembling fits. He needed a break to dry out for a couple of months.

As it happened, Piet didn't go back to underground work again, but he returned to the mine as a surface electrician. The wages and bonuses were a lot less than he was used to, but Piet had changed. His normal ruddy complexion was now hollowed and grey. Even the cash-in-hand electrical work lay untouched, piled up in his garage. It was nearly a year later that I had cause to speak to him again.

It was one o'clock on a bitterly cold Highveld winter night when an electrical transformer blew on the mine substation. I was called out, as I had the night shift crews working underground and all the power had gone down. No lights, no ventilation and no way out of the mine but a long, long walk. I drove across to the substation and parked my car on the gravel apron that served as a firebreak. Piet had been called out as the stand-by electrician. He had sent out his aide to get more tools from the truck when I asked him how long he thought it would take to repair. Before he could reply, I thought I heard the aide behind me, dragging something heavy across the gravel.

Scrape. Scrape. Scrape.

Piet yelled out; 'Pick the bloody bag up and carry it you lazy bastard!' Then he turned and stared past me, out onto the gravel surround.

'No! No! Get away from me!' Piet screamed in terror. As he turned away in panic, his out-flung hand fell across the exposed contacts of the live busbars.

There was a blinding light, like a huge flash bulb exploding. The scene burnt onto my retina, so I could see the same image imprinted in the negative. In that microsecond surge of blinding energy, I could see Piet and another figure. They were both in silhouette; one with arm outstretched, the other apparently grappling the other. Piet slumped to the ground in a crumpled, smouldering heap. His aide rushed in substation yelling for help, but I was too stunned to be of any assistance. I sat on the cold floor staring into the gloom as the vision of the two ephemeral figures slowly faded from my sight.

How Piet wasn't killed outright that night, I don't know. He recovered consciousness in hospital, but no one would say he was lucky. The doctors tried to save his arm, but it was so badly burnt, it had to be amputated below the elbow. Then gangrene set in and the whole arm had to be cut away; but it was too late. Piet was dying inch by flesh-rotting inch.

I last saw Piet when I had to go to head office in Johannesburg. I dropped by to see him in the hospital ward and as it was outside normal visiting hours, his family wasn't there. Despite the liberal use of strong antiseptic, the room smelt unwholesome; rather like decaying meat.

Piet opened his eyes. It took him a little time to recognise me.

'You saw him didn't you, Meneer? The night at the substation, you saw the Boss Boy – you saw him then?'

I don't suppose Piet knew his name was Restless Mbuzo any more than I did until a saw the death certificate.

'He came to finish me, you know,' Piet said flatly.

'Come on Piet, don't talk like that,' I tried to reassure him. 'You've been through a rough time. You've been hallucinating, that's all; it's probably the painkillers you've been given.'

'It wasn't like I said at the enquiry. It was my fault,' he continued, 'the boss boy did sound the whistle - and sure, the driver stopped the winch. But the gully was full of reef, Meneer, I wanted to pull it clean so that we could carry on. I told the winch driver to start up and keep going. When he hesitated, I grabbed the lever and started it myself. The boss boy must have thought we'd stopped and climbed down right in front of the scraper. When it started suddenly he was probably knocked off balance. When I heard the whistle again, I thought one of the boys was getting impatient and was too bloody lazy to walk down through the narrow stope. I guess he must have struggled back out of the gully. He just lay there using the wire to signal for help.'

I started to interrupt, but Piet ploughed on as if I were his confessor.

'It was quiet for a while. Then we saw him, he was dragging himself across the stope using his one arm.'

Scrape. Scrape. Scrape.

'I'm telling you; if he could have got that one arm around my throat, he would have killed me for sure. You were there, you heard him babbling on. The winch driver was from the same tribe; he told me afterwards that the Boss Boy had cursed us. He said that, by his name, he would kill us both.'

'It was "Restless",' I said. 'Restless Mbuzo, that was his name.'

'I don't know. Whatever his name was; I don't care, but he got to the winch driver first, the poor bastard.' Piet sank back into his pillow. 'Then it was my turn. But it's over now. Thank God, it's nearly over.'

'Don't give up hope, Piet,' I muttered for something to say.

Piet didn't reply. He lay back exhausted and closed his eyes.

I attended his funeral ten days later. We bowed our heads at the graveside as we listened to the final internment prayer. The words seemed distant, punctuated by the sound of the cemetery worker's shovel lashing the sandy earth back into the grave.

Scrape. Scrape. Scrape.

Those are memories from over thirty years ago now. Solomon and I have since retired. Solomon went back to Lesotho and he lives in the same village where he was born; high up in the mountains along with his children and grandchildren. My wife and I moved down to a smaller house on the South Coast. My special retirement present from the mine was a highly polished piece of gold reef with a clock face mounted in it. The inscription reads: *'Time For Those Golden Years'*; which is quite neat when you think about it.

The reason I started to think about Restless Mbuzo again after all these years; is that a new mining outfit has purchased my old mine and its rock dumps. They are going to remove all the underground pillars and sweep out the workings to remove every last bit of gold. Of course, they will eventually come to the place where we stopped mining and rub their hands with glee; laughing at the old fools who left some of the richest gold reef behind.

I've thought about writing to them to tell them what happened to Restless Mbuzo; but I know it would sound plain crazy. Even if they knew the story, they won't hear the scrape, scrape, scrape, above the noise of the machines. The patient drip, drip, drip of the bloody iron-stained water will be swept away with high pressure hoses as they wash the last grains of gold from the workings. The old mine will be stripped and scoured of all the gold; the sweat, the blood and the bad memories. It will be spotlessly clean; but somehow forever tainted, like the freshly washed hands of Pontius Pilate.

Well, that's their problem now and I've got other things to occupy my mind. Tomorrow I'm getting up early to start concreting over a gravel path that runs around my house. Lately I've been woken up by sounds below my bedroom window.
   Scrape. Scrape. Scrape.
   It's probably only the neighbour's cat using the gravel path as a damn litter tray; but still, it's annoying.

You need your rest when you reach your golden years.

BRIMSTONE

The Pilgrim's Regress

'Come along, Mr. Benz! It's time for your medication.'

'It doesn't work; why go to all the bother?'

'We've discussed this all before, Mr Benz,' said the nurse in a matter-of-act manner. 'You've an infection which is resistant to antibiotics, so we are trying this sulphonamide to clear it up.'

Percy Benz groaned, 'I didn't have any infections until I came into hospital. I was only here for a heart valve replacement.'

'That's as maybe, Mr Benz. But you still need the sulphonamide. It will clear up the infection so that you will be strong enough for the operation. It's really wonderful stuff this sulphur, nature's own remedy. They used long before modern medicines were available.'

'If this sulphur-what's-it-called, was so flippin' marvellous; then why did we need antibiotics in the first place?' Percy moaned.

'Now come along, Mr Benz, don't be difficult.'

Percy struggled to sit up. He knew resistance was useless with the nursing staff. He spoke to the nurse as she went about her task.

'I used to manage a factory making sulphuric acid. We made it for car batteries and fertilizer manufacture.'

The nurse told him that as he knew how useful sulphur was; he should be grateful and accept it without making such a fuss every time.

'The smell of the fumes, it never leaves you. That foul smell of rotting eggs, it all comes from sulphur compounds: did you know that?' Percy asked, but the nurse was too busy to pay much attention.

'You know what Booker T. Washington said? He said: "A sulphur mine in Sicily was about the nearest thing to hell he expected to see in this life." He was damn right! I used to get our sulphur from the mines in Sicily before I could buy it cheaper from tar sand dumps in Canada. Believe me; I've had enough of the stuff to last me a lifetime.'

After reluctantly submitting himself to the inevitable, Percy slumped back on his bed. Without the nurse to distract him, Percy focused his weary eyes on the television, virtually the only source of colour in his bright, white private hospital room.

The television programme was a natural history documentary on the Galapagos Islands. The pictures showed a bleak and rugged volcanic island landscape. Some of the volcanoes were still active, producing pure sulphur which sublimated around the steaming vents like lemon-coloured snow. The narrator went on to say that sulphur-feeding bacteria were first discovered in hydrothermal volcanic vents under the seas surrounding the Galapagos.

Percy was initially puzzled as to why he'd just been given sulphur to kill off the bacteria, when there were billions of the little buggers thriving on it. He was about to press the buzzer and call the nurse back, when he heard the voiceover explaining these were very special bacteria. In near boiling seawater, these organisms obtained their energy from the sulphur, rather than devouring organic material. It was an example of life adapting to an otherwise hellish environment that might have fascinated the Victorian naturalist, Charles Darwin; had he but known. The programme turned its attention to some of the island's larger inhabitants with which Darwin was certainly familiar: the marine iguana. Percy looked at the pictures of the lizards. The slow moving, ugly-looking brutes lounged on the jagged rocks on the shore or swam around grazing on seaweed. It seemed a relaxed life style to Percy; a bit of sun bathing, splashing around in the sea looking for lunch, snort out gouts of salty seawater and then back on the rocks to warm up in the sun again.

The narrator's voice became more serious; there was trouble looming on this paradise's horizon. The Galapagos Islands had become a must-see natural wonder and thousands of eco-tourists and environmentalist pilgrims visited the remote islands every year. Ironically, those most interested in preserving the biodiversity for future generations were the ones damaging the ecosystem by shear weight of their numbers. The documentary said this was having a negative impact on the marine iguana numbers. Other threats came from the climate, predation from invader species, disease and so on. Percy thought it was going to be the least of the iguanas' worries if one of those volcanoes erupted again. Nevertheless, nearing extinction himself, he felt a brief pang of sympathy for the hapless reptiles before dozing off during the advertising break.

He awoke later to hear on the evening news that a minibus on an outing to London had driven off the Tower Bridge and plunged into the River Thames. All the passengers were presumed dead. This was followed by another gloomy and ironic story; crematorium workers on strike had refused to go back to work even to allow the funeral of "Red" Bill Botham, a well-known union leader. He had sustained minor injuries on a well-publicised picket line. An ambulance had been called, but as it approached the scene it was mistaken as a capitalist subterfuge to smuggle the strike-breakers in to work. The jeering crowd had pelted the ambulance with paint. The unsighted driver lost control, careened into the demonstrators and mowed down "Red" Bill. The damage to the ambulance was only slight; the damage to Bill was of a permanent nature.

Dying iguanas, dying tourists, and dying trade union leaders. What was so utterly fascinating, so incredibly newsworthy about death? He was dying and it had long since lost any fascination for him. He felt he was being slowly run down like one of his own car batteries; his reserves of energy slowly draining away. The television announced a forthcoming religious broadcast, but he switched it off to prevent hearing further details. The words future, forthcoming and even tomorrow, had ceased to hold any real meaning for him.

He awoke suddenly. A twinge, and then a soaring pain in his chest made him gasp. He struggled to reach the emergency call button, but his limbs refused to move. The alarm never sounded and the room remained as soundless as the silence within his ribcage. The pain subsided as he slumped to unconsciousness. He wondered if his life would flash before his eyes. It did.

It was one of those well-lit, hazy, fuzzy-at-the-edges, days in eternity, instantly recognizable from the set designer's handbook. Clouds of dry-ice vapour wafting at knee-height, spot lights centre stage, stentorian voices of immortals booming out from loud speakers. There was a narrow path leading toward some very large and expensive-looking gates. As Percy approached closer, the impressive doors slowly closed shut. Percy looked around but there appeared to be no one around. Not knowing what else to do, he knocked loudly on the door several times.

A small wicket gate opened up in the main door. A stout man with shoulder length hair and a full, pointed moustache stepped through the gateway. He dusted down his plain black jerkin and offered his hand in greeting.

'Blimey – are you St Peter?' Percy asked.

'No!' The man started to laugh and then, remembering such laughter was a sin of the frivolous; he stopped. 'No, I am merely privileged to deputise for St Peter on occasion. My name is John Bunyan.'

'John Bunyan – I've heard of you! Didn't you write…?'

'Ah, modesty forbids me to say, Sir. But do come in: oh, but firstly, what is thy name?'

'Percy Benz.'

Bunyan consulted his parchment: 'Oh forgive me; this is most awkward.' He eased his finger around his starched white Puritan collar in embarrassment. 'I see thy name is not found.'

'Are you sure? Perhaps my surname has been spelt "Bends" instead,' Percy asked, 'It's a common mistake.'

'There is no doubt, Sir; thy name is absent.'

'Why? There must be a mistake. I didn't do anything wrong!' Percy looked at Bunyan's perplexed expression and tried again loudly and slowly as if explaining something to a foreigner: 'Listen, thou hast made a bloody administrative cock-up, right? I did my bit for charity – I visited the sick - and I never went to prison.'

'Though thou payest large sums for "playing the lottery" as I believe it called; t'was no generous act of charity. Also when thoust did visit thy workers who were ill, it was no mission to bring Christian comfort, Sir! It was to ensure they were not simulating the sickness!'

'Well, a lot of them buggers used to take time off and try to claim sick benefit for no reason...'

Bunyan looked at his scroll before continuing: 'And furthermore, thy lack of incarceration was due to the strenuous efforts of thy worldly-wise legal team, rather than, as He hast judged, on the innocence to which thoust profess.'

'Now look here, Johnny-boy! I worked hard; I ran a successful business, I made damn good products! Did you know our factories supplied over sixty five percent of vehicle batteries in the United Kingdom? Where would the economy be today without modern transport; you tell me that, eh?'

Bunyan looked unimpressed; so Percy tried a different tack.

'I employed lots of people; put bread on hundreds of families' tables! And I travelled a lot to other countries to open up new markets; gave opportunities for those less fortunate in the third world as well. I mean, when it comes down to it – that's what life is all about isn't it? It's about your fellow man - and all that. I'm really a peoples' person at heart.'

John Bunyan sighed: 'When thou talkest of thy journey, and of what thou hast heard and seen, thou art inwardly desirous of vain-glory in all that thou sayest or doest.'

'Oh I see! So really what your saying is; it's because I wasn't a good Christian, isn't it?'

'At one time that wouldst clearly have been my guide. But no, Sir, I am afraid thou art deceived. See thee now; out of all the world's many faiths; thoust participated not.'

'So I can't enter heaven? Bugger it!' Percy muttered under his breath.

'I'm sorry,' said Bunyan with compassion. He stroked his moustache in a pensive manner and then added, 'Still, as I am want to quote on these tragic occasions: "Admittance is based on regeneration, not merely on an affirmation of a creed or doctrine." And so my poor Sir, happenchance we meet a while later.'

'What do you mean - later?' Percy asked. He heard no reply as the vision of the pearly gates and their temporary guardian faded away.

Percy found himself gazing out across a dark river. The river exhibited all the required mythological characteristics; wide, deep, eternally flowing, and so on. It was the river Jordan, the Styx, standing between the "here-and-now" and the "now-and-forever"; a flowing boundary between life and death itself. There was a fog gathering on the water. Percy recognised the rank smell of sulphur as the clouds drifted across to him. The smell grew stronger, and the river turned from water to blood red, molten brimstone. Percy sat on the bank and watched miserably as a lone hooded figure propelled a small boat across the bubbling expanse to meet him.

Of course! The ferryman! Percy was amazed at how much he already knew of the after-life from folklore, legend and a smattering of religion. He racked his brains. I mustn't take the oars, however much he complains, he thought. I mustn't pay him until we reach the other side - the other side? Oh my God, the other side!

Percy lifted his eyes to the opposite bank in dread of what awaited him there. It resembled the skyline of Manhattan thrown up in anger against a glowing, lava-red sky. In the foreground crouched a grotesquely disfigured structure. Its size and predatory manner mocked the absence of any symbol of liberty that might have welcomed the poor and oppressed to another city a whole lifetime away. However, as Percy looked at those other souls gathering on the bank beside him, it seemed as if the poor and oppressed must have been welcomed elsewhere.

The ferryman pulled to the shore. He stood up in the boat and flicked back his hood. Percy gasped. It was "Red" Bill Botham!

'That's it, Brothers! I'm on strike! No one crosses this picket line to Hell!'

"Red" Bill placed the same inflection on "Hell" as "Work", as being a devout atheist and devoted trade union leader, he had never really believed in either of them. "Red" Bill then went on a rant about the hours he was expected to work (Eternity) the pathetically low wage (Nothing) the miserable conditions (Absolute Hell) and his newly formed union's demands (Just About Infinite).

'It's all a crypto-fascist plot! If we'd been paid a living wage, we wouldn't have had to work overtime on Sundays to earn decent pay! We could also have gone to church and given money to charity in a meaningless gesture of middle class, bourgeois conscience appeasement! It's wrong Brothers! And we won't put up with it! As such, here we are, and here we stay, united until our just demands are met!' He planted his feet firmly and brandished the oar in a gesture of menace.

Percy glanced nervously across the crimson river that seemed to pulsate and spark as the huge structure began to move. Clouds of sulphurous fumes bubbled up as the monstrous shape disentangled itself to reveal the loathsome figure of Satan himself.

'WHAT?' Satan belched out, the smell of his breath enough to bring tears to a skunk's eyes, 'You worthless microbe! Fetch the rotting pile of putrid dross over here; right now!'

'Not until our demands are met,' said "Red" Bill.

'Your demands?' Satan roared, 'YOUR DEMANDS? You miserable, insignificant heap of amoeba dung! I'm the only one to make the demands around here!"

'Brothers! You see how management responds to our grievances! I urge you to show solidarity and support your new union's stand!'

The Devil roared on. He swore, he cursed and he stomped around in his lake of steaming brimstone. His foul and fetid bodily eruptions reached apocalyptic proportions, but it was to no avail. "Red" Bill stood his ground and would allow none to take the oars from him.

Percy's hopes started to lift slightly. If "Red" Bill wouldn't ferry them across, they would be unable to enter Hell, a fact that seemed to displease few people. Few people, that is, except the lately deceased members of LAMS, the Luton Amateur Masochists Society. On a pilgrimage to see the London Dungeon's new torture chamber exhibition, they had attempted to ramp over Tower Bridge as the bridge was being raised. Their society's old minibus was in a pitifully decrepit state (even as a vehicle for masochists) and it failed to make the leap. Like lambs to the slaughter, they had met their newsworthy demise in the River Thames. The members were now frantic to cross over another river to suffer the pleasure of an eternity of pain and anguish. Only the oar-wielding "Red" Bill stood in their way.

The Devil calmed a little and peered over the miasma of bubbling sulphur at the gathering throng. He extended a talon and beckoned to Percy.

'Come on over, Percy Benz. You've certainly earned your place over here with me. Pick up those oars and get rowing.'

Percy resisted the Devil's invitation: 'Why me – what have I done?'

'Why, Percy! You took advantage of Free Will to fully indulge your insatiable appetites! The wheedling corruption and greed, the wanton gluttony, the joyous abandon to bacchanalian excesses, the fornication, the orgiastic revelries…!'

'Eh?'

'Your foreign "business" trips, Percy! The epitomes of depravity - and all paid for on your company expense account – Marvelous!'

'Well, I might have let off a bit of steam after work,' Percy admitted reluctantly, 'But still; where's the harm in that?'

'Quite so – all fun and games at the time - and so - here you are!' The Devil chuckled diabolically. He stopped gloating when he noticed a moody teenager picking his nose and flicking balls of dried snot into his unholy river. He growled and turned his attention to the bored youth: who turned out to be a failed Buddhist.

'You! Yes you, kid; the unenlightened one! What's your name?' demanded the Devil.

'Rodney.'

'Well then, Rodney, why don't you stop excavating your nostrils: reincarnate as a fish, and swim over here?'

'No ways!' Rodney replied with a sneer.

'Listen, Pal! You get your spotty backside over here pretty damn quick or I'll reincarnate you as a, a marine iguana!'

It was possible the Devil's choice of animal was a reflection of his earlier television viewing. He made a point of watching television regularly as the adverts inspired him to greater heights of jealousy and avarice.

'I've already been an iguana,' Rodney muttered.

'Really? How the Hell can you screw up being a beach lizard?' asked the Devil in genuine surprise.

The masochists stopped their whining as Percy and the others in the crowd strained to hear Rodney's reply.

'Oh, I did the lizard thing all right; even the other reptiles and primitive mammals. It was just the more advanced stages that were a real pain in the arse. I've been an orangutan nine times, and humans; I've lost count.'

'Two hundred and sixteen times since the last Ice Age,' the Devil calculated with some malice.

'Two hundred and sixteen?' Percy queried, mindful of John Bunyan's "later" comment. 'What religion were you?'

'I did all of the major religions at least a dozen times; even some of the obscure ones during my earlier attempts. None successfully though,' answered Rodney dismally. 'Like it's all such a schlep.'

'Wait a minute,' said Percy who had yet to grasp even the rudiments of eternal time scales, 'You mean to say, you can re-incarnate into what ever you want and as many times? You can just keep going?'

Rodney shrugged his shoulders: 'Yeah, so what?'

'Because it's getting a new life, exactly like recharging a car battery!' Percy said in amazement.

'Well, anyway, you still have to succeed at one life form; you know, before you can upgrade to the next one.'

'Sure, I can see the sense in that. But what if, let's say, we were to go back, like, regress to an iguana for instance? Can anyone do it?'

Rodney looked confused: 'Yeah, suppose so. But what's the point?'

Percy looked at the Devil who had begun to gnaw his filthy finger claws anxiously.

'The point is this, my lad. Only by way of an example; but we could be sitting on some tropical island munching seaweed, rather than watching Old Nick here turn up the thermostat for the next trillion years. With any luck, each of us will eventually come right and then - off we go!'

There was general agreement that this idea was more appealing than the current and apparently eternal and infernal situation.

'Red' Bill, however, was adamant. He would never abandon his picket line. The Luton Amateur Masochist Society had a brief but violent discussion, which only ended when all had received their fair share of a painful thrashing. They decided they just couldn't lose if they stayed and tried to cross the picket line. They would either be constantly beaten back with abuse and swipes of the oar blades by 'Red" Bill, or they would eventually break through to a land of eternal torture and humiliation.

Meanwhile, Rodney, motivated at the prospect of being a success at something at long last; proceeded to demonstrate the art of reincarnation: 'Okay, watch me, then do exactly the same, Okay? Marine iguana! Here we come!'

He did a bit of a shake, a sort of a twist, and a couple of intricate passes with his hands, and then he was gone like he had never been; let alone been two hundred and sixteen times before.

Percy and the others were stunned. The idiot boy hadn't explained what to do if you wanted to be reincarnated as anything else but a butt-ugly marine iguana!

'HOLD IT! Just hold it right there! Where do you think you lot are going?' Satan roared trying to re impose his authority, 'Don't think you get off that easily...'

Percy wasn't going to hang around: anything was likely to be better than this.

'Marine iguana! Here we come!'

'Get back here, you puny scumbags!' bawled the Devil. 'You'll all be reincarnated as a fungal infection between a sloth's toes if I have anything to do with it!'

Fortunately, he didn't.

It was another of those well-lit, hazy, fuzzy-at-the-edges, days in Eternity. The squeals of pain and pleasure from the Luton Amateur

Masochists echoed across the river as "Red" Bill repulsed another charge with an appalling lack of physical restraint. This was followed by the now familiar diatribe condemning the strike-breakers as "self-centred, neo-fascist, hedonistic, gratification seekers", contemptuous of the legitimate aspirations of, well; mainly himself.

The Devil tried to splash them with sulphuric acid and yelled at them to shut up, but the opposite bank remained just as noisy as before. Satan clenched his many teeth and tried to concentrate on the television news which nearly always cheered him up. There was, however, an upbeat item on the Galapagos Islands. A dramatic and unexpected increase in the fertility rate of the marine iguana had pulled the reptile population back from the very brink of extinction.

The Devil snorted and let loose a variety of disgusting sulphurous bodily exhalations as he recognised a number of iguanas; including Percy Benz, as lost customers. He watched irritably as an enthusiastic conservationist lifted a lazy, dumb-looking marine iguana into the camera's view.

'It's lucky they're not all like this one!' remarked the conservationist. 'He's simply too stupid to run away. We call him Rodney!'

The Devil stared at the television screen and groaned. Now he remembered. Oh yes, it was Rodney all right. Rodney: the one and only failed Satanist of the 14th Century.

GREENSAND

Slipped away

'How'd it go today, Honey?' he asked over his shoulder then turning to see my face, he answered his own question; 'Oh right, as good as that?'

I propped my bulky art portfolio against the wall and flopped down on one of the kitchen chairs.

'It was really slow. I only sold two paintings all day. I even had to knock down the price of the last one,' I said.

'Congratulations! You sold more paintings today than Van Gogh sold in his whole lifetime! What about a glass of vinho to celebrate?' Jamie asked, proffering the glass he'd already poured for me.

That was my man, full of ironic encouragement.

'Thanks,' I said, 'but it's hardly a celebration. It's just not going to be enough, is it? The summer holiday season's my busiest time of the year. A few more weeks and then the tourists will leave. I'll never be able to make a living like this.'

I took a sip of the chilled white wine and reflected this wasn't quite how I'd pictured my post-university career as a young, up-and-coming artist. Unfortunately, my attempts at becoming Hampshire's answer to Frieda Kahlo ended when the folk of the south coast declined to part with their money for my surreal mementos of introspection. The passion I had for my painting was perfectly counterbalanced by the despair I felt, day after day of that first summer, trying to convince the public to buy my art. I'd even considered doing animal face painting for the countless kids that ran shrieking up and down the promenade; I would probably have made more money. Things had been pretty bleak until I'd met Jamie.

It had been a really hot day. Lurking in my shady spot, I'd observed the skin colour of the beach goers change from 'flesh pink' to a shade just short of 'boiled lobster' - or 'carnelian', as we artists prefer to call it. I'd also seen Jamie. He sauntered casually back and forth along the seafront past my pitch. After several passes, he stopped and struck up a conversation. He asked about me, my paintings, and me again. He left after a few minutes and returned with a pint glass of ice-cold passion fruit and lemonade he had bought me from the pub across the road. Then, unexpectedly, he dug into his short's pocket and pulled out a roll of banknotes bound by an elastic band. He looked distinctly embarrassed and muttered something about; 'I don't know much about modern art, but I like this one.' And he pointed to one of my less *avant garde* paintings.

We met up regularly over the next few weeks, sometimes at my stall, or for a couple of sundowners in the evening. Then, as the summer drew to a close, he'd persuaded me that he'd like to have an 'artist in residence' to share his home. I didn't need much persuading and the spare room had quickly been converted to become my studio. I'd lived there with Jamie ever since. To make some small financial contribution to living costs, I'd pushed aside any pretence of artistic integrity and turned to painting more conventional scenes to adorn living room walls; landscapes, seascapes, children on the beach or paddling in rock pools. At least they brought in a little money.

'Yeah, I know it's not easy,' Jamie sympathised, 'Let's face it, Honey, it's expensive to bring a family on holiday, what with ice creams and amusements for the kids. There's not a lot of spare cash around at the moment. Just as well there's only the two of us!'

I was glad there was just the two of us as well, although my Varsity friends thought of us as being a very odd couple; me, slightly built, in my mid-twenties, a bohemian and an impoverished (but I may say, not unattractive) artist and Jamie; a bit too chubby to be called rugged, early thirties, sports crazy, steady income, removal man and part owner of a second hand shop.

Jamie sat down across the table from me. 'Look, I don't know much about the art world – I leave all that to you fancy college types. But if you want to be more commercial, you've got to think more like a businesswoman.'

'Businesswoman? How do you mean?'

'Well, you only sell the painting on canvases or boards – they're not framed. And, to my eye anyway, they don't look finished. Anyone buying it has to think – oh, now I'll have to get a frame for that picture when I get home.'

I sighed; 'Yes I know, but good frames are so expensive.' I wiggled my empty wine glass in Jamie's direction, hoping for a top up.

Jamie obliged with a refill and then continued; 'So, just frame a few so you can put them on display. Give the punters an idea of the finished article. Like the painting with the sea mist rolling in on the promenade you did a few weeks back – that's got a bit of an old-fashioned look to it; it would look really smart if it was properly framed.'

'Old-fashioned? It was my attempt at an Impressionist-style,' I said.

'So, that's right, isn't it? I bet those old French painters would have put a nice frame round their stuff. I reckon your painting is just as good – it deserves a good solid frame; don't you think?'

Pleased as I was to have Jamie compare my paintings to the Impressionist masters of the 19th Century, my budget was very limited. I hardly contributed anything to the household costs as it was and I'd feel guilty about reinvesting what little money I'd earned into buying expensive picture frames.

Jamie could tell what I was thinking. He said when he did house clearances, they often came across old pictures. Along with any furniture that was in reasonable condition, they would be taken back and sold at the business' second hand furniture and bric-a-brac shop. Jamie had yet to find an undiscovered 'old master'; but they'd sell them on for a couple of pounds or so. He said he'd look out for any pictures with suitable frames.

'You could pick up a frame for a couple of bob, knock it about to give it an antique, distressed look. It would look dead right on one of your Impressionist pieces.' He sat back and patted his slightly protruding stomach. 'Now then, just to get in the right frame of mind so to speak; what do you think them Impressionists ate for supper?'

'Who's a clever boy, then?'

'Einstein? Dali? Copernicus? The bloke who invented chocolate?' I ticked off the names although, of course, I had anticipated the intended answer; and so I saved it until last; 'Or could it be ... you?'

'You're darn right, I am!' Jamie boasted. 'We were clearing out a cottage over in Lymington today. It belonged to an old lady who'd died a month or so back. No close relatives, so she'd left her estate to a local charity. They'd already taken away anything they thought was worth auctioning, but it's the house that's got the real value. It's in a really nice area too.'

'You're not thinking of buying a house in Lymington are you? Seriously, it will cost a fortune! And besides it's a bit, you know, geriatric around there now, isn't it?'

'You're not kidding! God's waiting room! Even the neighbour who popped around with an offer of a cup of tea must have been at least a hundred in the shade herself. The old dear said it seemed like the person who had lived in the cottage, Miss Carlin, had been there for ever – certainly as long as she could remember.'

'It must be all the good sea air,' I said.

'Funny you should mention it,' said Jamie in a puzzled tone. 'I've done a lot of house clearances and you come across some odd stuff from time to time, but I distinctly remember thinking one of bedrooms smelt just like you were standing by the sea. There was even sand over the carpet as well, it was all a bit weird. I pointed it out to the evaluator in case he thought we'd tramped it in, but he wasn't bothered. He said someone had probably knocked over a cactus pot. Anyway, they would get the house professionally cleaned and aired out before putting it on the market.'

'It was an old person's house; it is bound to smell a bit musty after all those years. So, getting back to this stroke of genius ...?'

'Right, it seems the late Miss Carlin, bless her, had loads of pictures. They're prints and some enlarged old-fashioned photo's, the walls were full of them. Mostly large size, but some smaller family photo frames – good quality too; must be nearly fifty of them in all.' He sighed, 'No original masterpieces though – more is the pity.'

'What sort of pictures are they?' I asked, guessing they would consist of country landscapes, still life and maybe cute kittens.

Jamie rubbed his chin. 'I didn't take too much notice really, nothing of any obvious value. There were a few oil paintings, but mostly figures and photographic portraits, even those really old sepia types. Perhaps they were of long-gone family members. Anyway, the evaluator didn't want them, he just wanted rid. I think he was keen to get the stuff cleared out and then sell the house for a quick half a million quid.'

'And so you think some of the old frames might suit my paintings?'

'Definitely! I brought them all back to the store. Why don't you come down on Sunday morning and have a look for yourself?'

I wasn't particularly hopeful, but as Jamie had gone to the bother to put the frames aside for me, I said I thought it would be a great idea.

-

The following Sunday found me squatting on the floor next to the stacked pictures and flicking through them. The frames were of surprisingly good quality. Not sure of my budget, I planned to stack them in piles as to their desirability: 'Definitely', 'Perhaps' and 'No!'

I tried to look at the frames in isolation and imagine my own painting sitting in the centre, but inevitably I was drawn to the images they contained. Jamie, who was rearranging second-hand furniture elsewhere in the store, had been accurate about the subject matter. The pictures seemed to be nearly all figures or portraits. There was a common resemblance to the women in them, so much so I assumed they must have been family members. There was also a couple of dozen photographs or paintings of young men. They didn't appear obviously related to the women or each other. The pictures showed the men standing or sitting alone, in various settings, a mountain path, some in army uniform, one on a boat. There was one portrait I particularly liked; something attracted me to the handsome young man and his setting. Wearing only shorts, he was seated on a rock beside the sea. He looked as if he had turned to face the camera just as the picture was taken. I put it aside, separate from the others.

Jamie wandered over to see how I was doing: 'Any good?'

I pointed to the ones in the 'Definite' pile. 'How much for these?'

'Right-oh, let's say a fiver each – but you can pay me when you sell the painting.'

'And these?'

'It's your lucky day, lovely lady! Buy one, get one free.'

Later the same Sunday afternoon, with Jamie stretched out on the sofa with a beer watching the cricket on the television; I was up in my studio, sifting through the pictures. I should have been on the seafront trying to sell more paintings, but frankly I was glad of the excuse to stay at home. I measured up the ones I'd selected from the store. As I had decided to acquire all of them, it was taking some time.

I was curious about the older pictures and how they had been made. They were all securely mounted behind glass panes which were in need of a good polish. It was difficult to tell whether they were realistic and very detailed paintings, or if they were old photographs that had been hand-tinted with colour. I guessed that some of the older, smaller ones must date from around the mid 19th Century. There was none of women and men in the same picture, which I found puzzling. No grandfathers, no fathers, apparently no older brothers or uncles. I flipped through them again and realised that although the staid and posed pictures showed the women at different ages, there were no similar pictures of older men. It struck me as rather odd. Posed family portraits had been a staple since the birth of photography. Peering through the dingy glass, I was again drawn to the subjects of the picture, especially the solitary young men whose times seemed to span the decades. I gazed at my favourite again, the one of the rather athletic-looking youth perched on the rock. It too was mounted behind cloudy glass and a tightly fitting frame. Despite my art training, I couldn't decide how the painting or photograph, or possibly a mixture of both techniques, had been achieved. I heard Jamie lever himself from the sofa and shout up if I wanted a cup of tea now that the cricket had stopped for the afternoon tea interval. I took the picture down to show him.

'I think there's better frames than this, Honey,' he said.

'Maybe; but look at the picture. What do you think, Jamie?'

'Er, well, it's a bloke sitting on a rock – probably taken by his girlfriend. Or boyfriend, you can't tell nowadays, can you?'

'Why did you say 'nowadays'? It looks like a really old picture to me.'

'Yes, fair enough, but he looks modern, doesn't he?'

'I'm not sure; he's got longish dark curly hair and men also wore their hair longer in Victorian times too.'

'Yes, but he wouldn't be wearing bathing shorts like that in those days. Perhaps the photo's been mocked up to look like an old-fashioned shot; like those photos you can get taken down on the pier.'

'On the pier?' I looked at him curiously.

'You know! You get dressed up – put on a top hat and an Edwardian frock coat or a bonnet and a crinoline dress and then they take a couple of photos. They print it out on sepia paper while you wait – and then you've got a photo looking like it was taken a hundred years ago.'

'The picture certainly looks detailed enough to be a photograph, but the colours are muted. Do you think it could have been hand coloured later?'

Jamie peered at the picture: 'Yes, possibly. It looks textured though, especially in foreground. Perhaps it's one of those early photos – we come across them occasionally. But then, as I said – his shorts look just the same as you'd buy from any modern beach shop.'

I wasn't convinced: 'But look at it closely. Doesn't it seem to have a slight three dimensional look about it to you?' I angled the painting slightly to show him. 'It's as if there's a depth to the image.'

Jamie agreed: 'Yes, a bit – but you get that effect on some of the old-style pictures, before they had the paper print type. The solutions were printed on glass and the picture came out as a positive print. They were only one-offs though, not like a photographic negative that you can run off hundreds of prints. Still, I've not seen one as large as this before – usually they're a standard plate size to fit in the back of the camera.'

'You seem to know a lot about it,' I said a little surprised.

'I know a lot for a removals man, you mean?' he mocked. 'Well, as it happens, yes, I do. A few years back an antique dealer in Brighton was asking around us house clearance businesses. He said he had clients who were interested in collectables of all the early photographic methods. He wanted us to be on the lookout for good quality examples, daguerreotypes, ambrotypes, tintypes.... '

'Yes, those names sound familiar. I did a module on the history of photography as part of my Art degree at Brighton.'

'... so anyway, the dealer explained to me about the different types and the sort of stuff he was after.'

'And what was that?'

'Ah! He seemed to be particularly keen on naughty Victorian nudes; early pornography, I guess you would call it. But failing that, anything related to any historical events.'

'Well, he's definitely not having this one,' I said, feeling protective of my scantily clad beach man. 'I think he looks quite dashing. He's got an iconic, almost Byronesque quality to him.'

'Hmm, I saw a film on Lord Byron once,' Jamie chuckled again. 'He was a right character! He put it about a bit, didn't he?'

'He was polyamorous, if that's what you mean,' I sniffed.

'That's exactly what I mean. But with us poor serfs, it's "he's always chasing after skirt"; but it's dandy for these romantic aristocrats because they're just feeling a bit 'polyamorous'. Where's the justice in that?' Jamie said in a wounded tone.

A curious sensation came over me at that moment. As much as I loved Jamie, I had the curious feeling I wouldn't mind getting a wee bit polyamorous with the good looking man captured in the picture.

'Are you all right, Honey?' Jamie asked.

'Yes,' I said quickly, feeling the colour coming to my cheeks. 'I'm just puzzled by the way it was made. I've not seen anything quite like it before.'

'Well, if you are going to take it out the frame, you'd better be careful. If it's an ambrotype and you separate the glass plates, you'll destroy the image – and your 'Handsome Harry' here will be lost.'

I decided that I wasn't prepared to risk spoiling this picture. I'd first have a look through the others, may be a small one, and see how they had been mounted. There were plenty of other frames to look at and besides, this particular frame wasn't right for my own pictures anyway. I would keep it as it was, at least for a while.

-

Over the next few days I carefully removed some of the pictures from the frames so I had some thing to work on. I noticed on the back of the pictures that there was a place or date written in pencil on the brown paper backing. The oldest photograph I found was of three seated women in the 1870's. The group of women and possibly their descendants appeared in pictures spanning over 150 years. And then there were the pictures of the men; the oldest in 1880 appeared to be one of a solitary solider, looking relaxed, leaning against a craggy hillside outcrop. Jamie thought his uniform might be from the time of the first Anglo-Boer war in the old Transvaal. And yet, I couldn't get over the uneasy feeling there was something odd about the collection. I started to spend more of my time looking through Miss Carlin's old pictures than I spent on my own artwork. I grouped them by age. The group of three women became two and then one. The pictures of the women were all carefully posed, looking at the camera and dressed in the finery of the day. The earlier pictures saw them seated outside. Jamie pointed out they would have needed strong sunlight as the film was not so sensitive, the sitters would have to hold the pose without moving. The interior shots were taken later, formal poses next to solid looking furniture or an imposing ornament.

The images of the men were very different. They appeared to be casual, not posed at all. Following the Anglo-Boer war image, there were more pictures from the First World War; an officer standing and looking across a battlefield, an enlisted teenager crouched down in a trench, writing a letter. Not all the men were in the military, though. Some seemed from a more peaceful era. There was a strapping young farmhand, looking as if he was walking down a country lane after bringing in the harvest; a lone hiker with his backpack, a sailor in a small dingy, and of course, my favourite, the man on the beach. None of the young men looked directly into the camera lens, only the lone hiker seemed to be in the act of looking upwards, as if encountering someone else on the path ahead of him. Even my Lord Byron lookalike was only partially turned towards whoever was taking the picture. And yet – was I really looking at a photograph?

I'd cleaned the glass covers so the images were now more easily seen. I'd been particularly careful with my beach man picture. I gently rubbed away at the glass like Aladdin might have polished his magic lamp; sadly no genie materialised, but bringing the image to life was enough reward.

When the glass was clear, I was astonished at how sharp the image was. Yet despite what I assumed to be its age, there was an incredible amount of detail visible in the picture. It was so life-like. I fetched a magnifying glass and the image revelled even more features. It was all there, the bubbles on the crinkled seaweed, a sand fly on a pebble. I was sure that it was only my cheap magnifying glass that prevented me from seeing every grain of sand or each individual hair on his lovely head. This couldn't be just any old photograph, there had to be more to it than a superb technique and the highest quality camera lenses. Was it even a photograph? Even on the closest inspection, the slightly three-dimensional perspective remained.

Is there such a thing as too real, or was it all a clever optical illusion? I'd seen an exhibition of 'super-realist' artists when I was student. The paintings were astonishing in their exquisite detail, ranging from stunning portraits to even the most mundane of objects, a collection of bottle caps, raindrops on blades of grass, even ornaments wrapped in crumpled newspapers with each word of print perfectly legible. You'd swear you were looking at a high definition photograph. Then there were other artists who worked on the smallest of scales; intricate scenes painted on a coin or a sunflower seed, perhaps using a paintbrush with only a single hair. Even if it wasn't to your taste, you had to admire the artist's technical ability and their patience. Perhaps it was a combination of the two techniques, although I struggled to imagine Miss Carlin, the little old lady from Lymington, could have been the artist responsible.

'What do you make of it?' I said watching Jamie's expression as he studied the picture with the magnifying glass.

'Dunno; not seen anything like it before. You're right. Everything looks like it's been done in minute detail.' He frowned in puzzlement, 'But like, what's the point?'

'What do you mean?'

'What I mean is; for all its cleverness, it's not exactly a masterpiece of composition for a serious artwork is it, Honey? You know more about it than me – but it's not what I would call balanced - the setting of the figure in the picture, the rocks, that bush on the cliff, it doesn't come close to the artist's 'golden ratio' thingy – does it?'

Jamie could see I was about to protest but carried on: 'Yeah, I know you're quite taken with the young master Byron clone, but what about the rest of it? The background, the foreground it's all pretty boring. And the colours – sure they look realistic, but it isn't – what can I say – an inspiring picture, is it?'

'It isn't conventionally classical, if that's what you mean,' I said.

'Classical? Let's be honest – it's not exactly 'The Last Supper' is it? The composition could be typical of any amateur snapshot; 'Here's a picture of me on the beach at Hastings'. Then slap it on Facebook – job done!' Jamie said. 'See what I mean?'

Jamie had a point, much as though I was reluctant to admit it.

'I'm just thinking aloud,' he said with a shrug, 'but for what it's worth, Honey, even if it was hand colouring on top of a photo; it must have taken ages to produce something like this. And if you were going to go to the trouble to get it as near to nature as God himself: why struggle to get every little bit exactly right on what actually turns out to be a pretty average picture? Surely, if you were going to put in that amount of effort, you'd want to go all out for something really worthwhile?'

'I agree its not a masterpiece, but may be it's about the person depicted. Perhaps he was important to the person who did it. I'm intrigued to know more about how it was done. Perhaps I could use some of the techniques in my paintings.'

'Well, I've not come across anything quite like it before. I could take it over to my antique dealer…'

'I'm not selling it!' I blurted out more forcefully than I had intended.

'Okay, Love; calm down! I meant to get some expert advice. May be you should show it to your old art Prof at Brighton University?' Jamie suggested.

I said that I might, but I'd try and work it out myself first.

After practicing on a couple of the other frames, I'd worked out these images were not old daguerreotypes sandwiched between glass plates. The dirty glass covering turned out to be just that, dirty glass. The covering had a smeared appearance all windows on the coast displayed; caused by a sheen of microscopic salt carried inland by sea mist. I plucked up my courage and carefully removed the glass to look at the image underneath. A distinct smell of old seaweed emanated from the picture, but that faded quickly. Thankfully the image remained. And there he was perfect; and perfect in every detail, as was everything that surrounded him.

I studied the materials typically used to compose such an unusual work. I've seen a lot of materials used as medium for art; oils, acrylic, ochre, blood, plant extracts, food dye, even elephant dung; but I had never seen anything quite like this. I couldn't decide whether the surface was very old or freshly created. The incredible detail was more evident now that the glass had been removed. I could see there was a slight tan line on the man's wrist as if he had just taken off his watch. Perhaps Jamie was right, it was a modern picture after all.

I turned the picture over and removed the brown paper backing. There, previously hidden away on the back of cardboard mounting, was a pencil inscription, 'Adam Blake, Briar Chine, IOW' and a date. My heart jumped with the realisation that it was this year's date, in May. My mind reeled. The picture I had thought must be from the last century was only a few months old – and taken not far from where I was now, somewhere across the Solent, on the Isle of Wight.

How had this amazing image come into old Miss Carlin's possession? Was this a relative of hers? Perhaps he was a grandson or great nephew? And of course, unlike the other young men captured in their prime over the preceding decades, 'Adam' would still be very much alive. I decided to take Jamie's advice and contact my erstwhile professor, Henry Harris, at the University of Brighton. It was only a short journey and I convinced myself that it was purely in the interests of a serious artistic enquiry.

-

I told the professor a little about the painting and about how I had initially thought it was old, Jamie's view that it was intended to be faux vintage, and so on. I suppose I was gabbling on a bit and before I had finished saying why I thought it was so important, the Professor held up his hand to silence me. He then beckoned me to hand over my precious object.

I watched as he studied the picture. He massaged his brow; he pulled on the lobe of his ear and then stroked his nose thoughtfully between thumb and forefinger. Finally, he looked up towards the ceiling and stroked his grey, Trotsky-like beard.

'Really quite intriguing!' he said after a period of thoughtful silence.

This was, I thought, a good sign. I'd been half-afraid of a; 'You stupid girl! Did you learn nothing whilst you were here?' if it turned out that I had missed something obvious.

Professor Harris cleared his throat: 'It is – unusual. My best guess would be the artist has used some mineral pigment that has been ground down extremely finely. There's no obvious trace of binding agent that I can see, but it's probably some kind of tempera.' He paused, 'Follow me, young lady.'

I dutifully followed him down to a basement room in the university department.

'We'll need to carry out some tests; see what compounds the artist has used...'

'No, I don't want anything scraped away for a sample,' I said firmly. 'I don't want the picture damaged!'

'No, don't worry; we don't have to spoil anything. Let's see if Norman, our technician, is still around. He can operate the thingy-me-bob better than me.'

The 'thingy-me-bob' was one of the University's art department's analytical tools. Norman explained he didn't need to remove any of the paint material from the picture. It could all be done *in situ* with non-destructive analytical methods. He'd try the portable X Ray fluorescence unit or XRF as he called it. He said it was just like the machine they used on the space rover to analyse rocks on Mars.

I wasn't so confident. After a few moments hesitation, I agreed, insisting that the technician try it on a small corner of the painting; the cliff in the background behind where Adam was sitting.

After a few minutes Norman came back with a print out: 'Yes, definitely mineral – it's got iron, aluminium, silica and a bit of potassium in there.'

'So, what mineral is it?' I asked, hoping it might be a pigment name I would recognise.

'I don't know, there's hundreds of minerals or combinations of minerals which have those elements in them,' Norman replied. 'And there could be more, the XRF doesn't detect any of the lighter elements.'

He sensed my disappointment; 'Look, to get an idea of the actual minerals; we could always try our X Ray Diffraction kit on it. That is; if Professor Harris says it's okay?'

Professor Harris nodded his ascent.

'Okay, I'll set it up on the frame and let it run. It blasts X rays at the paint's surface and then any crystalline material will diffract the beam. The different angles of the refracted beam are specific to the crystal structure.'

We watched as Norman as he set the painting firmly onto a tabular frame and carefully lined up the X-ray source. Then he brought the arm bearing the detector over the painting. He motioned us to retreat to a safe distance and started the equipment going. With maddening slowness, the detector started to edge along the arc of the arm, a fraction of a degree on each click.

'You might want to go for a coffee,' Norman suggested, 'The XRD runs a lot slower than the XRF. It's going to take at least an hour.'

When we returned, Norman was hunched over a computer screen looking at a graph with numerous peaks on it. 'That looks about right,' he said and hit the print button.

The chart was overprinted with various vertical coloured markers aligned with the peaks.

'Best I can do in the time,' Norman said. 'If we let it run overnight you'd get more detail, but I think this is what you're looking for.'

The Prof reached for his reading glasses and peered at the small print at the bottom of the printed page.

'There's a little quartz and some calcite. Ah! Now that makes sense, the main ingredient appears to be glauconite. Thank you, Norman. Good work.'

'Glauconite?' I queried.

'Yes, interesting someone should use *'terra verte'* in this day and age. I'm sure that it must be the pigment responsible for the greenish colour of the rocks behind the figure.' He noticed my puzzled expression.

'In paintings before the ubiquitous use of oils; glauconite, or *'terra verte'* as it was called then, was commonly used as a green pigment. In antiquity, it was widely used for murals and religious icons.'

'And the pigment would be mixed and stabilised with say, egg tempera as a binder?' I added dredging my recollection of history of art lectures.

'Exactly! The yolk can give off a rather unpleasant smell for a while.' He winked at me, 'That might have been a bit disconcerting for the holy brothers – their icon of a revered saint smelling like bad eggs, don't you think?'

I told Professor Harris about my initial impression of the smell of seaweed when I first removed the glass covering.

'Ah! Very interesting! The artist could have used alginate as the binding agent for the pigment; it's a gum made from brown seaweed such as kelp. The commercially available stuff is odourless. But, if it was a homemade extraction, they might not have managed a totally successful separation of the dissolved alginate from the rest of the seaweed gunk.'

'But why would anyone go to the bother of making the gum themselves?' I asked. 'There's plenty of binders or pigments available from any artists' supplier.'

'Quite; this is where I find myself agreeing with your paramour, my dear. The painting itself, its composition, is utterly mundane. But perhaps the artist wanted to create a local scene using only the local materials. It is a seaside scene, so the 'Art' is all in the use of local materials; the seaweed as a binder, coloured sands such as glauconite for the pigment, and so on. The art of sand painting was briefly popular in Georgian times, 'Marmotinto' it's called. The technique is revived from time to time by craft enthusiasts.' He sniffed dismissively, 'I suspect that, for the amateur hobbyist, collecting and mixing the material is half the fun.'

He paused for a moment. 'There are cliffs of different coloured sands all along the south coast – the Isle of Wight is particularly famous for its variety of 'earths'. Glauconite occurs in cliffs all around the south coast of England, in the so-called 'Greensand' rocks. There you are; Greensand, *terra verte*, the name says it all, really.'

My heart skipped a beat at the mention of the Isle of Wight; I hadn't mentioned the location before the Professor had cut off my explanations. I told him another reason for my visit, that was, the super-realist nature of the painting.

Professor Harris squinted at the painting and studied the intricacy of it for the first time. He carefully detached the painting from the analytical equipment and carried it across the corridor to another room. He put the picture under a binocular microscope and switched on a powerful light, focussing it under the lens.

'Good Lord, that's incredible!' he said after a few moments. 'Your eyes are sharper than mine. Tell me what you see.'

It was obvious what had impressed him. In the microscope's field of view were limpet shells attached to the rock on which Adam was sitting. As I increased the magnification, I could see the individual striations on each shell. Even more astonishing was the limpet, insignificant as it was to the scene, had even smaller barnacles growing on it. I zoomed in to the maximum the binocular microscope would allow and there, on the minute barnacle, I could clearly see the individual plates and the tiny closed operculum that made up its protective shell. Awestruck, I wondered if we had a more powerful microscope, whether we would be able to see mites crawling over the barnacles. Fanciful nonsense of course, but this was clearly no ordinary painting. I didn't mention the even finer features that my old lecturer hadn't picked up.

'Have you ever seen anything like it before, Professor Harris?' I asked. 'How was it done?'

The Prof shook his head. What he at first had thought was a fairly routine enquiry from a curious former pupil, had now deeply intrigued him.

'We would need to do further tests, look more carefully at the materials and so on. If we could reach some conclusions as to the techniques employed in creating the image, well, I think that it would be worth publishing an academic paper on it. With you as a co-author, naturally.'

I was flattered by his suggestion. A co-author on a publication with an authority like Professor Henry Harris! I was secretly pleased as it would give me a valid reason to spend more time studying what I now thought of as Adam's picture.

Professor Harris continued; 'I know you mentioned that you obtained it from a house clearance, but if you could find out more about the provenance of the work, the owner, the artist; that would also be an important first step. An academic paper on Unknown Painting, by Unknown Artist, of Unknown Subject in Unknown

Location: Date – Unknown; is hardly going to grab the attention of the art world. Why don't you see what more you can find out?'

I eagerly agreed. For reasons I can't explain, I didn't reveal I'd already seen the annotation with this year's date and the Isle of Wight location. Despite the Professor's kind offer to look after the painting in the meantime, I returned back home with Adam's portrait tucked safely in my bag.

-

Later that evening over a glass of Frascati, I told Jamie all about my visit to the university and what we had found out about the picture, the seaweed and greensand pigment.

'Remember, Jamie, you said the house smelt like the sea? Could that have been the smell? Maybe she had brewed up some kelp for a binding agent,' I suggested hopefully, 'And you said something about sand – perhaps she'd gone and collected bags of different colours for her art work.'

Jamie shook his head: 'I doubt it was actually Miss Carlin, Honey. I had the impression from the evaluator that she was a very old lady. Not the sort to be beachcombing for buckets of sand and seaweed. I didn't see any other artist's stuff lying around either. Perhaps she had a lodger; although what sort of person would be crazy enough to want to have an artist living with them....' he tailed off looking at me pointedly.

I smiled weakly at the joke, but then asked him if he knew anything about Miss Carlin, or maybe her relatives.

'No, I haven't a clue. But because she left everything to charity, I assumed that she didn't have anyone close to her.'

'Jamie, you said you spoke to her neighbour. You remember where the house was, don't you? So we could go back and ask her?'

Jamie muttered that he thought I was spending too much time on this picture and I should be concentrating on my own art works. He was right; I hadn't picked up a paintbrush for a while. I defended my inactions:

'Look, Jamie, this is an amazing picture! It's not a brilliant composition, you're right about that; but if I could find out how this was done, maybe I could apply the technique to my own paintings. With the slight 3-D look, the detail and using local materials and a more serious subject matter, it would be something really different; wouldn't it?' I appealed to him, 'It's got to be worth a go. And it's better than trying to flog clichéd seaside scenes to tourists year after year.'

'Well, *I* like your seaside pictures,' Jamie said huffily.

'I can still do those in the meantime, but this could be a whole new discovery. It's important to me Jamie. And who knows? I might be able to start paying my share around here, at last.'

'Okay. I'll drop round and call in next time I'm in Lymington. I'll check with the neighbour to see if she knows whether Miss Carlin had any relatives; or arty lodgers.'

Over the next few days, I found myself unable, or unwilling to paint my own pictures. My earlier motivation to make more of a contribution had temporarily deserted me. With Jamie working out of the house during the day, I had plenty of time on my hands. I spent most of it looking through Miss Carlin's former gallery. My attention was drawn time and again to young Adam's laconic pose on the beach. The painting could have been used as the perfect illustration of Byron's own words, the 'rapture in the lonely shore'.

I even dreamt about the same seashore. Submerged in the shallow waters, the long strands of balmy seaweed moved against my naked body, caressing me with the gentle sway of the waves. Rejuvenated, I emerged from the glassy sea; a Venus reborn. I stepped out onto the beach, feeling the warm sand of his world beneath my feet. I approached him, anticipating the moment when he would be aware of my presence and turn that beautiful face toward me. I murmured his name...

I woke with a start, quivering with tension and my heart pounding. Oh God! I prayed I hadn't called out Adam's name in my sleep! Undisturbed, Jamie dozed on beside me, oblivious to the frisson the dream had caused.

In my student days I had, of course, experimented with surrealism, the juxtaposition of the real and the fantastic, dreams and wild imaginings in my earlier, ill-fated artistic attempts – so why should this banal scene now infiltrate my subconscious? I examined the picture, turning it this way and that. Surely, there was more to it than the male subject, attractive though he was? I tried to identify what cryptic symbolism it might contain, but failed to find any Freudian clues which might trigger my dreams.

It came to me eventually, in a slightly delirious moment during another sleepless, sultry summer night. It was not what was contained within the scene, but what was missing.

Me. I was meant to be there; alongside the man on that beach. The message of the painting was startlingly clear.

'Come to me.'

A few days later and after a little research on the internet, I told Jamie that I going to the Isle of Wight to sell some of my artwork there. I was also honest enough to add I was going to be doing some research on where the painting or photograph or what ever it was, was made. I'd taken a photograph of the image and I carried that with me, leaving the original at home.

The huge crowds had departed from the Cowes week festivities, but the island still had plenty of tourists enjoying the last week or so of the summer weather. I'd located Briar Chine on the southwest of the island and driven to the spot. Unlike the beaches near Bournemouth, the seafront was largely undeveloped. I left my old car in a car park at the top of the cliffs and made my way down the steep footpath to the beach. Miss Carlin would have had to be a very sprightly old lady to have made this short journey. Jamie's theory about a younger artist friend suddenly seemed a lot more likely.

I wandered along the beach trying to identify the place where Adam's picture was taken. I saw limpets, barnacles, stranded strips of Kelp. I even identified the abundant greensand rocks composed of the tiny glauconite grains. I picked up a rounded pebble to take back and show Jamie. Fanciful as it seems – I had been half hoping to see Adam there; taking up his relaxed Lord Byron pose on the same rock. There was no sign of him. It was a small beach but even so, I couldn't pick out where the picture had been taken. The cliffs behind Adam didn't match the photo I held in my hand. I'd intended to take another photograph of the same spot so that we could have put in the publication as a comparison. Perhaps the 'Briar Chine' name was wrong. There were dozens of these chines or naturally eroded cuttings through the cliffs on the Isle of Wight. I didn't have time to search them all. Disappointed, I walked back up the wooden steps to the car park as rain began to fall.

There was no point in setting out my paintings, so I went to the nearest pub for a quick lunch. The rain also seemed to have put off the tourists and I noticed there were very few customers. I struck up a conversation with the landlady who was serving behind the bar. During the course of my ploughman's platter lunch, I told her about my itinerant art sales quest. I also asked her about the local area and Briar Chine. I remarked that the beach seemed smaller than I had expected from reading about the area.

'Oh yes, the beach used to be longer, but there was a landslip. A whole section of the cliff slumped right down into the sea. It was on the TV news even, they warned people to stay away. It cut this part of the beach almost by a third; the trade hasn't been so good since.'

I was curious as to why that should be.

She told me that it was easier to access the beach from the west side – it was where the larger car park was – but families would walk along the beach and climb up for a pint or a bite to eat. Since the landslip though; it was risky to climb over the unstable jumble of rocks unless it was low tide.

'You might be better selling your paintings down at the lower car park,' she sighed. 'Most people stay the other end now, since it happened last May.'

Last May? When my picture was dated? Curious, I asked my chatty host about the events of that time. She cast my mind back to the really wet spring we had suffered earlier in the year.

'It's to with all the rainwater. As I've been told - the rain drains down to the clay layers, and it makes the rocks above it unstable.'

She made a stacking motion with her hands. 'The water builds up and up, and then - without warning...' she slid her hands across each other quickly, making a slight rasping sound, 'the rock slips on the clay and the whole cliff collapses into the sea.'

'Was anyone hurt?' I asked.

'Aye, it was tragic – a young local lad. They reckon he was on the beach when the cliff collapsed. Terrible it was – people were digging with spades and their bare hands, but it was hopeless. You can see how big the slip must have been, even now. It took them a couple of days to get those mechanical diggers on site because there was no road access to the beach.'

I was shocked, 'And did they find him?'

The landlady shook her head sadly: 'No, not a trace of him, the poor dear. He must have been buried instantly and swept into the sea with all the mud and rock. It happened so quick they say. Your heart goes out to the family. Poor lad, still in his teens, he was.'

My mouth was dry and I struggled to swallow the cheese I had been eating. I managed to wash it down with a mouthful of juice.

Trying to sound casual, I asked: 'The boy's name – it wasn't Adam, was it?'

'Yes, I think it was. So you've heard of our tragedy after all, then?' she asked.

I replied I vaguely remembered something from the news from a few months back. I tried to find out a little more about the events of that day without sounding too morbid; then I paid for the meal and went back to the car. The weather had not improved and I sat in the car alternatively staring out at the grey sea through the rain-streaked windows or looking at my photograph. Was it the same man, the same Adam? If it was, then the handsome man was no more alive than the soldier boys in Miss Carlin's older pictures.

A feeling of sadness and self-pity overcame me. I wasn't destined to meet Adam; to have a romantic adventure, sell any of my paintings or even solve an artistic puzzle. I was left to sit in a crappy old car, on a miserable day, sniffing back tears at my feelings of disappointment and failure. I looked down at the photograph I'd brought with me. It was only a picture of a man on a beach. I could look at it without any of the yearning I'd felt when I was transfixed by the original version from Miss Carlin's cottage. As Jamie had pointed out, it wasn't such a remarkable picture after all.

I thought about Jamie and wished he were with me. I hoped he'd had better luck on his trip to Lymington. Although I was feeling down, I knew Jamie would go and talk to the old lady on my behalf; not because he was fascinated by the picture, but because he loved me and I'd asked him to help me. I could hardly go back and say to Jamie I'd given up so easily, it wouldn't be fair.

I could still find out more about Adam the subject of the picture, in honour of his memory if nothing else. Perhaps locals might know if he'd modelled for a picture or who was with him – perhaps the picture was taken earlier on that fatal day. But wait – the painting couldn't possibly be done in an afternoon at the beach. It was probable that someone had taken photographs, and then later produced the image from that, even intended it as an 'in memoriam' tribute. A thought crossed my mind. Were Miss Carlin's pictures of soldiers also memorials in some way? I decided to find out more about the circumstances of that particular day. I started the car and took the road inland to Newport.

The rain showers had cleared by the time I reached the town's main library and curiosity had replaced my earlier despondency. I asked the Librarian whether they archived copies of local newspapers. She said that they did, but, it might be quicker to look on the library's computer as the Isle Press also published a selection of articles on their website. I quickly found the item I was looking for and then located the full story in the newspaper from the middle of May. The photograph accompanying the article was of Adam Blake, the same person as in my picture.

The report said an eyewitness had walked past Adam as he'd come out of the sea from his swim and then turned back a minute or so later when he heard the rumble of the rock fall. It seemed Adam must have been killed instantly by the landslip, buried under the rubble as the cliff collapsed into the sea. Despite an intensive search, no body was ever retrieved.

It seemed Adam was well known locally. A gifted student, he was studying for a degree in marine ecology. He'd worked the previous summer as a lifeguard in the area and had rescued a child who had got into difficulty in the strong currents. The newspaper reported that Adam was in the habit of going down to the beach in the afternoon in order to get in some early swimming practice. His friend said he wanted to get in shape for this summer's beach patrol work.

I surreptitiously took out my photograph of the painting to compare again to the newspaper article. Miss Carlin's picture had better captured the essence of the young man; athletic, brave and intelligent, everything you could wish for in a local hero. Now he was gone, not even a proper grave to mark his passing.

I made a copy of the newspaper on the library photocopier, carefully aligning it to get the newspaper's date in the corner. I planned to use the information as a supporting evidence for the publication with Professor Harris. I also wanted Jamie to know what had happened to Adam, a few days after Miss Carlin's picture had posed. I hesitated, something wasn't right. The date on the newspaper was when the Isle Press was published, once a week on a Friday. I scanned the newspaper article and it gave the date of the fatal landslip. Goosebumps broke out on my skin as I realised it was the date written on the back of Miss Carlin's picture.

I sat down heavily at the reading desk and studied the article again to check there was no mistake. Could Adam have sat on the beach and had his picture taken on the same day? Or was the picture taken before and then had it been reconstructed in remembrance of Adam? It might mean the date on the back of the picture was not of the image's completion, but the date of his passing?

I studied the picture in the copy of the newspaper again; Adam was looking straight at the camera, a slight smile – no hint of reticence or lack of confidence in his face. And yet in Miss Carlin's picture he appeared to be looking slightly away, more a three-quarters profile. The strange thought struck me that all the solitary males in Miss Carlin's picture collection were represented in a similar fashion. Did she, or some artist friend; preferred their subjects in a more natural, less self-conscious pose than you might achieve from a 'smile please!' photograph? I felt a pang of guilt that I hadn't paid much attention to the other subjects, many still resided behind their original glass frames. I had spent my energy on Master Adam Blake, only to find he too had joined the ranks of soldiers, sailor, the mountain hiker and others from days gone by.

I packed up my bag with a sigh. I left the library and drove to catch the ferry back to the mainland and Jamie.

-

Jamie put down a mug of tea on the table in front of me and then proceeded to slurp noisily from his own.

'So that's the neighbour's story, make of it what you will. Personally, I think she's getting a bit confused with the different generations,' he said.

'So let me get this straight, Jamie: she says Miss Carlin lived next door for many, many years? And at one time 'old' Miss Carlin lived there?

'I think the neighbour is mixing up the years and remembering when Miss Carlin was there as a young woman, maybe eighty years ago?'

'Well, the photographs of the women do look remarkably similar in appearance. Really, it's just from the clothes fashion that you can tell what generation they were. Did you ask her anything about the history of the various Carlins?'

'Yes, but she was very vague. I even asked if they had been buried in the local churchyard. You know; I thought you could look up the records - but she took umbrage even at the suggestion ...'

'How do you mean?' I asked.

'She replied, 'Oh no! Miss Carlin *never* went to church," said Jamie, mimicking the neighbour's quavering tone, 'Very disapproving, she was.'

'And did she remember any visitors, like artists or lodgers?'

'She thought Miss Carlin had young gentlemen visitors at the house from time to time; but she was *never* invited around to meet them. She seemed miffed by that as well,' Jamie chuckled.

'So Miss Carlin entertained young men alone at her house. Would it have been so outré for a spinster back in those days? Anyway look at this.' I showed Jamie the copy of the newspaper article and told him what I had found out about Adam's tragic death and the coincident date on the picture.

Jamie scratched his head and said he vaguely remembered hearing about it – the storms had caused a number of landslips around the coast earlier in the year.

'We don't know how the marmotinto style has achieved such high definition, or how it came into Miss Carlin's possession. Still, I'm convinced that it was intended as a tribute to Adam.' I said confidently.

Jamie scowled at the original painting and then at the article. 'Avert your gaze from 'Mr Beef-cake' for just a moment and look at the shadows.'

'Beef-cake! I don't know what you mean,' I said flushing with embarrassment; but I knew exactly what he meant. Seeing Adam in the original picture had re awoken the sense of yearning I'd experienced in my dream.

Jamie tut-tutted, gently mocking my denial: 'Anyway,' he continued, 'the paper said the landslip occurred at ten past three. The angle of the afternoon shadows in the picture show it must have been mid afternoon; so about the same time. The template could have been taken only minutes before the whole cliff came sliding down.'

'So if it was a photograph taken at that time; what happen to the photographer? The eyewitness didn't mention any other person nearby.'

Jamie grunted and sat down to read through the article again while I went upstairs and looked at the other pictures from Miss Carlin's collection.

Firstly, I looked at those of the men. Peering through the dull glass covering, aided by the magnifying glass, I could pick out similar features on all the other portraits, the same accurate rendition. No detail was too miniscule to be missed; grains of grass seed on the officer's gaiters, strands of fibre on the fisherman's rope, even the words on the young conscript's letter. Every aspect was shown: 'warts and all' as Oliver Cromwell had insisted for his own likeness. Still no wiser as to how this effect had been achieved, I turned to the mounts of the women. These were clearly different types compared to those of the men. They were all conventional photographs, either printed on plate or paper depending on their age. In one of the earlier sepia tone ones, the woman I thought was 'our' Miss Carlin or her younger self, was posed sitting upright on a high backed chair. Unlike the male subjects, she stared directly out of the print. Miss Carlin looked a strong, determined person; perhaps one of the suffragette generation. I could make out the large framed pictures hanging on the wall behind the woman, some of those I now had in my possession. The word 'possession' struck a chord within me. There was a fierce pride in her expression, almost as if she was posing amongst her trophies.

Was that it? In defiance of the mores of her time, where these young men her forbidden lovers? Perhaps Miss Carlin had been of a polyamorous persuasion in her youth. Still, how would that explain my Adam's portrait? So it could not be; there must be a seventy, even an eighty year, age gap between them. It was more likely her pictures were her equivalent of male pin-ups, a harmless fantasy for a lonely spinster. She might have acquired them furtively, which might explain why some of the subjects were three quarters turned in surprise towards the camera when the image was taken.

'Naughty Miss Carlin!' I thought; relieved to have found a solution to what had been vexing me. But my smile dropped when I realised that was less than half the answer. I couldn't imagine Miss Carlin being a battlefield photographer, or out at sea on a small boat, or lying in wait for a solitary mountain hiker on the off-chance of snapping a photograph of an adventurous youth. The artist who had constructed the Marmotintos might have worked from a photograph, but it still didn't explain the astonishing accuracy. The art showed features even a modern camera might struggle to define.

Still puzzling on the issue, I heard Jamie call me and I went downstairs.

He was squinting at the original Adam Blake image.

'Honey, you mentioned the Prof tested the picture and the green colour was made by the mineral, glauconite. And that's the stuff what makes up the greensand: is that right?'

'Yes, that's what Professor Harris concluded.'

'And you tested the picture up here on the cliff? Did you test any other parts of the picture, like on the sand, or the man?' Jamie asked.

'No,' I said, 'there wasn't really enough time – it took over an hour to do just the bit in the corner. Of course, we'll do more tests if the Professor thinks we can get a publication out of it though.'

'That's a pity. The newspaper talks about the accident and a warning, because the geology of the Isle of Wight makes it prone to coastal landslips; on occasion with tragic consequences. It says the worst affected areas are those of greensand sitting on top of the clay.'

'Yes, the landlady said that as well...'

'So, what I'm saying is this; the cliff that killed Adam was made of greensand, and you proved that it's greensand as what makes up the colour in the picture. Not just to match the colour, but exactly the same material.' Jamie looked at his fingernails, 'And then there's this.'

He held out his hand; 'I scratched the tiniest bit of the paint on the cliff. Some of it came off under my nail – look!' He scrapped the dirt out onto some paper.

I was dismayed – how could Jamie be so careless as to damage the picture? I started to shout at him for being so thoughtless, but he cut me off short:

'Look at the painting, Honey! There's not even the slightest scratch – go and get the magnifier if you don't believe me. Now watch this.'

To my horror, Jamie reached forward and gouged a line across the cliff with his finger and then rubbed off a blob of dirt onto the paper.

'What are you doing? Stop it! You're ruining it, you idiot!'

Jamie snatched up the painting and held it like a shield before my face. I thought it was to stop me from lashing out at him, but then I saw. There was no mark at all, even though Jamie must have scrapped away a deep layer of the paint.

When I had calmed down, Jamie pointed to the clay smeared on the paper.

'This stuff's greensand, as well, right? If I'd walked up to the cliff and rubbed my finger over it – it would look the same as that, wouldn't it?'

I was too stunned to say anything. Even though I thought I'd seen the clay scraped off the picture with my own eyes, there wasn't a scratch on the painting.

Jamie turned and opened up a kitchen drawer and pulled out a teaspoon. Without saying a word, he waved the spoon and nodded his head at the picture.

I nodded my agreement: 'But just on the edge,' I said in a quiet, hoarse voice. I swallowed as I watched Jamie lower the spoon onto the picture and then dig it in, twisting it slightly as he did so. Impossibly, the spoon disappeared below the surface of the flat picture.

Jamie pulled the spoon back. It was mounded with damp, greenish clay. There was no discernable mark on the picture.

'That's not funny, Jamie, really!' I said indignantly. 'You had me going then. You've swapped spoons with one you'd dug into the garden while I was upstairs.'

Jamie shook his head. He wiped the spoon, and then like a mime artist, he slowly, deliberately pushed the spoon into the painting; once, twice, three times; knocking a small pile of dirt from the spoon each time. We both stared in silence at the evidence before us.

Jamie straightened up and rubbed the back of his neck.

'Well, I'm no art expert, but I tell you what I think. It's not just the pigment of the cliff; it's not only made from the same greensand as the cliff. It *is* the cliff, the whole, real, actual cliff, before it all came tumbling down.' He picked up the spoon. 'I reckon if you got hold of that fancy microscope at your university and looked at the same spot on the picture really closely – you'd find there's teaspoon marks in the clay.'

'It can't be true!' I protested. My mind reeled trying to grasp what this meant. 'Yet, the smell of seaweed! And you saw sand all over the floor when you were at the house. It didn't come from any pot plant...'

Jamie dug the spoon into the lower part of the picture and this time retrieved a heaped spoonful of pale beach sand. The dry grains spilled over the paper next to the clay.

I swallowed hard. 'But that means - you could collect the seaweed or pull a limpet from the rock! My God! If you knew how, you could even...'

'...even liberate young Adam Blake,' Jamie finished quietly. 'Looks like you could do with a drink, love.'

We sat and drank our wine in my studio, trying to come to terms with our discovery. Surely, the other pictures must tell a similar story. I told Jamie it was as if, somehow, the enigmatic Miss Carlin had captured the image, the true essence, of each of these young men moments before their death. In a way, it was a kindness. She had preserved them for prosperity, they remained with her, even as the world moved on and eventually forgot them. What else could it be?

Jamie sniffed: 'I think it was more than remembrance, Honey. The neighbour said, 'Miss Carlin had young gentlemen visitors, but she was never introduced to them."' He waved his hand at the other pictures. 'No wonder! There's plenty of strapping young lads shown in these pictures. I think that she had a more sinister motive.'

'It's certainly bizarre – but why sinister? After all, she was rescuing them. Wasn't she?'

'The whole thing's bloody odd; but it's an even odder coincidence that the Miss Carlins or their accomplices, knew exactly when these men were about to die from some disaster – and then turned up and snatched them away.'

Jamie drained his glass. 'I think it's Miss Carlin who's responsible for their disappearance. If we checked up on the history of these boys – I'll bet their bodies were never found – and they were all eventually presumed dead.'

'But people can't just disappear off the face of the Earth,' I said.

'Oh, but they do! Especially daring types, like these lads. The sailor-boy? He went out alone to sea and never returned. I bet there's a report somewhere they found pieces of his boat washed up on the shore. Well, the bits that aren't shown in his picture, anyway.'

'All of them? But there's dozens or so such pictures! They span over a century.'

Jamie bent down and picked up the painting of the man walking up a mountain pass and glanced at the writing on the back. 'So, you might want to research what happened in 1932 to Duncan Forsythe, a solitary hiker in the Cairngorms. My guess? He was a presumed victim of a freak avalanche; and sadly his body was never recovered.'

'That's crazy! You think Miss Carlin kidnapped these men somehow? She stole their belongings, their bodies, even their souls...'

'...and captured everything around them as well, a perfect holograph. Exactly like the greensand we can dig out of a picture of a cliff. Miss Carlin might have even caused the landslip, the avalanche, the bomb blast, or whatever.'

'By taking a photograph?'

Then it dawned on me and I answered my own query: 'But, it's not really a photograph is it? It's not only captured the light reflecting from the objects – it's captured the whole damn thing; each grain, every microbe, probably each and every atom! Everything has been snatched from the landscape and encapsulated in a picture to hang on her wall.'

'Right, it's the same with the soldiers at the front. What happens when a crater suddenly appears on a battlefield? Anyone would think it was caused by an exploding shell.'

At first I thought it was madness. Then I realised it might be a bizarre explanation of what really happened at Briar Chine on that day.

'And I suppose, if you abduct a lifeguard, along with a load of rocks and beach sand from the base of an unstable cliff; then obviously, the whole lot comes tumbling down in a massive landslip.'

Jamie nodded thoughtfully: 'It's beginning to look like Adam Blake's body wasn't found through lack of trying, Love. I think he was transported into this picture the moment it happened. She took a fancy to him and spirited him away; same way as she, and probably mother and grandmother Carlin before her, took all the others.'

Jamie and I discuss the conundrum further, but even after a couple more of glasses of wine each, we were no nearer a rational answer. We searched through the internet to try and date the earliest images, the ones that Jamie had originally thought were the old ambrotypes. It might help us find out how long Miss Carlin and her female relatives had been carrying out their strange ways. It seemed the oldest picture dated back over a century and half. I shuddered involuntarily when I read the word 'ambrotype' came from the ancient Greek meaning, 'Immortal Impression'. Had these men been captured, suspended for an eternity? And if so; for what purpose?

The implications were too great, just too weird, to absorb. I intended to research the strange artefacts, the other men and their mysterious disappearances; but it would be another time, possibly far in the future. Although some artists encouraged others to accept their eccentricity, I could foresee how such a journey could descend into madness. I was a normal painter, not a paranormal investigator. I needed to go back to my seascapes and try and sell some more artwork before the summer finally came to an end.

Unsurprisingly, the thoughts of what happened to Adam and the other young men would not leave me so easily. Later that night lying in bed with Jamie, I thought of the bewilderment of the friends and families of the handsome young men who had inexplicably disappeared into thin air. They were plucked from their lives, only to reappear in Miss Carlin's occult gallery. I had an eerie feeling she occasionally summoned them from beyond their prison images to keep her company in her neat little cottage in Lymington.

Staring up at the ceiling, I found myself muttering aloud: 'So, who *was* Miss Carlin? I mean, who was she really?'

Jamie rolled over sleepily and put his arm around me: 'Not *Who*, Honey, more like, *What?*'

ROCK

A Very Big Rock

It was a nice sunny day.
'Mother, can I go and play with John?' said Janet.
'Yes, you can go and play with John,' said Mother.
Janet went to play with John.
Janet saw John's hands were dirty.
'Look John, look! Your hands are dirty,' said Janet.
'Yes,' said John. 'My hands are dirty.'
Janet said, 'How did your hands get dirty, John?'
'I dug a hole,' said John.
'Oh!' said Janet. 'Can I see the hole, John?'
'No Janet,' said John. 'It is a secret.'
'Is the hole in the garden, John?' said Janet.
'No, it is not in the garden,' said John
'Is the hole in the woods, John?' said Janet.
'No, Janet, the hole is not in the woods,' said John.
'Come John, come and show me the secret place,' said Janet.
'I want to play a new game,' said John.
'Let us ask Peter if he wants to play,' said Janet.
'Peter will not come and play,' said John.
'Why won't Peter come and play?' said Janet.
'There was a bad thing,' said John.
'Oh dear!' said Janet.
'A rock hit Peter on his head,' said John.
'Oh! That is a bad thing!' said Janet. 'Was it a big rock?'
'Yes. It was a very big rock,' said John.
'Oh dear!' Janet said.
'Now Peter cannot play any more,' said John.
'That is very sad,' said Janet.
'Yes. It is sad,' said John.
'Peter was my best friend,' said Janet.
'Peter was also Kate's best friend,' said John.
'I thought Kate was your best friend,' said Janet.

'Yes,' said John. 'I thought Kate was my best friend, too.'
'Come John! Let us see if Kate will come and play,' said Janet.
'Kate cannot come and play,' said John. 'There was a bad thing.'
'Oh no!' said Janet, 'Did a bad thing hurt Kate?'
'Yes. A rock hit Kate on her head,' said John.
'Was it also a big rock?' asked Janet.
'It was a very big rock,' said John. 'Kate cannot come to play.'
Janet said, 'I am sad that Kate and Peter cannot play with us.'
'Don't be sad, Janet. Come and play a new game,' said John.
'Yes, let us play a game. It will be fun,' said Janet.
 'Yes. It will be fun,' said John, 'now you can be my best friend.'

DIAMONDS

A Girl's Best Friend

Your expressive eyes closed, you smile faintly, dreamily, perhaps remembering some secret pleasure. It will be your last smile; this I know and I ache with sorrow and regret. I have sacrificed everything to be with you for these last few moments, to see a hint of that gentle smile. It is the same smile that would save a whole world.

You turn away from me now, naked on this sultry summer night. And yet, as if seeking some final warmth, you snuggle into the satin sheets. You are so vulnerable and young, so beautiful; and now so still. So sorry, my love.

Real Persons Inc., Time Frame Protected

'What? Now? Tomorrow is Fusion day...'

'It comes from the top. The Chief wants new talent and he wants it now. As you are still prancing around in your humanoid costume; you are ordered to go. Real end of story.'

'This is hardly a costume! What about under-time?' I asked hopefully. That way I could jump now, do the preparation and relocation and then come back at exactly the time I left.

'No, so sorry. No staff available. It's real time.' She gave an, 'I'm-only-following-orders' type of shrug. 'We'll credit you.'

'Come on! You can do it for me, surely -'

'Don't push me. Zuk! Just because we spent Procreation Remembrance Night together! If you went to integration now, and I do mean now; you might still get back in time!'

I was not happy, but then again, when was I ever? 'Okay, I'm going. Who's the lucky jock running Damage Control?'

'DamCon? Even you won't need them!' she scoffed.

I almost choked on my humanoid tongue. We couldn't be so short of staff.

'What do you mean?'

'Focus on this, you irritable pink humanoid. Planet Earth, five kilo years past. A female movie goddess.'

'A Goddess?' I queried. 'A deity? I didn't think we collected religious stuff.'

'No, it's make-believe. Movies are like holoscope, but only two dimensional, see? Not religious as far as I know, more a humanoid celebrity. You'll pick it all up in integration, if you ever get there real-time today,' she added pointedly. 'Anyway, the beauty of it is; the whole planet dies off ten real years later. So you ruffle a couple of continuum, who cares? You won't need DamCon. Here's the profile, now go on!' she urged.

I took the tablet and watched her retreating back. 'On some worlds people get on with the various other sexes you know!' I called after her, but she kept walking away. 'And a wonderful Happy Fusion Day to you too!' I added bitterly.

-

I headed to the integration section. File Earth. Five kilo years past, the tablet contained the languages, customs; the whole lot. Locals hadn't developed time travel and never would do. It was currently classified as 'Regressed Primitive'. The footnote mentioned it was of archaeological and invertebrate interest only. I checked previous Earth collections. Only a male called 'Alexander the Great' from two kilo years before this date. Cellular cast was under permanent contract to Ace Armaments Incorporated. Not much help. So it should be no problem. The designated subject was a humanoid female (Prime) Earth date 1962, Actress, Marilyn Monroe.

There were no holofiles available, so I scanned some 2-D plates. I flipped through the usual boring stuff and looked through the records. Famous people get written about, photographed, recorded a lot. There was plenty of gen on Marilyn. I batched some details over to the labs – they would need to be prepared and get ready to make her feel at home. She was a model, an actress, and did some singing. I watched a few segs. She sang 'Diamonds are a girl's best friend' in one of them. I didn't really get it – how could an allotrope of carbon be someone's best friend? Then I saw part of another seg where she was best friends, not with diamonds, but with a couple of males – who were dressed as women as a primitive disguise. Zuk! This was confusing; but you know what? It made me chuckle. Maybe this was going to be more interesting than I thought. Anyway, I couldn't hang around. I hurried to get on with full integration, class Human.

Earth Hollywood, August 1972 Time Original
In too much of a hurry, I summoned up the wrong year. Zuk-luck! Still, I decided it might be worth a look around. The entire planet is only days away from nuclear destruction, certainly the human life on it, anyway. It was difficult to think about. Being Humanoid anyway and having gone through integration, you tend to pick up nuances of pleasure and pain. These help you to react as a native of the host planet. I felt sympathetic and then depressed. I experienced a desire to imbibe large amounts of alcohol, which is a mildly stimulating poison. I went to a bar where they sell this toxin in various guises and watched the news on a 2-D set. President John Kennedy in his third term of office was explaining his decision to advance troops into China. A poisoned drunk next to me slapped the counter and yelled, 'Atta boy, Jack! Give those Commies Hell!'

I was going to tell him Hell was on the way all too quickly; but it would not be a wise move. I finished my drink and decided to go and collect subject Marilyn right then. It was only ten years later, no one would notice. But I do notice. When I found her, she was in the Jackie Kennedy Institute for chronic drug dependence. She is overweight, neurotic and mostly incoherent. The world blowing away will end her misery. It was a mistake to see her looking this way, I shouldn't have wasted my time. My feelings of depression increased and I nearly abandoned the whole project. Whatever, I jump to-

Earth Hollywood Fifth Helene Drive, 4 August 1962 Time Original

- and I entered the property 12305, Fifth Helene Drive, in Hollywood. This is where Marilyn lives at this time. An older woman approached me and greeted me as Mr. Kennedy. I recognise her from the files as the housekeeper, Unis Murray. She told me Marilyn was in. I knocked on the door to her bedroom and discovered a very different Marilyn to the one I left in the future. She greeted me with obvious delight. We were alone. I jetted her with Dreamatol, set the time and we jumped to-

Real Persons Inc. HQ Time Frame Protected
- and because of my unscheduled stop in 1972 it was Fusion Day, real time. No-one was around. Just Marilyn and little old, integrated, humanoid, me. She was convinced that this was just some delicious dream. That's the way it is when you are running on Dreamatol. I, on the other hand, was running on empty. My human form needed something to eat. I decided to retain my integration disguise. It wasn't too bad actually, a Caucasian male of about my natural height and build. As I had been in a hurry, I had modelled my facial features on a plate in the 2-D files. Someone called Robert Kennedy, brother of the President of the United States of America. For reasons I did not realise at the time, this made me especially attractive to my collector's item, Subject Marilyn.

We would have to wait until real-time tomorrow before the cellular moulding could be carried out and I could not allow her out of headquarters for obvious reasons. We walked arm in arm to a twentieth century Earth apartment which had been quickly assembled for the few real days she would be staying with us.

'Where on Earth are you taking me, Bobby?' she asked and laughed lightly.

I looked at her standing next to me. She was happy, almost radiant. A strange sensation started to take place inside of me. My human integration was responding to her presence, a kind of inner warmth and yet excitement. I suddenly laughed too. I was amazed to find I was actually happy. Me! Stuck with a five kilo year old alien from a dead planet in HQ on Fusion Day, and I was feeling - joyous!

Marilyn's Dreamatol had the effect of smoothing out the inconsistencies. The fact that she had been in her own apartment and was now walking around what she called the 'space centre' did not bother her at all. I explained that she was having a dream and I would be close by all the time. As we reached the old-fashioned doorway she giggled and nuzzled her face into my neck. I felt dangerously unsteady as my body started to tremble. It was a crazy, pulsing feeling. I could feel my throat drying and my face flush hot.

'Why, Bobby! You're blushing!' she said playfully.

This made matters worse; it was a terrible feeling, a wonderful feeling. I remember thinking if I didn't get out from human integration I would expire from happiness. Strangely, this did not bother me at all. I didn't realise at that real time, it was too easy to get addicted to these feelings. I was already losing control.

Marilyn opened the door and squealed in delight. She danced around, pointing and touching things. 'Oh Bobby! It's wonderful! Can we live here when we are married?'

I smiled: 'Sure, we can live anywhere. It's your dream!'

'Then we can be here together - forever!' and she leapt up, threw her arms around my neck and kissed me. I think I might have fainted from pure pleasure.

When I recovered my human senses and some of my own, I realised the Chief had made a breakthrough. Somehow, Marilyn Monroe (Prime) had the ability to make people feel good, to feel warm, but somehow, better. It was a brilliant concept. Instead of using cellular casts of Czararian warlords or Alexander the Great to subjugate clients or intimidate people into making purchases, this endearing creature could persuade people to do so. If my own experience was anything to go by, it was going to be a brilliant commercial success.

Eventually Marilyn succumbed to sleep. Although she would be perfectly safe where she was, I decided to stay with her. Not something I would ever have considered with any of my previous collection items. Perhaps it was me who had jetted the Dreamatol, but I stayed and watched over her while she slept. Sometimes I gently touched her face or stroked her blonde hair as if I needed to make sure she was real. My human integration meant that I needed rest as well. Content in my drowsy state, I curled up beside her. It had been a long real day.

Throughout the next few days I was with Marilyn constantly as she underwent cellular moulding. It is a harmless procedure and involves making a copy of living tissue down to molecular detail. This creates a perfect twin, closer than genetic cloning for Humanoids. Even the electrochemical pathways in the brain were duplicated giving the twin access to the same life experiences, memories and even dreams as the original. Upon completion, the copy or Cast would undergo a period of assimilation and modification before they were allowed to work. As 'organics' they were, of course, accorded full rights under the appropriate conventions. The captured subjects were always dispatched back to their own time and place original. They would remember nothing of the incident; only a continuum detector would be able to pick up whether there had been a breach. Frankly, the Continuum detectors were so tricky to operate that the usual standard was to rely on the archived reports.

So for the real time being, we were together. I sneaked away occasionally to the archive to have a look at more of her history and her film career. The diamond-best-friend thing still puzzled me. I asked her about it.

She laughed. 'Why Bobby, you know diamonds are what men give their special girlfriends.' She winked at me. 'I'm your special friend aren't I Bobby?'

What could I say? Diamonds had become very popular in Marilyn's time to signify lasting attachments between a man and a woman. And as Marilyn said; it was mostly the men doing the giving.

On one of my escort walk-abouts with Marilyn, the Chief called me over. He wanted to know why I was still hanging around in my human form. I deferentially pointed out to him that Marilyn was not the average 'Enslaver of Nations' and 'Destroyer of Planets' who I usually pulled in. These specimens tended to be confident and tough, and could generally look after themselves pretty well. I told the Chief (in the most flattering terms) that his brilliant idea had been to select someone of charm and vulnerability. However, this very vulnerability meant she needed protection and reassurance, and being in human guise, I was the obvious choice to provide it. The Chief eventually agreed; she would need special attention. He grudgingly accepted that I should carry on as her companion. I tried not to let my elation show, but got back to Marilyn as quickly as dignity allowed. I couldn't bear to be parted from her, everything seemed so much better when she was at my side.

I should mention I was not the only one to feel like this. Wherever we went from one section to another, Marilyn became the centre of attention. All the humanoids I spoke to were captivated by her warmth and personality. I know a couple who even did an unauthorised integration on the sly so that they could understand and speak her language better. Of all, she had the greatest effect on me. I had been integrated for four real-days now and it was sometimes difficult not to think of myself as 'Bobby'. In many ways I was Bobby, the senator Robert Kennedy of the future. And the most beautiful woman in the universe was in love with me. I watched her and talked with her, held her when no one was looking. I began to wonder who had captured who. I knew it was crazy, but I wanted to keep the pretence going.

I crept away to the company store. Normally you place a plasma order for the local stuff when you go on capture, it's useful for trade. It depends on the locality of course, but a costume, gold pieces, drugs, decorative breathing masks, salt, all have their worth at the right place and time.

'Man-thing, you wouldn't believe it! Plasma's on the blink.' I smiled at the clerk and flashed my ID, 'I need some diamonds.'

The bored clerk sighed and came back with a battered looking bucket. It was full of large, translucent pebbles.

It wasn't really what I was looking for, so I tried again: 'Nice, but I'm going to need the smaller, sparkly crystal kind – not the raw stuff. What've you got back there?'

I walked out a few minutes later with my prize. The clerk had asked for a requisition clip, but I'd given him a genuine autographed holotape of 'Jingquot the Berserker' instead, so he was happy to let it go this once.

The modelling was complete and Marilyn insisted on seeing her twin. She laughed and posed beside the inanimate cast. She mentioned Madame Tussaud's a few times. The Chief loved it, had the whole thing put on broadcast. Those of us who had been through integration embarrassed ourselves by applauding, and she blew us a kiss from those perfect full lips. The little human goddess from another world had acquired some new devotees.

It was time for relocation but we managed to grab a last few moments alone. I gave her the gold ring with the large solitary diamond I had purloined from the store. She put it on her finger and we kissed for a long time before heading to the departure lounge. Technical staff actually gathered round to say goodbye. That doesn't happen often. We went to the console room and jump pad. I started to feel bad, really bad. Something sickening was crawling in my belly. I was taking her back, hand in hand, to her certain death. I started to weep and -

Earth, Fifth Helene Drive, 4 August 1962 One Continuum disrupt

- we landed back exactly were we had left, in her bedroom, 12305, Fifth Helene Drive. Marilyn slotted into the spatial vacuum which she had left no time ago. She would remember nothing of our days together because no time had passed. I reluctantly removed the diamond ring from her finger. It was time for me to leave her back to the world, the room, the bed. Leave her to her miserable fate and to the planet's inevitable and final holocaust.

Click. Real-time

I noticed the bottle of tablets that was beside the bed. She had become addicted to these in later years, I was sure. I grabbed hold of the bottle and waved it in front of her innocent face, 'Marilyn, you must listen to me! It's for your own sake, these pills are no good...'

She was shocked. She kept interrupting me as I tried again to tell her what her life would become. She was hurt. She shouted at me and said I didn't love her. This was not good. It had been a mistake to try and change things. Normally, DamCon would have been buzzing around me by now, but of course, they had not bothered to assign anyone. Marilyn started to cry and yelled at me to leave. I jetted her a spot of Dreamatol just to calm her down a little and then turned for the door. I realised the real Robert Kennedy might have some explaining to do later as I had overstayed my welcome. I left in a hurry, catching a glimpse of Unis Murray in the passageway. I ran into the garden and jumped –

Real Persons Inc. HQ, Time Frame Protected
- back to the console room. No one took any notice of me, which was just as well. I looked like hell and I felt sick and miserable. How could she say I didn't love her? I had just tried to save her life, for a few years at least. The Marilyn I loved had died five kilo years ago, but that was no comfort to me. Perhaps I had made a difference. Instead of getting dissociated from Human form, I went back to the archives, Earth Section.

Funny. The computer files on Earth seemed to take up more memory space than when I was here before. Earth 1962, 1972, 1990, 2023 (what?) and further still. I looked at the storage for all the files. There must be another four or five kiloyears of data stored there. The Earthlings had not blown themselves away in 1972!

What had happened to Marilyn? Of her there was no sign. I searched all the way back until 5th August 1962. The day after I had left her. The media reported Marilyn Monroe dead, possible accidental overdose or suicide. The very night I had taken her back. What had gone wrong? The Earth had lived on, but Marilyn had died. What could be the link between the two events? I read on through the ancient reports as more details became available over the next few weeks. A drug overdose seemed to be the recurring theme. I was sickened as I realised what must have happened.

Marilyn must have taken some tablets before I had arrived. They had worked their way out of her system in Real Persons Inc., but when she was relocated they would be right back there again. Mixed with a jet of Dreamatol, she may have been confused enough to take more tablets, a fatal combination. I had accidentally killed Marilyn Monroe.

I held my head in my hands while the computer flicked through the years. I was too upset to care until I remember the death of Marilyn might somehow have prevented the war. Why had President John Kennedy not sent troops into China, starting the planet's final war which had ended with the push of a few buttons?

Kennedy never had a chance to push the button. A sex scandal had broken out just before the presidential election in 1968. A man named Richard Nixon, who had previously lost to Kennedy in an earlier national election had swept to power ahead of the discredited Kennedy administration. Free love was great for everyone in 1968 - except for the president and his running mate, brother Robert Kennedy apparently. Later reports showed that many of the allegations, some involving Marilyn and her friends, were part of a Mafia smear campaign to discredit the Kennedys and remove them from power. By then it was too late. The moral majority had made up their minds and voted.

So what had Nixon done to save the world? I read on, increasingly amazed as I found out that he had actually escalated the war at first, saturation bombing, chemical attacks and so on. I looked at the 2-D plates in dismay. Villages were on fire, wounded soldiers, burned children and refugees. I thought back to the soldiers and great leaders who we had collected for Real Persons Inc. I had always been in awe of them, all-powerful leaders, terrible tyrants, conquering and ruling by fear and death. I had thought of them as great figures, heroes of their time, just the sort of people to inspire our clients. We always pulled in a couple of galactic warriors for the office party to make it go with a bang. Now my human side was disgusted by their need for power and ever-expanding empires. Was Nixon one of these? He had just the same power to cause death and destruction in his enemy's land and yet, he had stopped.

Nixon, so it seemed; realised the futility of it all. Instead of dragging all of eastern Asia into the conflict, he had just ended it.

Following historic first visits by an American President to both Moscow and Beijing in 1972, the war finally ended for the Super Powers in 1973. No nuclear war! The Earth lived on! It was more important than ever to save Marilyn. There would be a world for her to live in. Her loveliness could entrance her world for years to come if I could only undo the damage I had caused. Somehow I needed to keep her alive, and yet make sure the war ended. I had to be with her again, so I went to the console room and –

Earth, Fifth Helene Drive, 4 August 1962. Time Continuum Second
– landed back outside Marilyn's house, just as I had left. It was impossible to recapture her and bring her back to HQ for treatment – I was in enough trouble. I went into the house to fetch Marilyn. I called for an ambulance and for her personal doctor, Dr. Greenson. In the meantime, I grabbed Marilyn and started to walk her around the house to try and keep her awake. As soon as the Schlaffer ambulance arrived, I laid her down in a small room near the front door, turned and –

Real Persons Inc. Time Frame Protected.
– walked as quickly as I could down to the library. I knew as soon as I saw the archives that something was wrong. The Earth files had shrunk back to their previous storage space. Kennedy had won the election and the war had started on schedule in August 1972.

What had happened to Marilyn? I read the reports, earlier back on that night in 1962, an ambulance man, Jack Hall, had managed to resuscitate Marilyn and had kept her alive. Dr. Greenson also arrived, but as it turns out, I had rung her psychiatrist, not her medical doctor. Between them they managed to get her to Santa Monica hospital where she recovered. Later reports by Louella Parsons, a 'gossip' columnist (whatever that is) reported Marilyn had been admitted to a rehabilitation centre. I suppose she must have slipped into the same addictive state in which I found her in 1972. What a mess. Perhaps the argument we had had led her to depression? Bewildered by the man she loved had predicted that she would turn into a hopeless addict, it had been enough to become a self-fulfilling prophesy. My human nature seized on the emptiness, the sadness for the loss of one I loved so. Guilt and a sense of terrible failure flooded through me as I gazed at the reports looking for answers. But there was no time on Earth left for a cure for my Marilyn. My lovely goddess was destined to be destroyed. I couldn't face the thought of it. I couldn't give up, not now. Someone, indeed a whole planet, needed me to do something.

As I said, I've met people who have destroyed planets, they had always seemed such magnificent, invincible specimens, powerful for all time. Now in my human frame, they repulsed me. I realised I had never once met anyone who had actually saved a planet, I didn't even know if it could be done. I had to try, I'd already committed enough serious breaches in regulations, so perhaps one more, just one more for Marilyn's sake –

Earth, Fifth Helene Drive, 4 August 1962 Time Continuum Third - Midnight.
I find her already sleeping. I look at her, child-like and so vulnerable, and I knew that I must do something. She needs more than medicinal help. I must give her the chance to know how much she is loved so –

Earth, Fifth Helene Drive, 4 August 1962, before Continuum Disrupt Third - 22.00hrs
- I call up her friends and colleagues anyone who might help her. Some I cannot reach but at least the word is out. I decide to call Dr. Greenson again as well. As I leave 12305 Fifth Helene Drive someone calls out: 'Just a moment, Senator Kennedy...'
  I ran for the garden and jumped –

Real Persons Inc. Time Frame Protected
- to the library. The Earth still dies in 1972. But something worked. Marilyn is receiving good reviews well into the 1970s as a mature and desirable actress. She appeals to a wide audience, even those too young to remember the naive and enchanting parts she played

before. Now I had only one task before me - to make sure her world continues for at least her natural life span. I started to think of it as my world too, Marilyn's and my world, and for all the humans who also loved her so much.

I noticed how my hands were shaking as I manipulated the files to give me more information. By now I was almost totally integrated into human form, with all its drawbacks and weaknesses. I was tired and troubled and time, my time, Marilyn's time, time everywhere, was running out. I knew if I were caught, I would be terminated. No question. But if I couldn't be with her, the woman I loved, then it didn't matter. I twirled the diamond ring around between my fingers, looking for inspiration in the sparking facets. There was no going back to the obligatory Procreation Remembrance Night celebrations.

My eyes blurred and my muscles ached as the hours past; flicking through reports for a glimpse of hope. There was not enough real time left on Earth to manipulate elections or persuade governments to abandon their deadly course. My own time within the company was also running out. The Company, slack as it had become with its own success, would still find out and destroy me before I could achieve anything lasting. I drove myself on, ironically calling to mind the feats of willpower of the murderous thugs I had previously regarded as heroes. Then I spotted it, a single historical incident that I might be able to manipulate to save the Earth.

The plan wasn't perfect, but it was all I had. There was no second chance. If I was found out, the Company would just reset the clock for doomsday and all would be lost. I went to the stores and after drawing the latest continuum equipment from two kiloyears in the future, I walked in to the jump room and surreptitiously adjusted the co-ordinates to –

Earth, Dallas, Texas, 22 November 1963, Time Continuum Third - Continuation
- the Texas School Book Depository. I made my way quickly and quietly to the sixth floor. I already knew what I would find there - a man holding a grudge and a gun. On such things history can be

turned. That's why a Captureman always has Damage Control looking over his shoulder of course. But not this one time, none had ever been assigned, nor would they ever be.

I looked past the back of Lee Harvey Oswald's head as he aimed the rifle towards a motorcade going slowly down a street in the midday Texas sunshine. He is here to kill Governor John Connally on a personal matter. Oswald had been discharged from the US Navy, possibly on the grounds he was sympathetic to communism. Oswald had appealed to Connally to remove his 'undesirable' tag from his Navy records, but Connally had refused. This, Oswald felt, had robbed him of any chance of decent employment in the future. He was about to settle the score. His quarrel did not concern me, but the man sitting directly behind Governor Connally in the convertible limousine did. He was President J F Kennedy.

I waited as Oswald breathed out evenly and started to squeeze the trigger. I froze him, just for a moment, as the cavalcade moved through the sights of his high-powered rifle. I released him and he squeezed the last millimetre of trigger movement as the cross hairs aligned on the President's head. He squeezed of another two shots and saw both Connally and the President hurl forward under the impact of the bullets. I think it was a few seconds before he realised he had also shot President Kennedy. The president's wife and a security guard scrabbled towards the back of the car, but I had no time to watch. I found out later that, although seriously injured, Governor Connally would survive.

Using the special equipment I had brought with me, I set the Temporal frame to create a time impervious shell. The traumatic events of the last five seconds are immutable. They are locked in an impenetrable zone. Regrettably, in all time scenarios, President Kennedy will always be assassinated by Oswald firing from the sixth floor of a building in Dallas. Any action taken to try and prevent the President from being in the car on that particular day, or Oswald being in the storeroom, would create a paradox and could not be installed. As the confused assassin rushed past me on the way out of the building, I jumped to –

Earth, Washington, 23 January 1973, Time Continuum Fourth
- a shop with a 2-D vision set. President Richard Nixon has just announced the American involvement in the Vietnam war is over. I look at the people around me. Although most Americans are sick of the war and the mounting body count, the withdrawal is a blow to a nation that had considered its self to be invincible. Nixon has shown great personal courage in negotiating with former adversaries and ending the war which would have turned into a planetary disaster. He has the makings of a truly great leader. I looked forward to returning to the library to catch up on what was sure to be his glittering political career. I decided to set another immutable time shell, just to be on the safe side. I had done what I could. I was now exhausted, a victim of my integrated human frailty. I needed to be back with my Marilyn. I missed her in a way I could never have comprehended only a few real days ago. I jump to -

Earth 5 August 1962, Time Continuum Fourth, 01:00am
- a confused scene at 12305 Fifth Helene Drive. My changes in the future could not have affected her past. What had gone wrong? I stood beside her bed on which she lay naked, curling up into the satin sheets. Had she taken the pentobarbital mixed with the Dreamatol I had given her, in Continuum First? When was I now then? I moved to towards the bedside table and-

Real Persons Inc. HQ Time Frame Protected
- I was left standing in a circle of intense blue light. With me on the pad were a bedside table and a pile of Marilyn's clothes left on the floor. As my eyes adjusted to the light, I noticed the table, it carried her medication bottles, a glass of water and a small red book. I couldn't believe it. DamCon had stepped in and bagged me and everything else within a short distance of where I had been standing in Marilyn's bedroom. They must have been desperate to be so reckless.

The Chief was sitting in a chair facing me. I quickly realised this was a set piece, obviously being recorded somewhere. I figured that

this would be as close as I ever got to a trial. The Chief spoke to me calmly and deliberately at first, as if speaking to a naughty child.

'And what the Zuk do you think you were doing?'

I was drained, sapped of all my strength and reason. I didn't know how much longer I could hold out. I rubbed my forehead as if trying to squeeze an answer out of my tired brain. How could I explain?

'I didn't want her to die! You saw her – you can understand that? The Dreamatol, it was an accident, just a stupid accident. I had to put it right.' In frustration I lashed out and kicked Marilyn's clothes from under my feet and across the floor.

The Chief was not impressed by my petulance: 'The whole damn planet dies off in ten real years, what's the difference? A simple job, it could hardly go wrong. Capture, collect, cast, and return - that was your job. But what happens?' He swung the chair to indicate the panels flickering away in the half-light behind him. 'I'll tell you. The entire temporal continuum network starts lighting up like Fusion Day. Huge, and I mean massive - gashes start ripping open through the temp fabric. And why?'

'I love her.'

'You cretin!' The Chief had decided that being calm was not the way of a warrior manager. 'The capture disc is formatted for one jump which you registered. Then, you jump again, and again, how many times? How many did you save? Register? Protect? Let me tell you. None! Not a single one! It's unbelievable!' He paused to glare at me. 'And yet, for some incomprehensible reason, you have put immutable time shells in 1963 and 1973 local time. Not even in the same place as the capture. That is way beyond your clearance level, Mister!' He turned to share the moment with his invisible audience. 'Well then, we all want to know; why? WHY? Why mess around with a world with a ten-year life span? Share your secret plan with us.'

'I saved the planet actually. It will go on for kilo years now,' I said in my human voice.

'You did what?!' the Chief exploded. I thought he would kill me right there and then.

'Marilyn brings joy. She's a goddess! I won't have her die! I won't let her die.'

'You won't? And who are you? Or have you seized power as a Time Master while no one was looking?'

'I did what was right ...'

'Listen to yourself, you idiot! Look what you have left behind.' The screen flashed out before us. 'Some-frames there was a scream and a doctor comes running, but some-frames he doesn't, some-frames an ambulance turns up to the house, some-frames it doesn't. Your collector's item dies in bed, in the hall, in the hospital and then, sometimes she doesn't die at all until decades later. Worse, certain persons are in two or more partial alternatives - time is breaking loose, ripping apart! And all you can say is, 'Actually I saved the planet'. Zuk!'

He shook his head. 'What a pity you could not save yourself.'

'I -'

'You better understand, Captureman, there is no more 'I' for you. And never was. The penalty is Death; post-dated from inception, naturally.'

He wasn't joking. The micro technicians would go right back, locate the exact male gamete that was to become half of me and vaporise it. Another one would be free to fertiliser the female ovum, but it would not be me. Not ever. Then they would go back and unpick everything I had fouled up and everything I had achieved. They would also un-save Marilyn.

The Chief regained his calm demeanour; he had progressed to the dispassionate "it had to be" management stage. Once he had passed the death sentence I suppose anything else was always going to be an anticlimax.

'Step off the pad,' the Chief ordered in a bored voice.

I feigned to move towards him, but then quickly snatched up the glass of water from the bedside cabinet and hurled it in his direction. I hit the pad hard and jumped -

Earth, Fifth Helene Drive, 4 August 1962, midnight, Time Continuum unknown

- to when I don't know. Real Persons Inc. must have tried to patch up the damage. I noticed the cabinet and the empty pill bottles came back with me. Marilyn's clothes lie on the console room floor where I kicked them, some five thousand years into the future. The glass is also missing, pieces of it §embedded in a wounded warrior-manager in another world. Marilyn is alive but she is slipping into unconsciousness. Thankfully, the Dreamatol and pentobarbital mean she is not in pain. She murmurs to me quietly in a dreamy, contented voice. She smiles and calls me 'Bobby' sometimes.

I have used the remaining power to place a time shell around us and these last few moments of her life. Immutable. They cannot take her away - and they cannot get to me whilst I am here. I destroyed the settings as a final precaution. I retain the jumper, but the range is now limited to the time shells I have set here on Earth. The last is here, in Marilyn's room, 12305, Fifth Helene Drive, on a warm night in August 1962.

For you, my sweet Marilyn, I broke into the coroner's office and stole samples from your autopsy; that will take place in a few days time. Part of you was with me as I made one last desperate jump back to my own time and world. My only remaining friend in Real Persons Inc. laboratories said there would be plenty of material to clone another Marilyn Monroe for another, perhaps more perfect world. He won't let us down. I gave him the diamond ring, he will gift it to your daughter, kiloyears in the future. There will be another Marilyn, and another for the next generation, and another. Forever. They will be as lovely as you are lovely. They will be loved, as you so needed to be loved.

I whisper to you of all these things as you drift into your endless sleep. And me, I am here now, a permanently integrated human. I will live out my real time in your world, returning to you here, in this room, at this special time. I write this down in your little red book of secrets that I took from coroner's office in a day's time. The book is now in a time loop and consequently, is lost to your world. You curl up on the bed. It will still be a few hours before Police Officer Jack Clements will be puzzled by what has happened here. He will wonder what happened to your clothes, or the glass of water that you would have used to take your tablets. He will not be the only one confused by these mysteries, which are, to my everlasting sadness, all my doing.

The fact that I am still here at your side means the Company have not been able to unravel my efforts, imperfect as they were. They will capture me if they can, but they will leave your Earth alone, of that I am sure. Perhaps your twin, or one of your many future daughters has captivated the hearts of those in power again, just as you captured mine.

I come back to see you on the same night, your last night, for more times than I can count. For all that I have lost, I have the lover's dream; eternal moments to be with you, to talk to you, to hold you, never to be parted from you. I gaze upon your face, and treasure every expression. I know every move you make by heart, but I can only guess at your dreams. They are perhaps of the few perfect days we will spend together in a future time. I see your lips move slightly and I know now this smile will be your last. It is but a faint reminder of the smile that led me to save your world and to risk my own. You turn to bury your face into the pillow, contentedly snuggling into the sheets. Gently, I move your arms so that I may lie closer to you and whisper to you of my timeless love.

The shell starts to fade. I must leave, but I will be drawn back to you again, to adore you and watch over you. Sleep now, knowing I am with you, for all time. Sleep softly little goddess.

PAST TENSE

Ochre

The findings of Drs Singer, Wyner, Klien, White and Voight have got me worried. No, they are not my medical practitioners, they are archaeologists and as archaeology rarely produces any stress-inducing reports, I think it best to explain. Sometime ago I read an article in a scientific journal. It was all about new archaeological finds in the caves at the Klasies River mouth situated close to in the World Heritage Site of the Tsitsikamma coastal park in South Africa. Their findings suggest that the caves were occupied by mankind's stone age ancestors for so many generations it brings a whole new dimension to the phrase: 'There's no place like home.'

The first inhabitants were *Homos erectus* (meaning erect man) but despite their virile sounding name, they became extinct. Occupancy then continued with *Homo sapiens* (meaning Wise Guys) and between them they kept the home, or cave, fires burning for over 130,000 years. [Author's note: To put some perspective on how long a time that really is: if a member of the tribe had partaken in the National Lottery ritual offerings, twice a week for every one of all those weeks; statistically, they would have been almost certain to win the jackpot nearly once.] So then, long time passing: and as Confucius say (yes, he really did say this one) *'Study the past if you would divine the future.'* On his advice, I studied their report of the past and now the future doesn't look so divine.

For a start the scientists discovered the Klasies river people didn't wear clothes, and that left plenty of room in the closet for skeletons – lots of them!

Now I'm not overly perturbed by the thought of nude cavemen or women in South Africa; in fact it is comforting to know their rather short lives were not wasted by being constantly pestered to take up fashion store loyalty cards. They were also fortunate in other respects. The archaeologists who dug up the cave found the detritus of their feasting habits. From the variety of fossils, it seems that the cave dwellers had the best of nature's pantry next to their homestead. With a wide variety of shellfish from the coast and plenty of meaty springbok and buffalo – the cave provides clear evidence of the planet's first ever 'Surf and Turf' dining experience. Clearly this was good news for our ancestors, because as you can imagine; they didn't have to spend all day searching for scraps of food to fend off starvation. That meant the early citizens could relax a bit; ponder the meaning of life, carve a bone; decorate the place with some ochre paintings, that kind of thing.

However, they didn't do any of those things. According to the authors of the research:

'Their remains reveal little cultural progress, even after hundreds of generations.'

Meanwhile around the Mediterranean, the primitive folk were into pottery and the prehistoric leather look whilst Peking Man was already using chopsticks and probably setting off firework displays.

Why so little progress? The archaeologists don't really have an answer apart from the observation the members of the Klasie Cave club *'were a bit dumber and slower'* than their cousins, but otherwise the scientists say they: *'were indistinguishable from us – they were modern men and women.'*

I have to disagree here, because there were no reports of empty tranquilliser bottles, discarded lottery tickets or chewing gum stuck on the cave walls. Still, even archaeologists make mistakes – remember the Piltdown man hoax?

I looked through the article searching for other slip-ups, but came away with positive proof that the Klasies River people were the genuine forebears of man today: *'there was also evidence of cooking – or at least charring by fire.'* The perfect description of a

Sunday afternoon braai in South Africa; or indeed, a barbeque just about anywhere else in the modern world.

So far then, the archaeologists have described the cave peoples as uncultured, meat-burning primitives who were not very progressive in their outlook. What else did they find out? Oh no! *'Evidence on the frontal bones (of other cave dwellers) indicates intentional defleshing by other hominids wielding a sharp stone tool.'* They go on to describe this as *'distinctive signs of hominid butchery.'*

'Surely; there must some mistake?' I hear you say, 'They already had a great choice of a la carte dining at their seafront apartment.' You would think so; eating your fellow diners for a snack between meals smacks of excessive gluttony, but I'm afraid not; there's no mistake. Forensic examination of bones shows that sharp stones leave lots of easily identifiable sub-parallel scratches on the skull bones, whereas carnivores and porcupines are less concerned about the subtleties of geometry and just munch away. The archaeologists conclude: *'there is reason to presume that cannibalism occurred.'*

Cannibalism! No only are mankind descended from cultural midgets with an IQ that would make a goldfish blush, but they also devoured their society's less acceptable members. The Klasies Cave gang: pariahs of the prehistoric world.

I'm sure some well-meaning members of other more advanced hominid groups (under the auspices of the United Natives perhaps?) tried to get them to change their ways, but they didn't succeed. We know of this collective failure because the scientists say: *'the site may represent the longest continuous occupation of one site ever known.'*

Now, understandably, none of these other primitive groups fancies forcing the brutal Klaises River mob to change their ways, let alone trying to talk things though over an informal lunch. So with force or negotiation out of the question; it appears as if the rest of the world turned to economic sanctions. Morally, it must have been difficult to justify selling blunt instruments to people who might use them to tenderise Granny after an unsuccessful hunting trip.

The sanctions seemed to have been pretty wide ranging, because as the scientists discovered, there was no evidence of new technology (and here we are talking about latter day 'state-of-the art' stuff like bone needles, clay pots, the wheel, and so on). How did the Klasies group react to the situation; regret, contrition, even reconciliation?

No. We know from the (lack of) evidence our enquiring researchers dug up; they stayed exactly the same! Not a flicker of change. They continued to eat shellfish, antelope and anybody else who, against the odds, had exceeded their 28-year old life expectancy.

This life style choice naturally impeded the cultural progress, but life went on, and on and on. The men hunted and the women gathered. It was likely that all were invited to the meat charring rituals on Sunday afternoon, even if some were never to leave afterwards.

Something about our African cousins still doesn't ring true though. There must have been someone at Klasies River Cave who wanted to be part of the world picture? Surely, there must have been local voices of dissent, even if only from vegetarians and anyone approaching their 28th birthday?

And then, buried deep in the research paper, I came across a small clue. The scientists uncovered the most chilling fact of all: *'It was much hoped that traces of painting might be found on the smoother walls of the cave'*.

Sadly, to this day, no artwork has been found, despite a local abundance of mineral red ochre. Not a solitary picture or a splash of colour, no daubed clay handprints; not even a single streak from a charcoal stick. Why not?

I have a theory that could answer the question posed by the original researchers. Klasies River people didn't decorate the place with ochre murals; not because they didn't have the materials or because they couldn't; but because they were not allowed to! Even in their uninterrupted isolation, the Klasie River elite did invent and manage to preserve a dark art that has lasted through the centuries to this day – Censorship!

As Alphonse Karr was to remark about 129,900 years later: *'The more things change, the more they stay the same.'*

Roll on the next 100 millennia!

AMBER

La Résine d'Être

Sturmbannführer Reinhard Gorman was jolted awake by the sudden braking of the Opel Blitz truck. He turned and swore at the driver.

The ashen-faced driver apologised to the officer before he clambered out of the truck. He returned to the vehicle a few minutes later looking bewildered: 'I'm sorry Sturmbannführer. I saw a man standing in the road. He was right there in front of me! I thought I'd struck him. There's no one there though.'

'You were half asleep, you idiot! You could have killed us all! It was only the sunlight flickering through the trees and you mistook the shadows for a figure. Watch where you are going in future,' Gorman commanded.

'Sorry, Sturmbannführer, it won't happen again. It is only a few kilometres to go to the camp.'

Gorman pursed his lips and looked out the window at the forest on either side of the track; the scenery had barely changed for hours. He would be pleased when they reached the remote camp.

A further fifteen minutes later the truck slowed and pulled into a turning circle. A small painted sign stating, 'Ahnenerbe Staff Field Offices' indicated he had reached his destination.

Gorman climbed out of the vehicle and stretched his back. Denied a staff car, he'd spent six hours in an army vehicle; the last three trundling along dirt roads through the forests of West Prussia, the former north of Poland. The dank and gloomy atmosphere of the forest belied the summer heat experienced elsewhere in the German occupied territories.

Stiff-legged, he walked a few paces across the forest clearing and then paused to massage some feeling back into his lower limbs. The shrapnel he'd collected in his leg at the capture of Boulogne still pained him, even three years later. He cursed; only twenty-eight years of age, but he would be condemned to walk like an old man for the rest of his life. The medal he had received for his part in driving the Allied armies back into the sea from the beaches of France seemed scant consolation at times like these.

The driver retrieved Gorman's leather holdall from the rear of the truck and brought it to his side. Gorman hoisted it over his shoulder. Trying to disguise his limp as far as possible, he walked in a brisk manner to the tented accommodation. A small group of men in civilian clothing awaited him.

A bearded man, perhaps ten years older than Gorman, approached him and held out his hand.

'Doctor Otto Kistler; SS Scientific Corps, Ahnenerbe. Head of Archaeology for the Danzig - West Prussia Reich District.'

'Sturmbannführer Gorman; formerly of the Waffen SS. I have been reassigned to the Scientific Corp SS.' He nodded curtly and handed over a document to the archaeologist.

The senior archaeologist introduced Gorman to his assistant, Heinz Engelhardt and then to the other gathered junior officers on the scientific staff: 'We received notification that you would be joining us in this forested paradise, Sturmbannführer Gorman,' Kistler smiled wanly, 'but we were not informed as to the purpose of your attachment. Perhaps you would enlighten us?'

'It has been long journey, Herr Doctor. Where are my quarters?'

'Of course! Pieter here will show you to your tent. Can I offer you some of what passes for coffee nowadays - or perhaps something a little more restorative?'

Gorman accepted the offer of an ersatz coffee and followed the orderly along the walkway of planks to where the officer's tents were pitched. He noted there was no obvious security presence other than the single sentry he had seen on duty when he had arrived in the truck. This lax state of affairs would need to change.

After a few minutes, a theatrical cough drew his attention to the presence of Dr Kistler standing outside his tent.

'Settling in all right, I trust Sturmbannführer Gorman?'

'It is adequate, thank you, Herr Doctor.' The officer signalled the scientist to sit down on the second chair: 'I was a member of the regular Wehrmacht before I joined the Waffen SS. As I will not be leading 'storm troops' anywhere for a while, my equivalent rank of 'Major' is perhaps a more appropriate title for my position here.'

Kistler shrugged and agreed; 'Major' would be used in this less formal situation.

Gorman continued: 'I have been assigned here for your security in what is still considered occupied territory.'

'I understand that is the official explanation. May I know the actual reason you are to be stationed here?'

'Your recent report on the petroglyphs on the megalith has raised considerable interest in Berlin on this site. I trust you have studied the research of Professor Walther Wüst?'

'Yes, I have met Professor Wüst at the University of Munich, more recently in his Berlin offices, of course.'

'Professor Wüst has informed Reichsführer Himmler that the findings from this area could be the key to establishing the prehistoric migration routes of the Aryans into Northern Europe. This would establish beyond doubt that peoples of a superior culture used this as a gateway through to the Baltic and into Scandinavia.'

'Ah! I see, Major Gorman. But as I mentioned in my report it is rather too early to be definitive...'

Gorman fixed the scientist with a hardened stare.

'Doctor Kistler, there is a war on. While you stroll around these woodland glades, the Americans have entered the fray. They are pushing through the deserts of North Africa. Allied bombs are dropping on the Fatherland as we speak.'

Kistler looked nonplussed.

'Doctor Kistler; need I remind you? This conflict is no longer Germany against the world. It is a question of shared ideology, of shared heritage. The Waffen SS has recruited hundreds of thousands of non-German nationals as soldiers from the occupied territories. They are dedicated soldiers, brothers in arms essential to our war effort. If the Allies establish a second front in Europe, we will need to recruit thousands more like them.'

'Yes, of course. Nevertheless, those here in Poland appear to have been; let us say, less receptive to the Party's ideology.'

'Poland no longer exists, Dr Kistler. Yet you are correct, persons of Slavic descent in the West Prussia region have proved troublesome; but it is nothing the army cannot handle.'

'I'm afraid I still don't see the connection with the Waffen SS's international appeal and our archaeological excavations here.'

'With the enemy pressing closer; Aryans, no matter what nationality; German, Austrian, Dutch, or Scandinavian; must accept the racial and historic ties that bind us. As the Führer has said; we Aryans must fight to jointly re-establish the racial purity of our shared past. It is crucial the descendants of Aryan peoples emerge as a race reborn.'

'The master race! Yes, of course,' Doctor Kistler nodded and hoped his tone had disguised his ironic intent. He paused and stroked his beard thoughtfully: 'So Professor Wüst has informed Reichsführer Himmler that our excavations reveal this site was inhabited by Aryans?'

'Precisely Doctor! The Reichsführer will announce the bonds of our ancestral blood are greater than the national boundaries which artificially divide us.'

'If I may ask again; your role with us here?'

'I am to provide security for the discoveries of significance for the Fatherland and its Aryan peoples.'

'I see and will you also be reporting back to Berlin on our progress?'

Gorman curled his lip: 'Doctor Kistler, I am no Gestapo spy. Like you, I am an officer in the Scientific Staff SS. My duty is to protect the site and its staff.'

Kistler thanked Major Gorman and made his way back to the mess tent where he took his assistant Heinz Engelhardt to one side.

'What is he doing here, Otto?' Engelhardt asked. 'He's not a scientist; he's a spy!'

'Keep your voice down!' Kistler hissed. 'He's not Gestapo. He's a professional soldier.'

'What did you think of him?'

'He's not of a scientific persuasion that's for sure. Gorman's a 'True Believer'. He's an officer; he's seen action in France. Our blonde, blue-eyed boy has accepted the Nazi Party line on the whole Aryan genetic purity thing without a second thought. He's a fanatic. He must have lapped up old Prof Wüst officer's lectures; his indoctrination on the Nordic people's superiority, dating back to prehistory.'

'So what? All SS officers attend those lectures.'

'There's worse. Apparently, Professor Wüst has regaled Reichsführer Heinrich Himmler with tales of our prehistoric discoveries; no doubt exaggerating what we have found here. From the sound of it, Major Gorman is expecting to see rock art like the wall of an Egyptian tomb when we take him out to the dig tomorrow.'

'What?' Engelhardt said startled. 'That's ridiculous! Surely the Professor has seen the photographs we sent through?'

'He's seen them. However, it's his interpretation that's got the Reichsführer in lather.'

Engelhardt held his head in hands: 'Oh God! It will be like his meddling in Schäfer's Tibet expedition. Another scientific investigation turned into a mystical adventure by a bunch of useless quacksalvers. What's he after this time?'

'Apparently Himmler is convinced the petroglpyhs are not merely a seasonal calendar, but the marks represent some occult sequence used by our ancestors for summoning supernatural agencies,' Kistler said with a heavy sigh.

'Christ! What do you think?' Engelhardt asked.

'Two things. First and foremost, scientifically, we know that's total rubbish. Secondly, we've got a lot of digging to do; or we'll be joining your cousin on the eastern front.'

-

The following morning, Gorman accompanied the two archaeologists to the site, a short walk from the Ahnenerbe encampment. They made their way along a walkway of wooden planks to a clearing in the forest where the excavations were being carried out. Kistler pointed out the megalithic structures.

Gorman had seen the photographs in the archaeologist's report but it was evident that further excavation had taken place since.

'An impressive Hünengrab. But I think, not that uncommon, Doctor Kistler. I have seen similar structures in France.'

Kistler responded. 'Yes, they are called 'Dolmen' there. We have also found comparable structures in Netherlands, Scandinavia...'

'Yes, I know. And these tombs are linked to the Aryan people: how?'

Engelhardt started to answer, 'We don't know whether...'

Kistler cut him off and continued: 'We are still researching, but as Heinz was saying, we don't know whether each site is genuinely linked to our Aryan forebears. However, such megalithic tombs were all constructed in a similar way. They show a spread throughout Scandinavia, Northern Europe, Syria, even traced back to the Indian subcontinent.'

'And this ties in with the fact that the Aryan peoples, the proto Europeans, migrated from India thousands of years ago.' Gorman said.

'It is indeed a tenet of the Ahnenerbe Institute's research, Major Gorman.' Kistler replied without directly stating his own beliefs on what the origins might be. He turned in time to see Heinz shake his head behind Gorman's back.

'So! Show me what makes this site special,' Gorman commanded.

They walked closer to the crude stone building and Kistler pointed out the petroglyphs: 'You can see from the deep weathering, these inscriptions have been here a considerable time; perhaps at the very time the stones were laid down to build this table-like structure.'

'They are rather indistinct.' Gorman noted with some disappointment.

'They were made before the advent of any metal implements and the grooves would have been painstaking carved out by repeatedly chipping away at the same spot with a harder stone.'

Kistler summoned an assistant to bring him a scroll of paper, which he laid out on the field bench for the officer to see.

Gorman pored over the scroll: 'So these inscriptions, these runes; you think they could represent some of the earliest language of the Aryans? What do they say?'

'It is a work in progress, as you can see. Part of the dolman is still buried in the forest soil and stones, but we have discovered more as we have uncovered the full structure. Unusually, there are inscriptions on the underside of the table stone which are better preserved from the elements.'

Kistler motioned his field assistant to bring a torch. Gorman walked around to what he presumed to be the entrance to the structure. Cursing under his breath about his damaged leg, he knelt down and peered inside. As Kistler had said, the carvings seemed more obvious and distinct.

'Why is this unusual?'

Engelhardt stooped down beside Gorman and then lay down, shining the torch further down. 'We believe these structures were built to form a burial chamber. The only people meant to see these runes would have been the shamans carrying out rituals, or the dead. Unlike the carving on the outer surfaces, they were not meant to be seen by everyone passing by.'

'And these are the ones which have so enthused Professor Wüst,' Gorman concluded.

'Yes, we are uncovering further petroglyphs as we excavate further...'

'You are aware that Reichsführer Himmler believes that these carvings are evidence that these people were in contact with advanced beings and utilised their powers, including time travel?'

The two archaeologists looked at each other. Kistler replied: 'Yes Major, we have heard of similar interpretations from Professor Wüst...'

'And your view?' Gorman demanded.

'The carvings may indicate a certain prescience of future events.'

Kistler could see Gorman was about to interject and so he added quickly; 'It is possible they had rituals or shamanic visions; probably under the influence of hallucinogenic plants. It might have appeared to these primitive people as if they were genuinely experiencing another world or indeed, time.'

'I note you have deciphered symbols of the swastika and the double lightning bolts of the SS as an integral part of this ancient text.'

'Yes,' Engelhardt admitted. 'That's true, but it's a bit of a stretch to call it a 'text'. The stylised S or the lightning bolt as you call it is, as far as we can tell, actually a Nordic rune representing the sun....'

'Correct!' said Gorman, 'I need not tell you that the Sanskrit swastika from which our symbol is derived, is also a representation of the sun and its life force.'

'I see you have studied the research, Major Gorman – it's rare for to find a layman with an understanding of these matters,' Kistler said.

Gorman permitted himself a tight smile. 'It is of interest to me, as I am sure it will be one day to all people of Aryan descent. And now if you please, the sequence interpreted to show time travel.'

The archaeologists walked back to the field tent with Gorman walking slowly behind inspecting the surrounds.

'Who are they?' Gorman asked, pointing out a couple of figures, a blonde haired teenage girl and an older man, standing on the edge of the forest.

'They are a man and his granddaughter, I think. They live in a small hut in the forest. I think her parents sent her out from the city to stay here. It's probably safer.'

'And you allow them to wander around here – at this site? What about security?'

'They are just gathering firewood or setting traps – they're no threat to us,' Engelhardt said with a shrug.

'They could remove valuable artefacts from the site,' Gorman asserted.

'We have found very few materials, Major Gorman. A few stone tools, some shells and one or two amber beads. There is precious little to remove.'

Gorman grunted, 'Any others living nearby?'

'There's a few other woods-people live in the area, simple peasants. We see them around from time to time. The technicians said they saw a lone man occasionally when they first set up here. They thought he might be a deranged army deserter, a dishevelled wretch. The senior assistant fired some warning shots when he got too close to the camp; but no one has reported seeing him around recently,' said Kistler.

Engelhardt said: 'Members of the expedition last summer also saw a lone wild man, virtually naked, they say. Apparently he stole some food from the camp. They spotted him loitering around the dolman – it could have been the same man. The field assistants tried to catch him, but he simply disappeared back into the forest.'

Kistler carried on in a slightly exasperated tone: 'It was an incident of no concern, but unfortunately there is a parochial legend that these megaliths are haunted or cursed. The locals and their forebears claim to have seen this figure near here over the years. Except to them, he isn't a man, but an ancient spirit guarding the megalithic tomb. The fear of the place is probably enough to make them keep their distance.'

'This forest has a bit of a mysterious atmosphere; I suppose the superstitious peasants have let their imaginations get the better of them,' Engelhardt laughed.

Gorman did not see the humour in it.

'It would have been a damn poor joke if he had turned out to be a saboteur,' he said. 'However, site security will be stepped up from now on. I will need to familiarise myself with the location of any dwellings in the vicinity. They may be used to harbour dissenting elements or the resistance.'

Kistler and Engelhardt thought it was highly unlikely, but decided against arguing with the visiting officer.

The archaeologists returned to the camp office and showed Gorman their recent findings, laid out on strips of paper. They explained the dolman was larger than had so far been exposed on surface. Soundings had shown that a further section of a Hünenbett, or barrow, still lay buried.

Gorman prodded the plans with his finger and pointed out some of the common runes with which he was familiar: man, traveller, river, gift, a god, day and year.

Kistler filled in some of the other possible meanings, before Gorman pulled a small notebook from his pocket and glanced at the pages and then back to the plan.

'The interpretation of the runes from Ahnenerbe headquarters is they refer to gifts given to an immortal or a giant, who appeared at the site in the summer, possibly for one day in the year. The rendering suggests that it is the same figure that visits the tribe over the centuries.'

'Ah, hence the Reichsführer's time traveller theory?' Kistler queried, trying to keep a straight face.

'Yes, what else?'

'We are not sure – Nordic runes so far have only been dated going back for a period of around twenty centuries. These stones are far older, dating back to the Neolithic period, at least double that time span. Doctor Engelhardt and I had been working on a more conventional theory; a representation of a celebration, possibly at the solstice or late summer with a harvest, incorporating a water ritual, feasting and fertility rites.'

Gorman straightened up and indicated that the junior assistants should leave the tented office. When they had left, he lowered his voice and said; 'And how does the carving of an aeroplane fit in with this conventional theory?'

Kistler and Engelhardt looked at each other. Kistler cleared his throat before speaking in an equally hushed tone: 'The 'aeroplane' as you call it, is clearly not a runic symbol, it appears to be an older ideogram. It may represent a mythical bird, or a large eagle…'

Gorman pulled a loose sheet of paper from his notebook and smoothed it out on the table. It was a drawing transcribed from a photograph of their dig.

'Of course, an eagle!' Gorman said sarcastically. 'And precisely what sort of eagle has a cross on its wings with a swastika on a vertical tail?'

The archaeologist remained silent.

Gorman smiled: 'I believe that it was you, Doctor Engelhardt, who made the actual discovery? You found these ancient site dwellers; stone age people from thousands of years ago, predicted the existence of our Luftwaffe?'

'I did discover the ideogram, that is true. However, I am naturally reluctant to leap to such a startling conclusion without further supporting evidence…'

'And such evidence may still remain buried at the rear of the megalith chamber? Now you see the urgency to expedite the excavation.'

'Of course, Major. But scientifically this is something that cannot be rushed. As you saw for yourself, we excavate with a hand trowel and brushes, photographing each layer, sieving the soil for traces of artefacts. This takes time…'

'Reichsführer Himmler fully recognises the importance of such a find for propaganda purposes. It will show our ancient forbearers predicted a time, looking far into the future, when the various tribes of the Aryans would once again be reunited. Reunited under the leadership of our Führer; their future secured by our superior intelligence and military might.'

Kistler stammered: 'Possibly so; but scientifically, it is a lot to infer from a single site. There is still much to do...'

Gorman glared at Kistler: 'Reichsführer Himmler is a man who does not expect to be disappointed, Doctor Kistler. I suggest you and your team carry that thought with you in your coming endeavours. Heil Hitler!' The officer turned on his heel and left the office.

Engelhardt swore under his breath. 'Now what do we do?'

'Thank God you didn't mention the ideograms we uncovered earlier this week! That would clinch it. The Nazi Party stooges would be up here with a dozen bulldozers to get to the rest of it.'

'And here I was; thinking that you were a Party member?'

'Heinz, I had to join the Party to get the senior posting to the Ahnenerbe. I justify it to myself now as a way of keep some of these other pseudo-scientist clowns from indulging their political fantasies. We must hope that Gorman's crippled leg will dissuade him from crawling further into the dolmen to see the new carvings for himself.'

'But what if the carvings do predict the future?' Engelhardt asked. 'My God! What if it's really true?'

Kistler shook his head slowly and sighed: 'I won't care; I shall have gone completely insane long before we are famous for its discovery.'

Major Gorman looked at a copy of a map that he had requisitioned from the site's surveyor. He took out his compass and headed east down the track to the next dwelling. He had visited two wooden cabins so far, crudely built structures, barely deserving of the term 'house'. The huts were occupied by an elderly couple, and in another, by an old woman living on her own. The locals either spoke no German, or pretended not to understand; so even the simplest of questions was met with blank stares. He thought about going back to the camp and requisitioning one of the Polish labourers to act as an interpreter. Yet, his leg was sore from the walk and he didn't wish to return to camp and then retrace his steps. He decided to proceed to the next cabin.

As Gorman approached the cabin, he saw a blonde girl carrying a bucket of water. He recognised her as the teenage girl he had seen the day before at the site. She looked up and saw him and stopped, uncertain as to what to do. She called out and an older man came shuffling out from the cabin.

Gorman walked briskly up to the couple and nodded curtly to the man. He asked if they spoke German. The old man shook his head, but to his surprise the girl said: 'A little.'

The officer asked his questions and he heard enough from the girl to gather they had not seen any strangers and they lived alone here. She said they had lived in a village near Gdansk, but she had moved here 'out of the trouble'. She insisted that she was eighteen years old, but Gorman judged her to be younger. He also understood she was tired with the hard-working, peasant life and she missed living in the town.

Gorman liked the look of her. Unlike her grandfather, who was of a coarse and rustic Slavic appearance, the girl was decidedly more Aryan-looking. Pale skin, blue eyed with plaited blonde hair. Gorman knew there were fair-skinned Poles living in the North; but she was almost classically Nordic in appearance. Her simple brown skirt, an embroidered white, open necked blouse and amber bead necklace, would not have looked out of place in rural Scandinavia.

The grandfather moved to go back into the cabin and he beckoned her to follow him; away from the German officer. She seemed reluctant to go and then pointed shyly to the wound medal pinned to his uniform.

He shrugged carelessly and said he had won it in the battle for France.

'In Paris?' she had asked, agog.

Gorman implied that he had won the medal during the fall of the French capital. It sounded more romantic than being nearly blown to pieces trying to reach some god-forsaken beach.

She was clearly impressed: 'I want to visit Paris,' she said. 'It must be wonderful.'

Gorman found himself thinking he would like to be the one to take her there. He reigned in his thoughts as heard her grandfather call out: 'Agata!' to the girl again.

The girl reluctantly followed the voice, but as she reached the shabby wooden door, she turned and gave a secretive wave to the officer.

Gorman started to raise his hand in acknowledgement before he remembered with embarrassment he should have concluded the meeting with salute to the Führer. He shook his head and then retraced his steps; back to the archaeologists' camp.

-

In order to distract Gorman's attention from the latest revelations from the dig, Engelhardt had laid out a few of the artefacts which had been recovered from the site for his inspection. He showed him the hand stone tools.

'We think these tools were used to carve the inscriptions. These were probably used as a crude hammer.' He picked up one to show Gorman who hefted it in his hand.

'It's too small to grip properly in a man's hand,' he remarked. 'Were these people midgets?'

'The people may have been smaller, Major, but what we have are the broken remains of the hammer stones. When the stones broke, they simply discarded them on site.'

Gorman rubbed his jaw in thought. 'Each design must have taken much work – clearly whoever did this attached great importance to the symbols.'

Engelhardt agreed, but wanted to distract the Major from asking too much about the symbols. 'We found these pottery shards and pieces of shells as well, though nothing spectacular. And these; a few amber beads. As you can see they have a hole drilled through them so that they could have been worn as a necklace.'

'I saw the girl who lives in the cabin today. She wears such a necklace, the beads look almost the same.'

'Quite possibly. This kind of amber has been found at Neolithic sites across Europe. It washes up around the seashores of the Baltic today. This site is close to the coast; the stones have probably come from there.'

Gorman held the bead in his hand: 'Curious to think this orange stone has been valued in this area for nearly five millennia. I read the Ancient Greeks believed it had therapeutic properties.'

'Yes, Major Gorman, that is so. Local folklore also claims it is a protector against evil as well as disease,' Engelhardt commented. 'It seems you have studied much.'

'I had plenty of time to read during my convalescence. It seemed prudent to use the time to good advantage.' Still holding the amber bead, he paused for a moment, 'The girl; what do you know of her?'

Engelhardt looked confused. 'Who? The blonde Polish girl? I know nothing of her. I've only seen her when she has visited the camp on rare occasions …'

'What was the purpose of her visit?'

'I believe that she wished to swap home-made goat's cheese for some of our canned provisions.'

'I remind you, Dr Engelhardt, the provisions are the exclusive property of the Scientific Corps SS. Nevertheless, were goods exchanged?'

Even though Engelhardt knew full well they were, and on more than one occasion; he was suspicious of Gorman's line of questioning. He referred the Major to the camp's Quartermaster for an answer.

Gorman responded slowly as if talking to a child: 'You do realise, Herr Doctor, the ease with which the officers could have been poisoned by such a reckless action? The whole mission could have been aborted for the sake of a slice of goat's cheese? Unbelievable!'

Engelhardt felt himself beginning to sweat; not just from the July heat. The team had been posted to this remote spot for two field seasons now; left virtually to their own devices. They had avoided the military conflict, the political dogma, and a lot of the petty party bureaucracy. Looking at Gorman's red-flushed face, it was clear those days were over. He started to regret his discovery of the flying ideogram; whatever it really represented.

Towards the end of July, the Royal Air Force had broken through the Luftwaffe defences and fire bombed the city of Hamburg. In the event the Allies decided to carry out raids on Berlin, the Ahnenerbe Institute made the decision to move its valuable archives and staff headquarters to a rural area. The senior archaeological staff members were ordered back to Berlin from the field site to assist in the relocation of the mountains of materials and documents. Gorman's plans to keep a closer eye on the forest's local inhabitants, including the pretty young woman, had been frustrated.

After a week it was clear Gorman's services were not essential to the relocation. He made the case to his senior officer that, in the national interest, he needed to go back to West Prussia and resume his security duties there. Another tedious truck journey took him back through the forest to the Ahnenerbe site operations. There appeared to be no other senior staff remaining at the camp and so Gorman decided to patrol the wider perimeter that would take him past the humble dwelling the girl Agata shared with the old man.

It was late afternoon when Gorman approached the cabin. There was a wisp of smoke coming from the chimney but no sign of the occupants. Consciously trying to minimise his limp, he strode up to the entrance and knocked firmly on the door.

Agata answered and broke into a shy smile when she saw the handsome officer standing by her doorstep. She told Gorman her grandfather was out hunting, but that she expected he would be back shortly.

Gorman ducked his head and entered the cabin. The darkened interior was neat, but it contained only the most rudimentary furnishings. The girl explained in halting German they did not have much; but she could offer him some black bread and cheese if he was hungry. Although Gorman was not hungry, he decided to accept the offer. He also gained the distinct impression that Agata was flirting with him. And why not? This attractive young girl was probably starved of young male company in this wilderness.

Agata brought Gorman the food on a wooden platter. As she leant forward, the amber necklace swung free from the open neck of her blouse. The amber beads glowed as they reflected the light from the small fire. Gorman asked her where the necklace had come from.

'I found them,' she said. 'I saw some beads in the soil by a rabbit hole; near the big stones. I put them on a string.'

She mimed threading the stones onto a cord and putting it around her neck. 'Do you like it?' she asked with a flirtatious smile.

Gorman arrogantly reached out for the necklace to examine it more closely, his hand touching the top of her breast as she straightened up.

'Let me see,' he commanded.

Startled, Agata started to back away, but Gorman clenched the necklace. Aroused, he pulled the girl toward him. As she struggled to break away from his grasp, he pushed his mouth down on to hers.

The girl cried out, but he was not to be dissuaded: he backed away enough to strike her across the face: 'Playing hard to get, eh?' Gorman laughed.

He grabbed her necklace again and tightened it against her throat. Using his body, he pushed her up against the table, overpowering her; lifting her skirt with his other hand.

The cabin door flew open and the old man barged in. Taking in the scene; he dropped the two dead rabbits he had been carrying, and brought his hunting gun to bear on Gorman. Enraged, he yelled at Gorman in Polish.

Gorman wheeled round, half dragging the girl in front of him. Unseen by the old man, he freed his Walther P38 from its holster and fired three shots in to the man's chest.

The old man lurched forward, collapsing with a cry onto the floor.

Gorman turned and struck the girl again hard with the back of his gun hand. He pushed her back, his hands closing around her throat to choke off her hysterical screaming.

-

Gorman's eyes scanned the woods. He had the eerie sensation he was being watched, but there was no one else to be seen. He looked on as flames engulfed the wooden cabin. The bodies of the man and the girl would be wholly consumed by the time the hut had burnt to the ground. The evidence of his crimes would be turned to ash within minutes. He waited a while, turning over the girl's amber necklace in his pocket; it was the only thing worth saving from the miserable dwelling. Satisfied that the fire would do the rest, he turned on his heel and walked briskly back to the camp.

It was early evening by the time he returned. He saw Kistler and Engelhardt had also returned to the site. He walked over to the tent that served as the main office.

'Good evening, Major! I heard from my assistants that you returned here a few days before us.'

Gorman shook his head: 'No, your informant is mistaken. I only arrived yesterday. Look at this.'

Gorman produced the necklace and laid it on the table. He told them he had found it on one of the paths he had followed through the forest, pointing out the snapped cord. He mentioned he thought it looked very similar to the few beads that Doctor Engelhardt had shown him earlier.

Engelhardt looked at them carefully and examined them under a magnifying glass. He came to the conclusion that the beads were indeed very similar, and had been manufactured in the same way.

Gorman pointed to the necklace. 'Fossilised insects have been found trapped in amber and preserved for millions of years, isn't that so?'

Kistler agreed it was the case.

'But what of these?' Gorman pointed to the larger piece in the centre of the string of beads.

Kistler picked up a lens: 'Fibres; it could possibly be animal hair which has been trapped in the resin. It's very rare, but I have heard of such specimens before.'

'That's what I thought. What sort of animal?' Gorman had his own theory, 'A wolf perhaps?'

Kistler shook his head. 'I'm sorry to disappoint you, Major Gorman, but no, not a wolf. Wolves are a recent evolutionary phenomena; they came into the world long after this amber was formed.'

'What then; some other sort of predator?'

'I don't know, I'm not a palaeontologist. I believe there was a carnivore called a bear-dog that might have been around at the same time as the amber formed. They are extinct now, of course. Its more likely the hair might come from some kind of vermin; the ancestors of the squirrel or rat perhaps. They would likely have made their home in trees during the Eocene period.'

Gorman was disappointed. He had imagined he held the remains of some powerful beast that had dominated these forests eons before. The idea these silvery threads belonged to some low life vermin held no such appeal. He asked if the archaeologist wanted them for their collection, but they declined. Without knowing where they had come from it made them of little scientific value.

'Didn't you say the young Polish girl had such a necklace? Perhaps she dropped it when she was going through the forest? You could return it to her; she might be grateful!' Kistler said with a sly wink.

The major winced at the mention of the girl: 'I am an officer of the SS, not a Lost Property clerk!' Gorman said curtly. Gathering the broken necklace, he walked back to his quarters leaving the archaeologists smirking behind his back.

Not wishing to be drawn into conversation about the Polish girl or the fate of their cabin, Gorman dined alone in his tent. He sat for a while trying to determine the way to galvanise the archaeologists to speed up their investigations. Hamburg had been attacked, Berlin would surely be next, and even this precious site would be within range of the Allied bombers. He started to write a letter to his mother, but memories of what he had done to the peasant couple returned to disrupt his train of thought. He turned in early for the night.

Plagued by nightmares of the ghastly dead emerging from sacred stone monuments or burning pyres, Gorman slept fitfully. It was barely dawn when he got up, washed away his night sweats and then dressed. He thought to finish the letter to his mother, but was unable to find it, only the blank sheets of paper on his writing pad. Puzzled, he emerged from the tent and walked around the camp where everyone else still slept. On impulse he decided to go back to forest, to check if the cabin had been completely destroyed. He half expected to be able to smell the smoke and charred remains as he approached the area, but he could detect nothing. Perhaps the wind was in the wrong direction.

When he emerged into the clearing, nothing could have prepared him for the sight which confronted him. The wooden cabin was perfectly intact. There wasn't so much as a scorch mark and the only smoke to be seen was a thin wisp emanating from the chimney. He was so shocked that he staggered back slightly leaning against a tree.

His astonishment was compounded when moments later he saw the old man leave the cottage carrying his gun, and then the Polish girl coming out to speak to her grandfather before he headed off to the other side of the forest clearing.

Gorman carefully eased his way behind the tree and observed the cottage from behind its cover. What the hell was going on? Had he dreamt the whole episode; the rape, the killings and the burning down the cottage? The girl came out of the cottage again, sweeping the front with a broom. He could see her clearly, even the amber necklace she wore around her neck.

He felt in his trouser pocket, but the amber beads were not there. He was sure he had brought them with him; that was to be his cover story. He had intended to say he'd had a change of heart and gone back to deliver the necklace when he was in the area as part of his patrol. That is when he had come across the tragic scene of the smouldering remains of their cottage.

Gorman felt hot and lightheaded. He sat down at the base of the tree and loosened his tunic. Occasionally he would sneak a furtive glance over his shoulder and see the cottage was still standing. It was as if yesterday had never happened.

Checking around to see he was alone, Gorman got to his feet. He was thirsty and he knew he was not far from a small river. He would head in that direction and try to cool off for a while. When he reached the river, he scooped up some water to drink before he rested awhile. A thought occurred to him; he had experienced a terrible nightmare. He concluded the little Polish bitch must have drugged the cheese she had given him, the same suspicions he had shared with Engelhardt.

Gorman realised it must be late in the afternoon and got back to his feet. He walked back to the girl's cabin. Wait until he got hold of her, he'd teach her to play games with an officer of the SS!

As he approached the cottage – he heard three shots ring out and a girl screaming. Gorman ducked for cover, a terrible feeling of déjà vu making his skin crawl. Gorman turned and hurried to find cover of the trees. The screaming stopped. Perhaps ten minutes later, a figure emerged from the doorway, a tall man dressed in an SS uniform. The figure looked around and then as smoke emerged from the building, he limped to the opposite edge of the clearing. He stayed there intent on watching the cabin which was quickly consumed in the inferno.

Gorman sank to his knees on the mossy forest floor and shuddered uncontrollably. 'Christ!' he repeated and swore over and over again until even those words failed him. He had witnessed the impossible; he had seen himself re enact what he had done the day before. No – that was insane! He tried to be rational; he must still be suffering from the effects of some poison and was having hallucinations. He needed to rest.

Gorman awoke in the same spot early in the morning. He stretched his arms and aching leg and then barely able to bear the suspense, he crawled forward, only to see the cottage standing as it had before. Gorman thought he must be crazy. Surely, he would have been missed at the Ahnenerbe camp, the others must have noticed his absence. He must get back and take an antidote for what was afflicting him.

When he arrived at the camp he searched for the senior officers, either Kistler or Engelhardt. They were nowhere to be seen. He spotted Hans the orderly and asked where they were. The orderly looked confused and he told Gorman that they were still in Berlin, supervising the evacuation. Hadn't Major Gorman travelled with them himself?

Gorman took a deep breath and pointed out to the orderly that it was obvious that he had returned from Berlin, and yesterday, so had Kistler and Engelhardt. Where were the assistants?

Eventually, one of the junior staff arrived, but he told Gorman the same story as the orderly.

'Are you telling me that the doctors have had to return to Berlin?'

The assistant shook his head. 'I am sorry Major Gorman; I did not know that they had arrived here and then returned. No one told me; I was only expecting them tomorrow.'

Gorman muttered 'idiot' under his breath and returned to his tent.

The orderly turned to his colleague with a shrug and silently mimed taking a drink, implying Major Gorman had been at the schnapps a little early this evening.

Gorman awoke with the sunlight filtering under his eyelids. He sat up, not in a cot in his tent as he had expected, but lying on a bed of pine needles.

'Fuck!' he said aloud and lurched to his feet. His head throbbed as if he had a monstrous hangover. He tried to remember what had happened. After speaking to the dumb orderly, he had gone back to his tent to write a letter to his mother. He'd had a few Schnapps, but surely not so much? Had he gone blundering around outside the camp and got lost? Where the hell was he? He fumbled in the breast pocket of his uniform, but couldn't find the map of the area. He cursed again and headed off in the direction of where he thought the camp might be.

After what seemed several hours of painful walking he came across a dirt road. He sat down on a tree stump wondering which direction he should take. How had he got so lost? It would be better to walk along the road he decided, far easier than stumbling over the boggy ground or scrambling over moss-covered, rotting logs. He watched as shafts of evening sunlight shifted between the standing trees.

He heard a truck coming down the road. Getting to his feet gingerly, he limped to the side of the road and could see it was an Opel army truck – likely it was heading to the archaeological field camp. As it drew closer, he stepped out to wave it down. It seemed as if the driver only saw him at the last moment and Gorman was forced to jump backwards and tumbled into the roadside ditch. Everything turned black.

Gorman woke again to the sounds of voices. He looked around and realised he was not in the ditch which was the last he remembered. Recovering his senses, he listened more carefully and realised the voices were not speaking German. Slowly, he rolled over on to his front to survey the scene. He found himself looking at the excavation site at the dolman megaliths. He could see from the yellow diamonds sewn onto the men's overalls that it was the Polish forced labourers who were shouting to each other; there was no danger here. He stood up and instinctively brushed himself down. He was shocked to see the bedraggled state of his normally immaculate uniform; it was filthy. He was covered in forest debris and splashes of mud. He shook his head to clear his thoughts. He would have to explain away his appearance. He concocted the story that he had been ambushed by resistance fighters, then escaped and found his way back to the camp by travelling at night – or something like that; to explain his absence. Gorman straightened his uniform as best he could and started to walk towards the camp.

As soon as they saw him, the labourers started shouting and pointing at him; one even threw a rock at him. Stunned, Gorman stood there and tried to call out, but his voice, unused for what seemed like days, seemed to die in his dry throat.

A junior assistant Gorman recognised as the youth he had spoken to few days ago rushed forward and shouted at him to leave. He then pulled out his pistol and fired shots in his general direction.

Gorman turned and ran, crashing back into the forest as fast as he could. What was the lunatic doing? The assistant could have killed him; had he been drinking? Surely he must have recognised him, even in his dishevelled state. Gorman slid down a small embankment and hid out of sight of his pursuers, cowering beneath a tangle of overhanging roots.

As he tried to catch his breath, a thought came to him. The word 'dishevelled' reminded him of something the archaeologists had mentioned. Didn't Engelhardt mention a vagrant who had been seen around the dig? Had they mistaken him for that wretch and then fired shots to warn him away? He decided he would hole up where he was, he didn't want some maniac to fire off any more shots. He would wait until it was nearly dark and then follow the track back to camp. Once there he could use the ablutions and change into a clean uniform. He chuckled; he'd make sure his boots were in especially good condition, because he was going to use them to kick the idiot assistant's arse around the camp and back.

-

Gorman didn't make it back to the camp. In his exhausted state, he had sat down for a short rest and then fallen asleep, only waking with the dawn. Shit! He stretched out and stood up. What the ..?

He looked down at his uniform. Yesterday it had been in a poor state, but now... He looked at it, aghast. The uniform of which he was so proud was in tatters, pieces missing, his medals lost. The cloth rags were barely held together by his leather belt, but his holster and pistol were both missing.

He heard noises and peered through the bushes in that direction. He could barely comprehend what he saw. The excavations around the dolmen were no longer there, it looked as if all the soil had been back filled, the megalith restored to what it must have looked like when it was first investigated. He slumped back and cradled his head in his hands; what was happening to him? He'd been away from camp for what seemed like days. Yet he wasn't hungry and he'd grown no more than overnight stubble on his chin. He was obviously the victim of some powerful hallucinogenic drug that was bending his mind. He needed to put an end to it now, needed to get medical attention. He waited until one of the people, possibly a surveyor, was close to his position and then leapt out and ran towards him shouting out in German.

The man was startled and retreated, but Gorman caught up with him and grabbed at his clothes, shouting out his name, begging for help. The man tried to run away but Gorman launched himself at him again, bringing him to the ground. His spittle flying, he yelled and begged incoherently for the man to aid him. The surveyor was terrified and tried to fend him off. Eventually others arrived and pulled Gorman away then chased him away with sticks.

'You fools; I'm Sturmbannführer Gorman of the SS! I need help! What the fuck is the matter with you people? Is this your idea of a prank? I command you to assist me, you morons!' Gorman raved on, 'Reichsführer Himmler himself will hear of your subordination! You'll pay dearly for this; that I promise you!'

No longer able to bear the beating and kicks he received from group, Gorman fled back to the safety of the forest. He didn't stop running until his aching legs would carry him no further. He was in sight of a log cabin and paused to check out the situation. To his astonishment, a young blonde girl walked out the door followed by an older man.

The girl looked all too familiar, but it couldn't be the Polish girl he had… had met? She was barely a teenager, perhaps it was her younger sister? The old man set off, but the girl hesitated and looked over in his direction. The man called the girl to follow him, 'Agata!'

Gorman crouched down out of view. It couldn't be! The cabin was still standing, the man and girl alive, but looking younger.

A terrible realisation dawned on him. He wasn't sure how, but since he had killed the couple and taken the amber necklace, he had been going backwards through time. First a day at a time, then another, then a month and now; could it be a year? While he was awake during the day, he lived his life going forward; but at night, the clock was set back and he descended into the past.

He tried to recall his actions over the last few days. It would explain the reaction of the assistants back at the camp– Kistler and Engelhardt had not gone back to Berlin at all, they had yet to return. And then there was the army truck; he stepped out in front of the very vehicle which had first bought him to this accursed place. The driver had seen him, and braked, but not found any body; his body, because he'd slipped further back in time when he'd been knocked unconscious.

Gorman slumped forward in despair. He realised it was his self in an earlier time that had been the mysterious wild man of the woods, the one the archaeologists had described at the excavation site. They had also said something about a wild man or spirit who haunted the site and was part of the local legend. The locals were said to have spotted his appearances over the years: just how long far would he have to travel back in time? My God! He was a living 'Peter Klaus the Goatherd' from the folk tale. Perhaps he too would sleep for decades, but would only wake further in the past, not in the future.

He looked at the rags he was wearing – barely threads now. He had travelled back in time to a point before the uniform had been made, it would disappear completely. He was glad it was still in the summer; the air was warm. If he slipped back and re-emerged naked in some distant winter he would perish with the cold. Gorman tried to marshal his thoughts but was soon overcome with shock and fatigue. Fearing the next day, he tried to fight off the desire to sleep, but eventually he succumbed.

Each time Gorman survived through the night, he awoke after years, even decades, had retreated. He was hurtling at an ever-increasing rate into the past. Nothing survived with him on his journey through time.

The blonde girl who stayed in cabin had yet to arrive, he saw the grandfather turn into a younger man, who lived with his wife in the new looking log cabin. Then too, the cabin disappeared in the time before it was built. The forest regained the footing it had before the peasants had cleared the ground. There came the day when there were no more people to be seen.

The one constant in the ever-changing landscape of the forest was the dolman megalith, now partially concealed in moss and forest debris. Gorman had given up trying to make himself a shelter. A bed of leaves and branches, cut by a crudely fashioned stone with a broken edge, simply reverted back to their growing hosts. Any clay pot or stone axe he succeeded in fashioning before twilight had long since reverted back to its earlier natural state; each waking day he would start the process again. Gorman was naked and alone.

Physically, Gorman never seemed to change, his hair and stubble grew no further, he didn't become more youthful. Cuts or bruises he had sustained disappeared the next time he regained consciousness. Thankfully the shrapnel in his leg had also vanished, presumably the shell had yet to be made in future; the metal yet to be forged. He could walk without a limp again. He found that he wanted to drink water during the hot summer days, but he rarely felt hungry. Even without hunger to drive him, he would ambush hares or catch fish in the nearby river using a sharpened stick as a spear. He became skilled at making a fire for cooking and on one occasion, driving away marauding wolves.

His existence, incredible as it had once seemed to him, gradually became a routine. He had become practiced at selecting a suitable stone from the riverbed, breaking it against other rocks until he had a clean sharp edge. He would then set about cutting a straight branch and sharpening one end with the stone tool. The litter on the forest floor was always dry and with practice he perfected primitive techniques to start a fire. A walk, a cooling dip in the river, or hunting his small prey filled out the day. He would leave time in the late afternoon to excavate a passage into a part of the dolman structure and reset his fire near its entrance. He would take a sturdy sharpened stick and would some times drag brushwood into the opening if he feared wolves were prowling in the vicinity. He would lie there looking at the runes and ideograms in the fading light as it moved through the chinks in the stonework. He had plenty of time to think why this should be happening to him.

He lost all track of the days he had spent there and could only guess at what time had retreated whilst he slept. He estimating the time on one occasion by noting the size of a huge conifer near the dolman, then the next time he awoke, it was a mere sapling. His journey through time was accelerating, the tree would have taken many decades, even a couple of centuries, to reach the girth as he had seen it, yet all that time had passed in one of his nights.

One morning he awakened to a different sound. Human voices. He looked out through the gaps in the stonework and saw what appeared to be an old man, two women and a child. Gorman pushed his way out from under the table stone and emerged into the daylight. The group dropped to their knees and then fell, prostrate on the ground before him. Gorman tried to speak but only managed to croak out a few words before he realised these savages couldn't possibly understand what he was saying. He looked at the people before him. They were in a bad way. Half starved, scarred, filthy, with lice crawling in their hair and ragged clothes. Surely these couldn't be the proud progenitors of the Aryan race?

Gorman motioned them to follow him. He went through his usual daily routine. They sat in silence on the riverbank as he speared fish and made a fire to cook his catch. Not hungry himself, he shared the food amongst them. They were clearly ravenous, even eating the fish heads that Gorman would have discarded. They spent the day together, huddling around a fire as it grew dark. The older woman who appeared incredibly ancient (but was probably only in her late thirties Gorman guessed) gave him a gift, an amber bead necklace. Gorman's heart pounded as he recognised the larger piece – the amber encapsulated the strands of animal hair that he had shown Engelhardt, thousands of years in the future. Otherwise naked, he placed the crude decoration around his neck.

Gorman went to sleep that night wondering if his good deeds had earned him some kind of reprieve – was it his destiny to save the last remnants of the Aryans – who would go on and reunite with other members of the tribe? Would he be catapulted on to the future? The following morning revealed the answer – no.

There was no sign of the travellers and of course, the amber necklace had disappeared. Gorman laughed sardonically to think of the mystery it would be to them when they woke up; the tall blonde god had disappeared into the dolmen at night and the next morning – he was gone! Magic indeed!

A thought struck Gorman; what was it the archaeologists had said? A supernatural being had reappeared at the dolmen in the summer. He would go on appearing to the tribes people as he descended further back into the past – that must be how the legend started. At some point, because he would not appear every summer, the Aryans would carve the runes on the tomb to pass the message on to future generations.

As the time passed, Gorman appeared several times before the tribal peoples. Each occasion was marked with a sense of wonder as the gathering waited to see the apparent resurrection of their god. There were celebrations in his honour; rituals held on the banks of the river and around fires within the forest clearing. He was given the amber necklace and offered tributes of animal skins, food, fermented berries and yes, women too. As the festival proceedings drew to a close, an exhausted Gorman would retreat inside the dolmen, usually with a young female for company. He laughed as he imagined the gathering's amazement that, in the dawn of their next day, he would have vanished into thin air.

He came to believe that this was the reason he had been chosen. His periodic bouts of breeding would mean his genetics would be passed on to improve the racial quality of these primitive people. The idea appealed to his ego, but when would it end?

He noticed in the following days the megalith was becoming more exposed, he could crawl deeper inside, seeing by the light that filtered through the gaps in the stone or from one of his handmade torches. What he saw, or rather didn't see, shocked him. The runes on the outside had become less (presumably because they were embellished by later generations as his legend grew) but his favourite, the Luftwaffe plane with its insignia, had disappeared from inside the megalith. The rock wall between several of the other runes was completely smooth.

If there were no ideogram of Luftwaffe bomber, the swastikas, or the SS markings then the archaeological dig would have been just another site in the dozens that the Ahnenerbe had excavated. He would not have been sent on Reichsführer Himmler's orders: the whole chain of events would collapse, and he would not be there to improve the Neolithic breeding stock for the future benefit of mankind.

Gorman scrabbled out of the megalith and for once he was pleased to see this time there was no summer gathering of the Aryan clans. He rushed down to the river and selected various stones, striking them against each other until he had shards of the right size.

He returned to the Dolman and using wet clay as a guide he marked out the outline of a large aeroplane as best he could manage. Satisfied with his efforts, he hammered repeatedly on the clay line with his stone tools, eventually chipping out the entire shape of his attempt at a Junkers 88 bomber. The work was hot and exhausting in the cramped confines of the stone tomb, but he managed to complete the picture before lying down and falling asleep.

The next day, his carving of the aircraft had disappeared. Gorman was distraught; until it dawned on him the carving was firmly embedded in the dolman's future. Gorman puzzled over the phenomenon. He knew the archaeologists were uncovering more as they excavated the rear of the tomb structure. He had the feeling that Kistler and Engelhardt were holding something back from him. Actually, it didn't matter that he didn't know what those carvings were. In the future, they would discover whatever petroglyphs Gorman chose to carve.

Of course! That was it – this was his real reason for being, his profound mission. It was not breeding with the early people, but to leave a message for the future to inspire others to Hitler's ideal of a pure and unified Europe. Gorman set off for the river, which seemed closer than his previous excursions. He realised that the river must slowly change its course over an extended period of time.

And so Gorman's strange life continued in days of perpetual summer. On the occasions when the primitives and their shamans were not at the site to witness the arrival of their god from the tomb, Gorman spent his time hacking away at the chamber, using his recollections to carve a profile of the new Panther tank, or the distinctive swastika designs and the lightening bolts of the Waffen SS.

By the time the infill of the tomb had receded to reveal the original extent of the chamber, Gorman was well satisfied with his efforts. Although he could no longer see them carved on the rock - they had each been consigned to the future - the series of ideograms would eventually be interpreted to showing the all-conquering future of the Aryan race. He laughed out loud as he contemplated carving; '*Küss mein Arsch, Kistler*!' in the remaining space, but realised that would be enough to undo all his hard work. He contented himself with a simple 'HH' for 'Heil Hitler!' He was done.

The next day, Gorman woke with a start and a terrible stench filling his nostrils. For the first time, the tomb was fully enclosed and filled with animal skins, primitive weapons and pottery. Underneath him lay a decaying corpse of a man, a man wearing a large amber necklace on a leather cord.

Gorman turned around and tried to get out of the tomb, but could not shift the large rock slab blocking his exit. He thought he could hear voices and he yelled and screamed out until he had drawn a crowd around the megalith. After what seemed hours, the gathering had made its decision. A huge branch was thrust between the stones and with several men pushing it, they levered the stone away.

Gorman ducked back into the tomb, and seized the amber necklace from the corpse and put it around his own neck. As the stone fell aside, Gorman emerged naked, blinking in the strong sunlight. There were cries and gasps of amazement from the crowd. Gorman looked at them, or rather over their heads; they were shorter than he was. The murmur of voices turned to chants. Several men advanced menacingly towards him, holding their spears at the ready.

So this is how it would end, Gorman thought. He felt strangely calm. He had no regrets. He had completed his mission; no one could have done more for the Fatherland, throughout the past, present or future. He would die a soldier's death, his place in Valhalla assured.

Gorman stood his ground, raised his arms skywards and failing to come up with any suitable words, he belted out a chorus of the German national anthem as loud as he could.

The crowd were stunned into silence, the spear-carriers retreated a few paces. Eventually an old crone stepped forward from the throng and cautiously approached him. She reached out and touched his arm, then reached up and pointed to the necklace before standing up as tall as she could to stroke his blonde hair with wizened hands. She cackled out a command and someone brought forth an old wolf skin that he wrapped around his waist. Food and drink followed and then Gorman knew; this is how his legend had started. The dolmen had been built to house the body of someone of great importance to the tribe, a warrior chief or high priest. He had emerged from the tomb, a re incarnation, a spirit of their former leader.

If this was the beginning, what was beyond that, Gorman wondered. Determined to make the most of what might be his last day, he signalled to a young woman; picking out the least malnourished, smelly and lice-ridden female of the group. He led her a short distance to river. The rest of the tribe followed behind. On reaching the river, he undid the wolf skin loin cloth, snatched up the girl and jumped into the shallow water, ducking them both under the surface. The girl struggled, but Gorman used his strength to hold her with one hand and used the opportunity to scrub as much grime from her body as possible; laughing loudly as he did so.

The tribe came to realise this was a game of sorts. The strange blonde spirit did not intend to sacrifice the girl by drowning her in his watery kingdom. They joined in the laughter; although they edged away from the riverbank in case he should choose them next.

Gorman climbed out of the river, dragging the woman behind him. Excited by her naked and almost clean body, he pushed the woman down on the wolf skin fur. Encouraged by lusty cheers from the gathering, he wasted no time in mating with her. He would do so again several times before the day's festivities ran their course.

It was too good to last. Gorman opened his eyes and saw the dolman was no longer there. He had gone back to a time before it was built, possibly before humans had ever visited this area. The sight of a single large block of stone, which might in the future form one of the megalith structures, only increased his despondency. The amber beads that had been his companion over the millennia were also missing. They were lying on the Baltic seashore waiting for some Neolithic traveller to pick them up and make them into a decoration fit for a chief or a god.

So what now was his purpose – where would it end? He walked to the river and drank a little water. Miserable and dejected, he trudged back to the large stone and made himself a crude bower of branches and leaves at its side, then lay down to sleep.

Gorman's days passed, he lost count of how many. He wondered if he would eventually emerge one day in the time of the dinosaurs, or before the earth had cooled and he would be consumed in a lake of molten rock. For the first time he could remember he was truly afraid and prayed for a better day tomorrow.

There had been hot days with dry riverbeds, days when the forest was covered in volcanic ash, other days during the glaciation periods were so cold that he collapsed and succumbed to hypothermia within minutes, only to wake up again in a more moderate climate. The landscape, the vegetation changed around him. Over millions of years; only he stayed the same, an immortal being heading rapidly in the wrong direction.

-

He didn't know where he was. Even the large rock he had been used to seeing every morning had disappeared. The environment had changed repeatedly, strange trees and flowers abounded one day and disappeared again the next. Although Gorman's physical strength was renewed each time he awoke, he was mentally exhausted. Each day was another burden placed on his psyche. He had given up on his rituals of bathing, making a fire, or a spear, there seemed no point, nothing more to accomplish. He sought out a suitable spot and curled into a ball, occasionally rocking back and forth.

Gorman heard a noise, a chattering sound. He looked around and saw two small furry mammals bounding around in the branches of the odd-looking conifers surrounding him. They might be the very creatures whose hair had become trapped in the plentiful sticky resin that oozed from every trunk. As the archaeologists had supposed, they appeared to be primitive mammals, mere vermin. Out of disappointment and frustration, he picked up conifer cones and threw them at the creatures. They quickly disappeared in higher branches, beyond the reach of Gorman's missiles.

Gorman returned to his spot when he heard more noises in the undergrowth. Puzzled, he peered through the bush and then froze on the spot. Simultaneously, three pairs of eyes turned towards him.

These animals were much larger than the rat-like fur balls that frolicked in the branches above him. The large one looked a like a cross between a hyena and a wolf, the two smaller ones looked as though they could be her cubs. The adult issued a low growl and they slowly edged towards where Gorman was standing. They were the 'bear-dogs' that that Kistler had mentioned.

Gorman had made no spear or fire brand to defend himself. He backed up to a tree and then leapt for one of the lower branches, clawing his way up, trying to get out of the pack's reach. The bear-dog and her cubs bounded forward, snapping at Gorman's legs, until he pulled them clear.

Gorman edged along the branch. He was heavily scratched and the tree resin stuck to his limbs as he slowly manoeuvred his way to the more solid support of the trunk. Once there, he broke off small branches and hurl them down at his attackers.

His feeble weapons did nothing to discourage the hungry beasts. His size represented a good size meal; it was an easy prize for which they were prepared to wait. The bear-dogs settled down around the base of the tree.

Gorman lodged himself into an uncomfortable position against the trunk and a sturdy branch. Perhaps if he could sleep, even a few moments might be enough; he would awaken at a different time and the bear-dogs would be stranded in the future.

The yelping from the pack increased. Tired of waiting, the she bear-dog started to scale the tree; its lethal claws stabbing into the bark for better grip. Underneath, her progeny whined and milled around in anticipation.

Gorman was terrified. He ripped off another small branch that was too light for an effective club. When the climbing bear-dog was within range, he tried to poke it in her eyes with the sharper end.

The bear-dog paused, unfamiliar with the situation in which her intended prey tried to defend itself. The next time Gorman lunged forward the animal snapped at the branch with her jaws and tore it away. Gorman tried to climb higher, but the bear-dog raked her claws down his calf, shredding his skin. Her pups, smelling the blood for the first time, yelped and salivated expectantly. Within seconds, the bear-dog scrabbled up closer to Gorman's position and seized his lower leg in her jaws, shaking it violently.

Gorman desperately clung to the tree, his face pressed against the trunk, his hair matted by the weeping resin. He kicked and screamed, trying to free himself, begging any god that was listening to save him from the searing pain.

The bear-dog changed her grip and her jaws clamped down hard. Gorman screamed again as the bones in his leg shattered under the force.

Still with man's leg gripped in her maw, the bear-dog started to back slowly down the tree, dragging Gorman down with her. Gorman could no longer keep his grip; man and beast plunged the short distance to the forest floor. The bear-dog recovered first. She leapt on Gorman, clamping her jaws on his throat while one of her cubs sliced open Gorman's belly with its claw, disembowelling him as he breathed his last.

While the bear-dog family feasted on his body; large globs of tree resin dripped from the broken branches and scarred trunk. It dropped on the remains of Gorman's head, entombing his hair in a translucent, sticky mass. Rat-like creatures would eventually descend from the branches and gnaw away at the skull bones that the bear-dogs had left, but they would ignore Gorman's resin-matted hair.

-

Back in the summer of 1943, Major Gorman's disappearance from the archaeological field investigation site was a mystery. They found his tent with all his belongings and spare kit. On the small table was an unfinished letter to his mother that gave no clue as to his intentions. The broken amber necklace hung on a hook by the shaving mirror and unused washbasin.

Dr Kistler sent the assistants and labourers to search the surrounding area, but there was no sign of Gorman. Kistler gained the distinct impression that the search was not particularly diligent; it seemed no one was in any particular hurry to find the overbearing officer. Disturbingly, a report came back that one of the peasant's cabins had been burnt to the ground. Two charred skeletons were found amongst the ashes; Kistler knew they would turn out to be the girl and her grandfather. Still, there was no sign of Gorman's body in the ashes, or indeed anywhere else. It seemed highly unlikely that an officer like Gorman would desert, but there was no sign of him. After another day's fruitless search, Gorman's absence was reported to headquarters. Kistler ordered the site labourers to dig two small graves and inter the charred remains of the girl and her grandfather.

The Allied bombing raids came closer and the summer field season was curtailed with the camp dismantled earlier than planned. Despite the regular propaganda radio broadcasts, Kistler had the feeling that the course of the war was changing in the Allies' favour. He doubted that the Ahnenerbe unit was going to be back at this site again, or indeed anywhere else. He had been going to keep the amber necklace; yet, when he contemplated recent events and fearing how the girl's simple jewellery might have come into Gorman's possession; he decided against it. On a whim during the last evening in camp, he walked out beyond the megalith excavations and to the site of the peasant's graves marked with simple wooden crosses. He felt the short walk was a transit between the graves; the forest's ancient and more recent dead.

He dug a shallow hole in the freshly turned shallow soil over Agata's grave and pulled out the amber beads from his knapsack. He noticed again the larger amber piece with the hair strands that Gorman had first brought to his attention. Kistler grunted softly; fortunately Gorman and his deluded fanaticism had disappeared before he'd witnessed the other engravings on the dolman. The implications of the stone carvings were beyond anything the Ahnenerbe had previously found; beyond anyone's wildest scientific imaginings. Kistler broke out into a sweat at the thought of what would happen if Reichsführer Heinrich Himmler ever found out that he and Engelhardt had spent several days eradicating all traces of the Nazi petroglyphs from the dolman. He had taken photographs and had them safely hidden away. Perhaps at some future date, the Allies would see fit to reward his discretion.

Suddenly feeling apprehensive, he looked up from the two graves at the surrounding forest. He shuddered; and couldn't help but wonder again what fate had befallen Sturmbannführer Gorman.

Kistler placed the amber beads in the hole and quickly covered them over with soil. Despite his archaeological profession, he had the distinct feeling that some things should remain permanently buried in the past.

SLATE

Metamorphosis

Chantal stared in disgust at the large glass jar full of dirty water on the windowsill. Tadpoles wriggled around in the green murk. Despite her frequent objections to her husband David and his son Alex, it had stood there for weeks in her otherwise tidy kitchen. First it had held frogspawn, then tiny tadpoles, and now it was home to the few evil-looking creatures that still survived. Some swam around while others lay lethargically on the bits of slate that Alex had put in the water "to make them feel at home". The cannibalised remains of their less fortunate siblings lay coated in a jellified mess at the bottom of the jar.

She had hoped all her stepsons' experimental subjects would die quickly. Then she could empty the jar into the toilet with a clear conscience. But no, some continued to thrive, indifferent to the foul water and their deceased kin. The survivors' rounded bodies now sprouted miniature limbs in addition to their stumpy black tails. They were freakish, misshapen little aliens silently scrabbling to get out. They bumped into the side of the jar, seeming to look out at her with those pinhead golden eyes.

She was going to start cooking lunch, but the odour of decay had made her feel queasy. She sat down with a cup of coffee, the strong aroma of the drink replacing the stink emanating from the makeshift aquarium. This neat little cottage was becoming her prison. Her dreams for a new start in life with David would end up as dead as those mould-covered tadpoles. The image made her feel nauseous. She tried to fight back the coffee-laced bile that rose into her throat. What on earth was the matter with her? All right, she thought,

perhaps I'm being a little too melodramatic. After all, hadn't she agreed the change would do them all good?
-

Chantal was an attractive, flirty young woman who enjoyed a good time. Her life's passion was going out on the town with her friends in Liverpool. She had had more than one 'one night stands' and several boyfriends before she met up with Gary, a van driver. After dating for a couple of months, they drove down to the south of Spain in his van to make a delivery of some sort. They stayed over at his friend's apartment for a short holiday. Mixing with this affluent group, with their mirror sunglasses and loud Hawaiian shirts, she thought that they could all live like colourful butterflies; crawling out of their cocoons each day, blithely seeking the sun wherever they wanted. Life was a laugh, or it was, until whilst having rather drunken sex on a beach, Gary suggested his friends should join in. Tipsy or not, that was never going to happen; she was not going to become a "shared around".

The following morning she stole Gary's gold chain and sold it to pay for the next flight back to Liverpool. Her carefree life had turned into a bit of a mess. She needed to get herself straightened out before it was too late. Luckily, she soon managed to get a job as a classroom technician at a good school in Hale. Although it mostly involved clearing up after the pupils' art or cookery classes, the job had its advantages. With the long school holidays, she could go travelling on her own, without having to rely on a cockroach like Gary.

David was head of the school's science department. Tall and fit, he could easily have been mistaken for one of the physical education teachers, but outwardly showed none of their confidence. He was charming with the staff and a popular teacher with the children. Since the death of his wife a few years before, he had kept his sadness at a distance by working hard at his vocation and caring for his son, Alex. Occasionally he would stare unseeingly at a page in a textbook, puzzling over past memories. They were unsettling feelings, mostly about his wife's behaviour before she died and nagging suspicions that perhaps he might not be Alex's biological father.

'Time enough has passed', the women in the staff room would say to each other: 'He needs a good woman to take care of him and his little boy.'

Chantal would always remember her first meeting with David, 'the only good thing I ever got out of going to school' she would joke later. They had seen each other around the corridors, but it was late in the afternoon as she was clearing up after a cookery class when David came into the domestic science room. He asked if he could borrow some bicarbonate of soda for his science class tomorrow. He came over to her and looked down at the basin she was holding.

'Interesting,' he said and after a pause he asked, 'What have you got there?'

Chantal replied it was raw cake dough. She was flattered to notice that his gaze had wandered slightly from the bowl to her apron-framed cleavage.

'Not had that for years,' he said and then to distance himself from any sexual innuendo, he swirled a finger around the bowl edge to scoop up some dough. He scooped up a second portion of the sticky mix, but before he could taste it again, she had guided his finger to her own mouth, licking off the dough.

She looked up at him cheekily: 'Can I have some more, please, Sir?'

They kept their meetings a secret for a while, but when it became more widely known, there were mutterings in the staff room. Although his colleagues were pleased David was happy; Chantal certainly did not meet their definition of a 'good' woman. Here was David, possibly in line to be the school's next deputy head, going around with a feather-brained bint who had left school at sixteen. She must be ten years younger than him, what was he thinking? That attitude was firmly entrenched a year later, when David's pretty girlfriend became his pretty new wife.

Chantal was happy enough to give up her job. David's salary was more than enough and frankly she was better off than she had ever been before. She was proud of her handsome, clever husband and as much for his sake, she had tried to put aside the hurt when she realised David's colleagues thought very little of her. She stayed at home and helped look after her stepson when he came home from school. He was a lovely little lad. She expected he might soon start growing tall like his father, but actually he was quite short and even a little stocky for his age. They played games together and being quite childlike herself, she found it was fun, a lot better than working. In the evenings after Alex had gone to bed, she would pour a glass of wine for David and herself and they would cuddle up on the sofa. Occasionally she would think, with a shudder, how things would have turned out if she'd stayed with that loser, Gary.

In those first few months David was as content as he had been for years. He loved Chantal. He loved the way she genuinely cared for his son, her encouragement, her lovemaking, her cheerful, loving company after his day at school. The only discontent he felt was with the distain in which his colleagues held his wife. The invitations to them as a couple to gatherings or school functions just dried up. At first he put it down to his almost certain promotion to deputy head had made him a target for their jealousy. Then one day he was in the stationary cupboard when he overheard the head master and a senior teacher talking nearby.

'David's a fine teacher, excellent head of department - and he might have done very well in the DH's role. But I just don't see him and that wife of his as a good fit. Really, to this day, I don't know what possessed him to marry her.'

'Good looking girl, though.'

'Indeed! But surely he didn't have to marry her for – well, you know. I suspect she's a bit of a gold digger; snapped him up when he was still vulnerable, I suppose. Now David's first wife though; I don't think you ever met her? She used to collaborate on research work at the University. She was an ambitious, intelligent woman; someone who could hold a proper conversation. But really, this new wife of his! Can you imagine her doing the rounds with the school governors or at the PTA? I hardly think so, especially with that awful accent of hers!'

David went home and without ever mentioning the eavesdropped conversation, he talked to Chantal about the need for a fresh challenge. It was time to move out of his old house and the old school; time for a fresh start somewhere else. A 'clean slate' was the expression he used. Chantal readily agreed; she was pleased to leave the more dubious bits of her reputation behind for good. They moved to North Wales where David picked up as head of science at his new school.

After a few months of settling into their new surroundings things changed, or rather it was Alex who seemed to change. David had bought him a small microscope for his twelfth birthday. Alex was thrilled with it, more so when David said something like, 'perhaps you'll become a biologist, like your mother.'

Chantal didn't think anything of it at the time. Then she noticed Alex, on the edge of becoming a teenager (a time when she herself had started to become more rebellious) transformed into what she secretly regarded as a nerd. He became studious, endlessly reading, fiddling with computers and home experiments. He had swapped his love of television cartoons for never-ending wildlife documentaries. Alex squatted, toad-like, for hours reading with the books resting on his crossed legs. Where there had been plastic toys and models on his bedroom shelves, the space was now occupied by shells, fossils and dried insects preserved in little plastic boxes. Chantal felt sad to see the delicate butterflies pinned down on a board, but Alex insisted it was 'science'. Perhaps to make a point, he had even placed some of his mother's hand written university notebooks on his bedroom desk. Although he couldn't yet understand them, they were like a voice from the past, countermanding Chantal's more frivolous approach to life. Alex gradually withdrew from being Chantal's playmate. He seemed only to want to please his father, or (perhaps more weirdly, Chantal suspected) his dead mother. Occasionally as a family they played games together. That ended when Alex beat Chantal at Scrabble, and then turned to his father and complained smugly, 'she can't even spell properly'.

When David came home from his school, Chantal complained again about the jar and its moribund occupants.

'But it's nature! It's survival of the fittest, isn't that right, Dad?' Alex said, seeking his father's support.

Chantal insisted the smell and sight of it was making her feel unwell. She knew David thought she was making a fuss, but when she said she had actually been sick that morning, he looked at her more closely.

'Do you think you might be pregnant?'

Chantal buried her head against David's shoulder and they hugged tightly. The wonderful moment of comfort was soon lost as Alex had overhead the question: 'Are you going to have a baby? Why aren't you fat, then?'

David told Alex nothing was certain yet. He explained patiently that even if Chantal were going to have a baby, it would be no bigger than one of those tadpoles at the moment. Chantal looked over towards the jar and its slimy inhabitants. She felt acid pangs of fear. What if her baby was like one of the weak ones, struggling, fated to fall victim to their stronger siblings? She quickly pushed David aside and rushed to the downstairs toilet to vomit.

'Oh yuk!' Alex wailed in disgust.

'Alex, please! Chantal isn't feeling well. And I really think your pets are big enough to be released now. You can put them back where you collected the frog spawn.'

Alex objected, but for once David was firm with him. He would have to release them at the weekend.

-

It was a cool but sunny Saturday morning. David was scheduled to drive one of the school's minibuses to transport the athletics team to an "away" meet. He reminded Alex again to get rid of the tadpoles before he arrived back home. Chantal asked where he was going to release them.

'In some water, of course!' Alex sneered.

After David had reprimanded him sharply; Alex said he was going to put them in a pond in the old slate quarry. Even though it was only half a mile away from their house, Chantal warned him not to climb on the slate ledges. Alex scoffed and said arrogantly that he'd been there 'hundreds of times' before. David told him to put the animals back in a shallow pond, and stay away from the deeper pool at the end of the quarry.

Alex sulked in his bedroom, but sometime after David had driven away, he started to gather his stuff. Normally Chantal would have fussed over him, telling him to watch out for the traffic, don't stop and talk to strangers, and so on, but after his attitude today, she was too tired to bother. She watched him from her bedroom window as he prepared to leave. He strapped the jar to his bike's carrier rack, then put a knapsack on his back and tied the sleeves of his anorak around his waist. Chantal shivered. In profile he looked like one of those revolting tadpoles, bulbous body, little arms and legs, and the dark coat flapping behind him like a vestigial tail. She watched him as he pedalled away on his bike.

-

When Chantal awoke it was early afternoon. She'd only intended to have a quick lie down, but she must have slept for longer than she planned. She went downstairs and realised Alex wasn't in the house, he had been gone for several hours. It wasn't like him to stay outside for so long. Where was he?

Chantal left the house and drove the car a short distance along the road and then on to a gravel track which led to the disused quarry. It had only been mined to supply local building material for their village and was much smaller than the main Welsh slate mines that had been worked over the last few centuries. Just before the entrance to the quarry there was a wider area that served as a turning circle. She stopped and parked the car there. The rest of the track was blocked off with low mounds of dirt to stop people driving down and tipping garbage into the old pit. She had to walk down along a sloping path to the quarry itself. She saw Alex squatting on a pile of dark slate near the base of the manmade cliff. He was looking intently at something near the water's edge. He didn't notice her until she called to him to ask what he was doing.

He looked up at her. 'I'm investigating,' he said in the supercilious tone of his that had irritated her so much lately.

'Yes, and I'm investigating where you'd got to. Why have you been so long? I was worried!'

She walked down further to the small pool surrounded by boggy ground. She could see from the empty container he must have already released the froglets. Although she had been upset earlier, she was relieved to have found him. Maybe he wasn't such a bad kid. It was probably his teenage hormones changing, and as she was pregnant, her hormones had likely been acting up as well. She'd just have to make the effort and try and get along with him. She determined to make a start by showing an interest in what Alex was doing. Chantal walked carefully over some small heaps of slate scree that had fallen from the quarry face and stood alongside him. She pointed to the smooth slate walls.

'How old is this place?' she asked conversationally.

'Hundreds of millions of years.'

'Millions of years? Really? Were there people around so long ago?'

'Of course not! It was even before the dinosaurs! Millions of years ago, this was just a muddy sea. Then it was buried and the Earth's heat and pressure changed the mud to slate. It's a metamorphic rock. That's a big word for you isn't it? Met-a-mor-phic.' He sounded it out, mimicking her Liverpuddlian accent. 'I can't believe you thought there were people around then? Geez, you can be so thick sometimes!'

'Don't be cheeky with me! I meant the age of the quarry, smarty-pants! Not how old the flipping rocks were,' she said in exasperation.

'Oh, that; the quarry must be hundreds of years old. Mr Williams, the geography teacher, said some quarrymen were killed in a bad accident here. He says their ghosts haunt the quarry at night.'

It occurred to Chantal that the haunting tale was probably told to discourage the local children from playing around the precipitous edges and the deep pools. 'Who's the gullible one now?' she thought to herself as she looked around. The purple grey walls of cleaved slate were slowly being reclaimed by green grass and wildflowers. Water lilies, reeds, and tadpoles too, had colonised the small ponds dotting the quarry floor. It was so peaceful that it was difficult to imagine it had once been a noisy, dusty mine. In the afternoon sunlight and with the bird song amongst the bushes, the old quarry was transformed into a surprisingly tranquil spot. Actually, she thought, the only unpleasant thing was Alex and his "know-it-all" attitude.

'Well, I don't think it's haunted; that's just an old wives' tale,' she said to regain a little of her adult authority. 'There's nothing at all creepy about this place.'

'No? Look at this then!' Alex pointed to what he had been studying earlier. It was a dragonfly, its iridescence giving it an almost metallic appearance.

'It's been trapped and it's going to be eaten alive - by flesh-eating plants!' he said gleefully. 'That's pretty creepy, isn't it?'

Chantal bent down to look at the insect more closely. The edge of the boggy pond was mostly covered in different sorts of moss, but there were also small, rather pretty, reddish coloured plants with shiny droplets on their many stems. The brilliantly blue dragonfly seemed to be stuck to the plant. Although the insect still struggled, it only succeeded in brushing against another of the sticky buds and became further entangled.

'It's a sundew plant, called 'Lustwort'. You know what "lust" means - don't you?' Alex said in his condescending manner.

Chantal was too surprised to come up with a suitable reply.

'Lust means it craves flesh. The Lustwort catches the insect on those sticky buds and then wraps around it. Then, the plant secretes a special type of mucus which dissolves the insect's juices and slowly sucks it all out.' Alex made a revolting sucking sound between his teeth. 'All that's left behind is a dried-out husk. It can take hours.'

Chantal wondered if Alex had deliberately caught the insect to feed the plant for one of his 'experiments'. She started to feel physically sick again. She sympathised with the dragonfly; she knew what it was like to have the life sucked out of you, bit by bit. She stood up, shaking a little: 'Right, it's time to come home now. I don't want to spend my Saturday afternoon watching things being eaten alive by parasites.'

'It's not a parasite! Honestly; you're so stupid! A parasite is a lower life form that lives on its host without killing it,' he said.

Chantal could read the silent message conveyed by his cold, angry eyes: "Just like you live off of my father".

Alex smirked and turned his back on her. 'Sundews aren't parasites at all, they're –.'

A heavy piece of slate smashed on to the top of his head. The dense thud echoed back from the quarry wall. Soundlessly, Alex toppled forward, falling face down into the shallow water. Alarmed tadpoles darted for cover under the rippling water-logged moss.

Chantal looked at the large bloodied rock in her hand and then casually tossed it into the pond near Alex's partially submerged head.

After a minute or so; she took off her shoe, stretched out her leg and prodded Alex's limp body with her foot. A few air bubbles escaped from his clothes, but he remained partly suspended by the soggy vegetation.

Chantal quietly contemplated the situation. This is where he really belongs, she thought with little remorse. The precocious little toad-boy was now in his element, along with the changeling creatures he had come to resemble. Maternal instinct had saved her tiny tadpole baby from being devoured by the mutating Alex. It was only nature after all: the survival of the fittest.

Chantal reasoned that whoever investigated the circumstances would conclude that Alex's death was a complete accident. The poor child was only doing what his father had told him before he had left that morning. And hadn't she also warned him of the dangers in the old slate quarry? Tragically, Alex had ignored her advice; he had been struck by a falling rock and then tumbled into the water.

It was heart breaking, of course it was; but now she and David would start again with a new family and a nice, clean slate.

Chantal leaned carefully over Alex's prone body. Using a thin reed stem, she prised the struggling dragonfly from its sticky prison and watched it fly away.

EARTH

Tenant Trouble

The place was in a mess. The Landlord surveyed what had been the one of the most desirable properties he had ever leased and wept. The whole property was a complete shambles and to make matters worse the dissolute tenants had not only neglected the premises, but had also criminally neglected to pay the rent. The Landlord had seen enough. He turned to his henchman,
'Bailiff! Bring me the tenants,' he bellowed.
The appearance of the three metre tall bailiff floating just above the floor of the United Nations council chambers in New York caused considerable consternation, even among those diplomats who had been hardened to the vagaries and upsets of international politics of the 21st century.
The bailiff, despite his ferocious appearance, was not an insensitive creature and he allowed treatment for those whose hearts had malfunctioned during his unannounced arrival. He held up his hand in the universal manner to demand quiet.
'I am Grunt, Master bailiff to Landlord Graunch the two hundred and seventy third (Junior); hereafter referred to as 'Landlord'. I hereby summon you, in your capacities as duly appointed spokescreatures for and on behalf of the resident tenants, hereafter 'Tenants' of premises G1097/SS52/ P3/ C3, hereafter referred to as 'Earth' (very original!) to appear before the aforementioned rightful owner and registered Landlord (see documentation appended) to answer the following charges which are in contravention and breach of the letter and the spirit of the agreement G1097/SS52/ P3/ C3 part 7, Subsections 6 to 118; namely 'Obligations of Tenant'.

Grunt paused to let this proclamation sink home and then continued: 'In particular, your attention is drawn to the following clauses:

Rent shall be payable at a period of once in every 10 millennia being measured by Earth orbits around Sol – see Appendix 1: you are currently 6 periods in arrears.

The number of occupancy of the Tenant species, or sub species derived there from, shall not exceed three billion individuals;

Industrial solid, liquid, gas, plasma levels in soil, waters, and atmosphere may at no time exceed those laid down in galaxitical convention SD 5567 for class three planets;

Under no circumstances may the premises or its satellite moons be utilised for the production of elements Granthamium and Plutonium, both expressly prohibited by the convention SD 5567.

Harvest rights on indigenous species bacterial, botanical zoological or energal may not exceed those shown in appendix 12;

Improvements desired by the Tenants are the responsibility of the Tenants. The drainage or storage of water, or the removal of soil may not be instigated without prior permission of the Landlord who at his sole discretion will rely on the findings of a planetary ecologist appointed by the Landlord at the Tenant's cost.'

Grunt paused from the litany of misdemeanours to add his own observation: 'Anyway, it doesn't require an ecologist to point out that atmospheric CO_2 levels have exceed 400 parts per million for more than a decade and continue to increase. Yes – don't look shocked - I'm talking about your air – you still have to breathe this stuff do you?'

There was a brief scrabble for documents as delegates and ambassadors from across the world searched for the information in their latest "climate change" reports.

'I hereby caution you that failure to appear before the court to answer these charges will result in summary eviction of the Tenant species from property Earth. I further caution that if the Tenants are found in breach of contract in any or all of the above named clauses shall be deemed sufficient to nullify said contract with immediate effect and the contract shall be terminated. The Tenant will be evicted from all the Landlords property (s).'

Grunt drifted over to UN Secretary General and slapped a writ into his pale and sweaty hand.

'Er – could we have a copy of the original contract?' the Secretary General asked.

'What did you do with the laser engraved platinum original?'

'I expected we mislaid it somewhere. It's been rather a long time, you see.'

'Let me warn you that ignorance, feigned or real, is no defence. It is unacceptable to volatilize the contract and then try and claim racial amnesia. Believe me, others have tried.'

'Of course, understood.' replied the Secretary General meekly, 'But we will need to refer to it, so that we can clarify a few points.'

'Very well, we will provide an additional copy at your expense. Anything else?'

'Yes, it's about this Court, which you mentioned. How do we - you know - attend?'

'Same way you arrived. Interstellar transport and follow the signs.'

'Ah! Unfortunately, it would seem as if we have lost the technology to do so. It's probably down in Atlantis somewhere. Would it be too inconvenient to hold the hearing here on Earth? We'd pay for the plaintiff's accommodation, of course. Perhaps you and your fellow, er, fellows, could take in a few of the sights; stay for a round of golf over the weekend, maybe?'

Grunt raised his eyes to the heavens, or at least the Horse's Head nebula part of it. "What a motley bunch! They lower the tone of the whole neighbourhood," he thought to himself and anyone else who were telepathic.

'Why not?' he sighed. 'Let's get it over with.'

A shot echoed around the large auditorium. The North Korean delegate on hearing that not only had most of the world rejected Communism but the entire universe was owned by capitalist landlords and their fascist lackeys, had prayed there wasn't a God as well and then shot himself.

The bailiff waited respectfully for the deceased to self-vaporise. When this did not happen, he noted the curious fact and said: 'See you in court!' and vanished.

'Your attention please,' said the badly shaken Secretary General, 'Back to United Nations business. Now, does anyone here know a good lawyer?'

-

After much debate and quibbling over legal fees, it was decided that there would be a delegation of lawyers to be headed by the legal firm Goldstein, Goldstein and McRangle. The lawyers would normally retain a thirty percent of any award should they win the case, however, this posed serious practical and political problems. They eventually agreed to be granted the freehold of their New York, London, Paris and Tokyo offices and all of Greenland, pending further negotiations with Denmark.

During a global press conference on the crisis, one of the spokesmen mentioned suggestions would be welcome. These arrived at the UN by the planeload and ranged from 'We told you so!' from the Greenpeace organisation to 'Nuke the sons-of-bitches back to Hell!' from someone who signed himself 'Worried' of Switzerland.

Meanwhile, in their plush New York offices, young Solly Goldstein the third (and probably Solly Goldstein the last, he thought pessimistically) ploughed through the rental contract aided by the occasion grunting of the taciturn and ancient McRangle (the only) who was reading the same document.

'Laddie, if we dinna ken it afore, we ken it now. Humanity have broken every single rule in the book.'

Goldstein, although alarmed at a hint of pride in McRangle's statement could only concur. 'We're all doomed!' he said as he noted with dismay it was the Tenants responsibility to secure their own passage and new lodgings upon eviction. He flipped to the last page on the translated microfilmed document and gazed at the signature of the long forgotten person who had negotiated the rental of the Earth and moon premises on behalf of mankind. He was disappointed to see that the name on the engraved dotted line wasn't Adam.

There was a knock on the door and his attractive Personal Assistant entered the room.

Solly looked up bleary-eyed at her lovely face and figure that suggested to him the (so far) inaccessible pleasures of wining, dining, dancing, hot tub, and sex, although not necessarily in that order. He fought back the tears as he realized there probably wasn't enough time left on Earth to make it come true.

'Mr. Goldstein and Mr. McRangle, this letter came into our offices this morning. I believe you should see this urgently.' She handed Goldstein an envelope handwritten in copper-plate style bearing a London postmark and far too many postage stamps.

'Have a nice day!' she said and paused expectantly; but not asked to wait, she teetered out of the office felling that her perceptibility might, just might, have helped save the world. And - if Solly Goldstein the third did not ask her for a date very soon – well, she would have to ask him.

Solly started to mumble about "Why don't people use email?" but then became engrossed in the letter's contents. He passed the handwritten letter to the stoic McRangle without any comment.

McRangle read it, punctuating each paragraph with an 'Aye' or 'Right enough, Professor.' He spread the letter out on the table and smoothed out the creased document carefully with his wizened hands.

'Well, there we are, Laddie! I think there's an excellent case here for a substantial counter claim! Very substantial indeed!' and for the first time in several decades, he chuckled aloud.

-

'They did what?!' exploded the Landlord.

'The tenants have issued a counter claim for damages,' replied a rather nervous clerk of the court.

'Summon the Master Bailiff immediately.'

Grunt appeared and the Landlord regarded him closely.

'You delivered the writ and a copy of the contract?'

'Yes, Landlord.'

'What did you make of them? What sort of creatures are they?'

'They seem surprisingly normal; even despite the overcrowding and chemical pollution. They must have degenerated and then forgotten, or at least abandoned, their previous technology. Naturally, they claim that they know nothing of any planetary rental contract. The General Secretary said we are the only contact that they have ever had with an extra terrestrial species. Really, Sir, they are utterly parochial.'

'Anything else?'

'As you might have expected, Landlord, their society has regressed to the point where they go to war with one another on a regular basis. As far as I could make out, these wars are mostly over resources, but on occasions the wars have been to settle arguments about whose deity is the most powerful.'

'And who won?'

'There has been no final victory. It's not the winning; it's the taking part that counts, apparently. Or perhaps I'm thinking of something else.' The bailiff shrugged; 'Either way Landlord, it appears we have issued the court order just in time. Another few generations and they would have been eating each other.'

The Landlord shuddered: 'Feeding on each other – Black holes! Who would be left to pay the arrears?'

'Indeed!' The Master Bailiff agreed. ' But nevertheless, Landlord, they have launched a counter claim. I have an odd feeling about Humanity; something doesn't look quite right about these creatures. Are you sure you have the right planet, Sir?'

'Of course it's the right place! I own the damn planet!'

-

Presiding Judge Bletxh was worried. For a start his son, having barely shed his sixth moult had decided to life couple with a hermaphrodite exotic dancer from Kron. And although he did not believe himself prejudice in anyway, the 'it' was 200 revolutions older than his son. To make matters worse, while he was sat in this oxygen-shrouded cesspit he had a suspicion that his wife would not be visiting her various mothers but entertaining Senator Gauz in a more intimate corporeal fashion than would be called for in a normal business relationship.

Could he attend to these family matters? Not at all, he had to be dragged a 1,000 light years from home to listen to the whining of some bloated Landlord (who collected a hundred times more Boodles in rent than he earned in an entire moult) going on about his regressive tenants whom he had clearly conned into renting a crummy, slummy Class 3 planet that he and any other Black-hole fearing, ammonia breathing, child-of-the-universe would not touch with an interplanetary probe. Damn this place!

Judge Bletxh wheezed miserably on his imported ammonia supply while the Landlord's legal representatives droned on about the extensive catalogue of broken clauses.

The judge raised his pseudopods.

'Lets see if we can cut this down a bit, shall we? I understand the parties have agreed that if any one of the major clauses is not adhered to; the right to rent the planet is void and the Tenants are to be issued with an eviction order. I further understand the Tenants do not in fact dispute the facts that:

1. they have not paid the rent,
2. their species numbers a ridiculous 7 billion on the planet,
3. they have manufactured plutonium,
4. and finally, they have, in just about every conceivable fashion, severely impacted the environment of a planet from which they themselves cannot leave.'

The irritable judge paused and tapped the dial on his breathing apparatus.

'I take it therefore the defendants intend to enter a plea along the lines of 'dereliction of Tenants obligations due to prolonged insanity of the species'; the counter claim being that such insanity was brought about by living in this hellhole for the past 70 millennium.' The judge cast a malevolent glance in the direction of the embarrassed Landlord: ' A plea, I might add, with which I am increasingly inclined to feel some sympathy!'

There was an expectant hush as Lawyers to the World, Goldstein and McRangle tried to discern the best approach. Even though

Judge Bletxh had the appearance of a hairy squid locked in mortal combat with a dialysis machine, his mood seemed to have become less favourable towards the plaintiff.

Mc Rangle eyed the judge over his spectacles and noted the tufts of red hair that protruded from around the visor. His appearance reminded him of a great aunt with a bristly chin who he'd been forced to kiss when he was but a bairn in his native Scotland.

'Best leave this to me, Laddie,' he whispered. 'He looks like he might have a wee touch of the Celt in him.'

McRangle rose slowly to his feet.

'Your Fairness, our plea is 'not guilty' on all counts.'

'What?' Judge Bletxh groaned in exasperation. 'May I remind you, that you; as the defendants, have already admitted responsibility for all the derelictions of the property!'

'Aye, Your Fairness, that's as maybe. But we, that is to say the human race, never signed any such rental agreement with the plaintiff. With your permission we would like to call our chief witness; Professor Crandfort Plint, Head of Archaeology at the British Museum.'

McRangle sensed rather than saw the judge's increasing discomfort and continued: 'However, if it pleases Your Fairness; I could summarize his findings.'

'Yes, yes! By all means. Continue!'

'Professor Plint is prepared to testify to the fact the tenants who signed the rental contract in question nearly 70 thousand years ago were almost certainly members of the Neanderthal species. They may not have been aware that the planet was already occupied. It was occupied by another hominid group, an emerging and evolving species: *Homo sapiens*, namely; ourselves. Professor Plint will further testify the few fossil remains of these two groups from this period clearly show that our species had its origins on this planet tens of thousands of years before the arrival of the Neanderthals.'

McRangle removed his glasses and shook his head sadly before continuing: 'Of course, we must now regard the Neanderthals as interlopers; squatters even, aided and abetted by their Landlord.'

'I see! So you claim you had no contract with the Landlord and in fact the plaintiff acted illegally in assisting the Neanderthals to occupy...'

'Invade, Your Fairness!'

'Quite so; to invade your natal planet?'

'Precisely, Your Fairness.'

'Very well, but what happened to the Neanderthals?' Judge Bletxh asked. 'I must warn you, indeed warn all of humanity, that genocide is regarded as a very serious offence; even in the case of such primitives as yourselves.'

'From the circumstantial evidence, Professor Plint suggests that the climate was not as idyllic as they were lead to believe and they may have lost large numbers due to influenza and other viral infections. Their population was decimated and they were unable to sustain their technology. As supplies ran low, they may have turned to forage as nomadic hunter-gather tribes to gather sustenance. Over the generations, they were unable to compete with the emerging *Homo sapiens* and became extinct.'

'Tragic, utterly tragic. Surely though, your counter claim against the Landlord can not be made on behalf of the lamented Neanderthals?' Judge Bletxh queried.

'That is not our intention at all, Your Fairness. We have testimony provided by the US Army Medical Research into Infectious Diseases (USAMRID) and the Smithsonian Institute that the Neanderthal colonists brought with them a variety of diseases. Whilst these infections may have only been minor ailments to Neanderthals; large portions of the human population had little or no resistance to them. By way of example, these include smallpox, measles, and tuberculosis; which only now are we learning how to control. Scientists are continuing with the genome sequencing of other deadly diseases and accordingly, we may still discover more examples.'

McRangle paused to study his notes again. 'Furthermore, the blood sucking mosquito acquired a parasite, probably from Neanderthal blood; which even to this day causes the fatal disease malaria, a killer of millions of our species...'

'Stop! I have sensed enough!' interjected Judge Bletxh. 'It is sufficient to have the case against you, Humanity, dismissed. I further admit your claim for damages at a future hearing, however...' he cast both pairs of blazing eyes in the direction of the cowering Landlord, 'I would strongly entreat both parties to settle out of the courtroom; because if I have to drag my backsides out to this slum again (no offense intended) I will not be held responsible for any lack of impartiality on my part!'

The Judge leaned forward and beckoned the lawyers Goldstein and McRangle to step forward to his plinth.

'Now, to satisfy my curiosity only; what order of magnitude were Humanity thinking of claiming?'

'I have a document prepared, Your Fairness,' stated Solly Goldstein the third (who now felt that there could be a Solly Goldstein the fourth if he could pluck up the courage to ask his personal assistant for a date).

'In essence: access to new technology, interplanetary travel, restoration of the ice caps, facilitated cultural exchanges and any new computer games; that kind of thing.'

There was a loud thud as the Landlord fainted and hit the floor.

'Very reasonable, it seems the least you could ask for! Sort out the details and send me a copy. However, returning to this present case, I have no hesitation in declaring in favour of the primitives, er, you the defendants. The case against you is dismissed, with costs.'

The judge removed the translation communication device and motioned to his assistants: 'Now, let's get the hell out of here!'

-

The Master Bailiff helped the Landlord back to his feet and looked around at the jubilant throng of *Homo sapiens* dancing around the auditorium in celebration. He thought back to his initial impression that things didn't look quite right. He remembered that the now extinct Neanderthals did look slightly different. They were more solidly built and physically stronger. With their prominent brow ridge and sloped backed forehead, the Neanderthals looked altogether much more noble and intelligent than this primitive bunch.

One thing was for sure; they wouldn't have let the property get into such a disgusting state!

IRONSTONE

The Crossing

Frans Nieman looked at the old Afrikaaner homestead. It still needed a lot of work and would take him several years to fix to his ideal. That suited him just fine. He had bought this dilapidated farm to escape the city pressures. It would be pointless to exhaust himself in a frenzy of 'do-it-yourself' activities so that he could relax at some later date. The old farm was his retreat from the largely self-imposed stress of running his own business. Here, in the African bush, he was under no deadlines. Since his divorce three years ago, he had lived in a rented apartment, little more than a sub-divided bedsit, near the city centre. He had buried himself in his work and saved hard to buy this place, a hideaway to escape from the memory of her and the claustrophobia of town life. He had promised his two sons they could come and visit him when he had more time and was settled in on the farm.

In reality, the farm was a fraction of the size it had been over a century ago. What remained was an old white-washed building with a corrugated iron roof. The roof was once painted bright red, but countless Highveld hailstorms, heavy rain and sun-scorched days had flaked and faded the colour to a dull ox blood. The walls were solid enough and the wood had mostly escaped the ravages of termites and rot. Although the house must have provided several generations of farmers with shelter it was now virtually a shell, hollowed out of all but a few bare essentials. The good arable land nearer the valley had also long since been sold. Instead of hundreds of acres of land, the old buildings now only presided over a water borehole and some very rocky uncultivated ground against the hillside. A 'spruit' or stream flowed through the property from the hills and provided fresh water the year round. A few gnarled peach and orange trees stood guard around the house. They were well past their productive years. The only other sign of farming was a small plot in which the remaining farm worker's family grew some of their own maize and vegetables. There were no commercial prospects for agriculture here now. The farm was only destined to be his weekend and holiday retreat.

This particular Saturday morning, Frans decided not to work on more improvements to the old house. The onset of spring had prompted him to start building a 'bush camp' in a spot he had picked out a few weeks earlier. He had instructed Jacob, his African farm hand, to carry tools and several bags of cement to the place. Jacob had organised a couple of mules and had made the trip during the week. Frans asked Jacob what he thought of the site he had chosen. He was surprised at Jacob's indifference.

The concept was in fact, completely foreign to Jacob. Such things were not discussed with white people, but he considered the whole idea strange. Where you ate did not matter so much as what you ate, or whom you ate with. To Jacob, having lived his entire life in this quiet rural area, the evening meal was the social focal point, a gathering, a place to talk and laugh. On pay days there would be drink and music with his neighbours, friends and more family. In his whole life Jacob could not ever remember eating a meal on his own. The white man's attitude was therefore, a continuing puzzle. This white man, who claimed sons, never bought them here. And although he presumed the 'Baas' to be still sexually active, there was no woman either. Perhaps the white man had some young 'squeeze' in the city to tire him out. Either way, he came alone to this house and now wanted to get even further away, to a place of total solitude. Still, if the 'Bass' was going to pay him to move things here or there, what did it matter to him?

Frans misinterpreted Jacob's lack of enthusiasm as laziness. He decided to build a smaller camp by himself, rather than spend his precious weekends trying to extract work from an apparently unwilling Jacob. It would be good to work with his hands again and besides, he could do with the exercise. He would make sure Jacob had plenty else to do around the old farmhouse and barn.

Frans clambered from his truckle bed in time to see the first rays of sun filter through the dusty windows into his makeshift bedroom. Padding barefoot around the empty house, the only other sound was the coffee pot coming to the boil on the wood-fired stove. He decided to forego breakfast and left the old farmhouse shortly after sunrise. He called in on Jacob to give him some instructions and to tell him where he was headed. Frans told him he would be back before dark and he would look over Jacob's progress when he returned. Frans left the homestead behind him and followed a track through the bush that would lead to his destination. The dead-looking vegetation was brown and parched from the arid winter. Hidden beneath the dead and dusty exterior of the bare trees, a freshly broken twig would reveal its green interior, hinting that life was still buried inside. It lay there dormant, waiting for the change in season to reveal its vitality.

It was a dusty hour's walk up the red soil track before Frans reached the place along side the stream. Under a tarpaulin, he found the tools and cement that Jacob had transported. They were laid out on an expanse of smooth, almost polished, rock. This was the site he had chosen, surrounded by bush and yet high enough to have a view of the valley. He laid down his pack and paused to admire the spot. Running water could be heard tumbling over the rocks to the side of him. He went to the edge of the rock outcrop and scrambled down a short, steep bank to the waterside.

It was a natural wonder. The stream had opened out from the narrow ravine and poured into a series of clear pools. The pools were linked by stretches of shallower water as it flowed over the bedrock. On the banks and surrounding crags were ancient trees, their thick, contorted roots winding over the rocks. These tendrils clutched at the rock and prised deep into crevices seeking out the thin soil. Precarious as their situation looked, it had held them fast from the occasional roaring storm waters, and protected the bank from further erosion. Today, their branches and roots extended their protection to birds and brown lizards. A malachite kingfisher flashed to the water and returned to the densely wooded margin with its small catch.

Frans went to the stream's edge and crouching down, cupped the water in his hands and splashed it to his face. Its coldness surprised and pleased him, reinvigorating him in the already warm air. The spring day would soon get much warmer; he must get going with his tasks. As he stood up he noticed a pile of stones on the opposite bank which he had not seen on his previous visit. They seem to have been deliberately stacked into a mound. Perhaps it was one of the old property survey beacons fallen into disrepair. He thought that this was unlikely considering its position and went to investigate. The stream was far too wide to jump and there were no stepping-stones. He took off his boots and socks and cautiously started to wade across towards the stone pile. The cold water flowing around his calves made him gasp. Although shallow, the water was running quickly here in a place between two deeper pools. The streambed was smooth and slippery and Frans was relieved to find that it was only knee deep. He emerged from the water opposite the pile of large pebbles that was set against the steep bank on the other side.

He examined the stones. They were all of a similar type and size, no very large or smaller ones even though there were plenty of them lying near by. He picked up one of the stones. It was heavy but fitted comfortably into his hand. They were about half the size of a brick but had been partially rounded by water action. Although there were some flat surfaces, there were no sharp corners or edges. He took a stone to the water and dunked it in. When wet the stone showed a hidden beauty. The rock was layered in colours of ochre yellow and brown with some bands of a greyish, almost metallic substance. It was ironstone, the tough and resilient rock that formed the hills on the edge of his property. It was also the source of the striking red colour of the iron-rich soil in the area. There seemed to be no obvious reason for the pile of stones. They were not a boundary marker or survey point and certainly not an ancient grave marking. Perhaps some children long ago had made a game of building the stones into a pile at the water's edge.

The stone he held dried quickly in the sun. The layering was still visible now the dust had been washed away. Frans decided these stones would be perfect for constructing an attractive 'braai' place where he could cook food over an open fire. He picked up a couple of stones and waded back across to the other side. When he was there he noticed another stone pile that was almost hidden by the undergrowth. There would be plenty of rocks here to complete the fireplace, and more besides.

Carrying the smooth rocks up the steep part of the bank proved to be difficult. After a few attempts Frans rigged up a sling using the tarpaulin and some rope. He would load a couple of dozen stones in the tarpaulin and bundle them up, then climb up the bank and pull the load up after him. The ironstone was heavy and it was hard work, but it was considerably more effective than his first few attempts. As the sun climbed higher, a new pile of stones grew at the campsite near the spreading wild fig tree.

By noon he had removed all the stones from the pile nearest his camp. He paused to rest in the shade of the tree for a while, taking a cold beer and some biltong from his pack. He did not sit for long; he could already feel his muscles starting to stiffen after the unaccustomed exertions of the morning. He slid down the bank and took off his boots again. He crossed the stream at the same point, collected stones from the pile and carefully headed back again, this time making another heap by his path up the embankment. He decided to build a sizeable collection before lugging the tarpaulin up to the top again. He had completed several trips across the stream and was about to return for more stones when he was seized by a strange sensation.

He was being watched by someone. *Or something.* His scalp prickled and he suddenly felt uneasy. He turned around slowly, his eyes scanning the dense undergrowth. Something was there. He hunched down slightly, gripping one of the stones harder, his muscles tense. His senses alerted, he noticed the birds had stopped singing. The breeze which stirred the leaves and nearby reeds, had now fallen still. Even the burble of the running water seemed low and muted. All was shrouded in heat and silence; waiting.

Frans felt out of place, as if he was suspended in a living photograph. He realized he had held his breath to concentrate on the slightest sound. He let the air out of his lungs, his heartbeat pounding in his ears. He breathed in short tense gasps, his throat dry and constricted.

Despite the heat, he shuddered and felt the goose flesh on his tanned arms and legs. He was afraid. The dark gothic fear of stormy nights and guttering candles could not match this nameless dread that held him, almost paralysed, in the searing African sun of midday. He could see and hear nothing to frighten him in this way, but the fear did not pass. He spun quickly to face the bush behind him, raising the stone to defend himself. Only deep and silent shadows confronted him. No leopard waiting to pounce, no mamba reared and poised for a deadly strike. He yelled out and hurled the stone into a thicket, tensing for any retaliation. Nothing. He swallowed hard and edged back toward the water, still on the alert. The light breeze stirred again, cooling the sheen of the sweat that bathed his skin. The birds flittered amongst the reeds and the bush seemed alive once more. What had come over him?

Frans carried some more stones over to his new pile but after a few trips decided he had had enough. The feeling of unease persisted and had changed his previous carefree mood. He knew if he had flushed out a buck with the stone, the tension would have broken. He would have been left feeling rather foolish. But there had been something of which to be afraid. Something dark hidden in the full light of day. Something.

He tugged on his boots and repeated the process of hauling the stones up to his campsite. In the event, he would need the tarpaulin to cover over the cement. He rested again, longer this time, comforted by the panorama before him. He noted his shoulders and limbs had caught the sun. He thought he must have had mild heatstroke as he was unused to this amount of physical work. It was just a dizzy spell. He had to admit that he was getting older; younger men than him had died of heart attacks. He should take it easy, perhaps bring his sons along to help. He thought about them briefly and then dismissed the idea. They were not close to him and if it did not involve wheels or some electronic gadget they would have no interest. Teenagers! He wondered if either of them had a steady girlfriend yet. Not the sort of thing they would confide in him, that was for sure.

While he was resting, he noticed something sticking up from a shallow crack in the smooth rock. He tugged it free. It was a small piece of unglazed pottery with some faint yellow patterning. His curiosity aroused, he searched around for a while to see if he could find any other pieces.

It was late afternoon when he took a leisurely stroll back down to the empty farm. He was tired but contented with his efforts so far. He would do some odd jobs around the house tomorrow. Jacob could help out if he didn't have too much of a hangover.

-

Several weekends later, Hannes, one of Frans' colleagues from work, visited him at the farm house, ostensibly to offer advice on renovation, but more truthfully to get away from the wife, children and the neighbours for a while. After an inspection of the buildings, they took a hike up to the bush camp by the stream. More used to the rough walk, Frans carried the provisions for lunch. Dried biltong, cheese and bread with a few ice-cold cans of beer to fill up the space in the pack.

When they arrived at the site, Frans showed Hannes where he planned to build his 'rondaval' or round hut with a thatched roof that would be idea for this spot. He also pointed out his handiwork with the 'braai' area and fireplace.

Hannes studied the stone walls. 'Where did these rocks come from?' he asked.

'From the river bed, just down here, I'll show you.' He led Hannes down the bank to show him the spot by the water pools. 'They were here in a small pile, already been sorted. There was a mound here that I've taken, and another over there, you can see there are still a few left. I can't figure out what they were for. They didn't seem to serve any purpose.'

Hannes looked at the stones that remained. 'Is the water deep here?' he asked pointing to the area in front of them.

'No, it's probably the shallowest part. That's how I could carry the boulders back to this side.' explained Frans.

'Ah, I thought so,' said Hannes. 'The stones were to mark a safe crossing place in the river, they're common in old Bushman areas. They've been set up past the flood mark, do you see?'

'But why were the heaps so big? They wouldn't need so many just to mark a crossing place,' said Frans.

'True, but marking the spot is just one part of it. As I understand it, whenever the Bushmen crossed the water, they would add another stone to the pile. It was a sort of offering to the water spirits for a safe crossing.'

'What, here as well?' asked Frans incredulously. 'The stream is only a few strides across! What was there to be protected against here?'

Hannes shrugged. 'I think it's the principle; not just a fear of crocodiles. If you believe in a water spirit then you acknowledge him; whether it is in a small stream, or in the larger river in the valley. God takes as much notice of prayers said in a simple chapel as from a cathedral, don't you think?'

Frans was taken aback. 'It's not the same thing at all, is it? This is a pagan offering! It's just a superstition of primitive peoples,' Frans shook his head. 'Imagine having your whole life dominated by spirits and superstition. Every small stream you cross, you must leave a stone on the heap. No wonder they never advanced!'

Having expressed his opinion; Frans dismissed it all as nonsense. They decided the heaps must have marked the crossing place, as upstream were deeper pools and the steep sided ravine. Downstream there were more rocks and impenetrable looking bush-lined banks. It appeared that they had also served a practical, more secular, purpose.

They returned to the shady spot beneath the canopy of the ancient fig tree and settled down for lunch, which was mostly liquid as suited a hot day. Frans told Hannes about the pottery shards he had found. They decided this might have been an old Bushman site. The Bushmen would have lived here and possibly foraged on the valley plain below. They talked about searching some of the cliffs for Bushman paintings but, because of his previous experience, Frans was wary of over-extending himself in the heat. They could look for rock paintings another day.

When they returned to the house, Frans looked for the pieces of pottery to show his colleague, but Jacob had done a more thorough job of cleaning than usual, and had throw them out with the rubbish.

It was mid summer before Frans invited anyone else to visit the farm. Domestic problems prevented Hannes from joining him, so for company Frans suggested a weekend roughing it to his teenage sons. They were not enthusiastic and made excuses. He later found out that his ex-wife's boyfriend had offered to take them to watch motor racing at Kyalami. Not in the best of moods, he decided he would camp out on his own this weekend. He drove out to the farmhouse after work on the Friday so that he could make another early start on the following morning. Before he left for his camp, he sought out Jacob to tell him where he would be and he would sleep out there overnight.

Jacob kept his views on people who slept out in the bush to himself. It also meant they could have a good time in the farm workers' shacks without the 'Baas' moaning at them about the noise on Saturday night. It was payday after all; everyone would be ready to enjoy themselves.

Frans took the familiar track to his special place at a comfortable pace. He admired the bush that was full and green after good summer rainfall. Only a few months ago had looked as if life could never be revived from such a dry and brittle land. Trees that had looked fossilized now blossomed again. The soil, which was their seed's autumn grave, had become their cradle. The seasonal miracle had occurred again and the living bush was reincarnated.

Frans scrambled over the ironstone rock formations searching for evidence of Bushmen paintings. He took his time and conscious of his previous dizzy spell by the stream, did not over exert himself in the heat of the day. He sat down to rest on a ledge. He noticed that in places the rock appeared to have wavy lines criss-crossing the surface and recognised them as ripple marks, just like those on a beach. Some school geography came back to him as he recalled how these rocks had been lain down under vast lakes or seas, millions and millions of years ago. His fingers traced the grooves in the rock floor. He smiled. Just as he had remembered a distant lesson, the rock had retained a faithful impression of its own past. He searched a while longer for any signs of bushman art and found some curious markings under a small sheltered overhang. Although he was pleased at the discovery, he decided it was time to head back down to his camp. He still needed to collect brushwood for the fire and he wanted to leave himself some daylight in which to prepare his site.

-

The fire crackled in the grate, the flames throwing their orange glow over his stone fireplace and the flat rock floor. The light picked out the lower-most leaves of the giant fig tree and now they seemed magically suspended in the dark space above him. The chorus of crickets had been sounding out since twilight and was the only other noise he could hear. From his spot he could detect no signs of civilization. Nothing from outside intruded into the flickering sphere of firelight. He sat back and opened another beer he had kept cool in the stream waters. Staring deep into the glow of the embers he was mesmerized by their changing shapes and hues. The sounds of the fire began to take on a rhythmic, almost musical quality. Shades and deep shadows became figures walking in the fire, around the fire, of the fire. The crackling wood became the 'clicks!' and 'toks!' peculiar to the Bushman tongue. The shades sublimated to people; Bushmen, gathered around the fire.

Frans was suddenly among them, sitting around their hearth placed on the smooth rock before him. Stones arranged in a circle prevented the embers from blowing away. There were more Bushmen, or more strictly their women, gathered near the fig tree. Near naked, some were ancient, others at the edge of puberty, and yet all of them exuded a lively, almost child-like manner. He saw the figures closer to him, seated at his side. A small man, taut and lean, his yellow-brown skin transformed to amber by firelight, was talking to his son. The rapid clicking and animated gestures stopped only for smiles or giggles. For a moment, the Bushman father turned and looked directly at Frans. As if recognising a friend in trouble, a smile of compassion radiated from his innocent face. It seemed Frans was welcomed to his place at the hearth.

Frans noticed the Bushmen had few possessions. Some skin blankets, clay pots, curious sticks with decorative bangles. From tiny clay pots, the Bushman took some bright yellow powder and mixing it with his saliva, showed his son how to make a certain pattern on a strip of soft leather. Although Frans could not understand the speech he knew the father was teasing his son. He would point to the design on the belt and then mime something to the womenfolk, and this brought more laughter. The son would smile shyly and shake his curly short-cropped head in good nature at being the object of the fun. Frans found himself smiling. From the reaction of the girlish figures on the far side of the fire, it must be a present, a very special gift, to one of them from the Bushman's son.

As Frans watched them he thought how perfectly they fitted here in this place. They were part of a physical and spiritual mosaic, tessellated between the rock and sky. This delicate people owned nothing and yet possessed the earth and beyond. His place was in fact theirs. Mere paper proclaiming property could never confer the real ownership upon him. He stared into the fullness of the Bushman's world and ached at the desolation of his own. His home was without a family; his time without company or laughter. His days had become as dry and lifeless as the land in a long winter. He looked into himself. Had all the joy within him been hollowed away? Was there nothing left below the deadwood and dust of his life?

Lost in thought, Frans remained huddled by the fire, hypnotized by the incandescence. The topaz flames grew pale, till all beyond the stone hearth merged into the night and the chattering voices returned to the crackle of the dying embers. Saddened, but strangely comforted, Frans curled up and slept beside the ashes.

-

At first light, Frans awoke. His body felt stiff and his clothes smelled strongly of the wood smoke still drifting from the fire. He lurched to his feet and took a long drink from the canvas water bag hanging on the tree branches. He splashed the water over his face and rubbed at his eyes that were still smarting from the smoke. He walked back to the stone fireplace and sat in the same spot as last night. How could he have seen the Bushmen who had been killed or chased out of this area by white settlers or one of the Bantu tribes well over a century ago? He turned to look at the ironstone walls. He did not normally dream, or if he did, he could not recall them. And he knew this had been no dream. His visitants had been real people and yet in this place it was he who was the visitor. They had been here, but when? Could it have been three or four hundred years ago? The ancient fig tree could have been here a thousand years and still looked just the same, splitting the aeons old rock, then as now.

His fingers picked up the faint undulating structure of ripple marks on the rock. They recalled a captured memory of times long past. He looked more intently at the rocks that he had used to build up the wall. He saw again the dark grey layers striping the boulders. Iron, iron oxides to be exact, maybe the same compounds used to coat tapes to record messages for his answering machine or music for his old cassette player. The tape could not re play itself; it needed a source of energy, not electrical in this case, but perhaps the heat from the fire. And if lasers and light could reproduce solid-looking holograms from etched surfaces, could some image be brought to life here? The stones were a fundamental part of the Bushman's existence. They would have born witness to the Bushmans' lives and retained some magnetic imprint of their times. The ironstone had been a source of their paint and a canvas for their art. It was their hearth, bed, cradle and grave. The boulders formed a simple shrine, a thanksgiving to their gods for a safe crossing of a stream.

He was the newcomer, the intruder, with plans to change this place, to count it among his possessions. Next there would be a rondaval here, a small generator, a bar counter and a drinks fridge for sun downers, some lockable cupboards, and so the list would grow. It was not the place that needed to be changed. Remorse and sadness welled up inside him. He had blundered in to a memory of Eden and started to erase it. He knew the fire would have destroyed the magnetic record of the rocks and that the magnetism would reform when they cooled. What impulses would it record now? A solitary, lonely man hunched over a bush fire. This time there would be no scene of family intimacy or congenial gathering. Just a man who wanted to get away from it all; only to find it had all gotten away from him.

He went to where the tarpaulin covered his tools and picked out a hammer and cold chisel. Placing the chisel into the mortar he started to chip away at the stone wall around his fire. He was careful not to damage the smooth stones or scar their naturally polished surface. He prised them loose one at a time and stacked them onto the tarpaulin sheet.

The summer's heat built up quickly as he worked at dismantling the wall. Long before midday the work had become onerous, but still he carried on. Frans lugged the boulders to the bank and lowered them to the gully floor. He did not want to over-exert himself in the summer's heat but felt driven to continue. He slithered down the bank to his new heap of stones. He kicked off his boots again and picked up the first of the stones. He waded across the stream to the far marker and placed the stones on what remained of the original beacon.

'I'm sorry,' he said aloud. Each time he traversed the crossing place and added the stones to the pile, he would say, 'I'm sorry.' or 'Forgive me.' and then trudge back through the water.

Whether this was for his lost family, or in memory of the Bushmen, or to his own God, he made no discrimination. It was a general penance, reparation for past mistakes. He struggled with the load of stones, back and forth. As his ancestors had laid stone upon stone to build their churches, and more distantly, had laid such stones at sacred places; so Frans re-constructed the Bushman's beacon.

Rough patches of cement that still clung to some of the boulders chaffed away at his hands. The mortar abraded his skin and tore at his blisters in a way the water-smoothed stones had not when he had first carried them. Dark smudges of blood stained the rocks. Still he carried each of the ironstone boulders, each crossing transforming his burden to an offering. He too was changing, each crossing, every stone was another piece replaced in the pattern, a wound healed.

By noon, the sun blazed directly overhead into the river gully, banishing any shadow to the tree-lined banks. The rocks on the floor of the gully reflected the heat, till it seemed as if the pools of water must boil in this natural cauldron. From some magic of its own however, the water stayed cool and sweet, while Frans became overwhelmed and more exhausted. Finally, after hours of labour, he replaced the last stone and waded back to the other side.

An eerie silence fell over the gorge. The light zephyrs ceased to move the sullen air. He stood rooted in the searing heat between the sky and the earth. As before he felt the anxiety, the inexplicable terror, build in him again. Under his sweat-soaked shirt, his skin crawled with rank fear. He was being watched, scrutinized, by something ancient and powerful. He stood swaying slightly, blinking the sweat from his eyes, almost suffocating in the turbid air. He slumped to his knees on the boulder-strewn bank of the stream. Drops of perspiration fell onto the stones before him. Weakened, bowed and submissive, he watched and waited as the sweat dried from the hot, dark stones.

He had restored all he had broken down. And yet, there was something more it wanted. Something more it demanded from him. Leaning forward, he scrabbled away the packed sand from a lump of rounded ironstone. He dug around the rock, the sand stinging his cut and blistered hands. Struggling, he prised it loose and cradled the small boulder carefully in his arms. He lurched to his feet and crossed the silent stream again. Gently, he lowered the stone on to the mound and stepped back:

'Thank you. Thank you for my safe crossing,' he said aloud.

The weight of dread started to slip from him. He had made many crossings, but it was part of the same journey. He had travelled with the pain, but he had at last reached a destination, or perhaps this was to be a new place of departure. A cooling wind dashed the surface of the pools and carried away his sadness and guilt. Birds started to sing again from the nearby bushes. They celebrated the passing of the African witching hour in the fullness of the day. The deathly thrall was broken.

Frans was to come to the special place again often, with his sons, with his new wife, and later with his grandchildren and their friends. They would sometimes make a hearth on the large smooth surface of the ironstone and laugh and tell their stories around the fire. Whenever he helped the children to cross the stream, he showed them how to place a stone on the beacon. Frans always added a stone for himself. He had once been lost and then shown the way, a safe passage. Each of the many rounded stones was a small token that recorded his gratitude.

EMERALDS

Hidden Imperfections

'What?!'

'I'm sorry Senhor, the flight to Caracus and Miami, she has been delay for twenty four hour.'

I took off my glasses and wiped the perspiration from my face with an already damp handkerchief. 'Why has the flight been delayed?' I asked irritably, rubbing at the Amazonian mosquito bites on my neck.

The small Brazilian clerk lent back in his chair and smiled apologetically: 'Senhor, you are book on a Bolivian Airline flight to Miami, which also stop at Caracus, Venezuela.'

'Yes, that's correct.'

At the time I had booked the flight in question there was an air of unreality about being able to fly from Manaus in the middle of the Amazon jungle to Miami in the United States. Now, the unreality was being realised.

'It's the only flight to the States from here. That is why I booked a passage. Can you tell me why it is delayed?'

I slumped back in the chair opposite and the seat cover moulded to my sticky body like the plastic film on supermarket vegetables.

'The President of Bolivia, he wish to fly to Venezuela for a special meeting on Wednesday, but the flight she is only on Tuesday and Friday, so ..' he gave a typical South American shrug, 'he delay the flight of the national airline until Wednesday.'

'No wonder there's a revolution in Bolivia every fortnight! I'm not surprised they want a new President.' I said exasperated by the delay.

'Senhor, this is the new President! Come back and confirm your flight tomorrow. Everything be one hundred percent, A-okay. No problem!'

I stepped out of the office and was hit by the steaming Turkish towel that is the heat and humidity of mid-day Manaus. I lifted my arm and hailed a taxi. Rivulets of sweat ran down the inside of my shirt, anxious to form yet another tributary to the mighty Amazon. A paint-peeled blur slithered to a halt on the molten ribbons of tar that the locals here call roads. When the din from the jingling icons and saints that festooned the taxi subsided, we argued about the fare. He asked for ten American dollars, I offered four. He asked eight dollars, I offered four.

'You are rich American tourist, I just poor taxi driver trying to make living,' he whined.

'I am stranded British businessman, trying to make ends meet,' I whined back.

'Brazilians are mucho poor people,' he countered.

I replied that the Brazilians who mugged me two days ago were considerably better off than I was now.

He shrugged in the traditional manner.

I signalled for another cab.

He said 'five dollars', so I climbed aboard.

The short drive back to the hotel was an unexpectedly religious experience. I pontificated on the meaning of life, and life after death. I thought deeply about what to do with my hands. Initially, I dug my fingers deep into the crumbling, plastic coated upholstery. Then I clasped them together in prayer. Finally, I placed them around the throat of the taxi driver and squeezed until he stopped the taxi. As I disembarked, I noted that the St. Christopher statuette on his dashboard looked long overdue for stress management counselling.

As a bat searches for a cave, I headed for the deep shade of the shop fronts. Once there, I risked exposing my skin. I was not surprised to see a nervous rash competing with the mosquito bites that covered most of my surface area. Sunburn had further reddened my battle-scarred epidermis, but made no more impression than would a tomato thrown against the side of a fire engine. The itching lumps on my arm reminded me that if I had to spend yet another night in that dilapidated hotel, I would need to get some insect repellent. This was not how I envisioned my business trip developing.

This was a time back in the mid 1980s and the wives and girlfriends of yuppie brokers and wheeler-dealers in Tokyo, New York and London had temporarily grown bored with decking themselves in diamond jewellery. Deep in the far-flung jungles of the world, men lived and died to dig out the exquisite gem emeralds and get them to market without getting their throats cut. Perhaps that added to the vicarious excitement of wondering how many lives might have been lost for a necklace to adorn a lovely and un-slit, neck.

Emeralds were the new status symbol. So, naturally, I had come to Brazil to buy emeralds.

'Brazil for emeralds?' I imagine you querying. 'Surely, you mean Colombia?'

And you would certainly have a point. The truly spectacular (and spectacularly expensive) vivid, translucent green emeralds are from Colombia. The stone is actually a mineral called 'Beryl' with its brilliant green colouration caused by impurities of chromium. Brazilian emeralds are still the mineral beryl, but the green colour is caused by the presence of more vanadium. The colour is not so verdant, but the upside is that the stones have far less visible imperfections. A chemist told me that vanadium atoms fit into the gem mineral atomic lattice a little better than chromium. It seems you can't have the best green colour without some niggling imperfection. However, unlike diamonds, which as you may know, are examined by the gemmologist with a loupe or magnify glass to check for flaws, emeralds are only considered 'flawed' if the inclusions can be see with the naked eye. So, if you want almost flawless emeralds, you have to accept a slightly more murky-looking Brazilian gem. Murky – that's good word – I'll touch on that later.

My first foray into the emerald business had not gone well. I had been forced to move from the modern luxury of an air-conditioned, spacious hotel room to my present quarters due to a change in fortune. The fortune changed hands in a side street. That's what happens when you get robbed in Brazil. You exchange your cash, travellers' cheques, credit cards and the samples of emerald gems you had been carrying in return for the right to retain your vital organs in a reasonable working condition. The muggers seemed particularly pleased with the emeralds, but didn't seem surprised to find that I was carrying them. As I was only a short distance from the gem dealer's premises, I am convinced that the muggers had been tipped off that I was on my way. Remember, I told you to look out for that 'murky' word.

Of course, I had tried to claim back some funds on the missing travellers' cheques, but I had lost the receipts as well. The woman clerk was sympathetic but insisted on the receipts. She told me that I should have kept them separate from the cheques as stated on all the forms. I had kept them separate; cheques in my wallet, receipts in my briefcase. Unfortunately, being a businessman, I was carrying both. The muggers probably didn't realise that they were not supposed to take everything. I put it down to inexperience on their part. However their lack of professionalism meant another night in the company of *'Mosquitos dos Amazonas'*; something I relished not at all.

I walked slowly down the street on the shady side, until I reached a *'farmacia'*. As good a place as any to obtain pharmaceutical products you might have thought.

I went to the counter and pulled out my Portuguese phrase book. The muggers didn't take that – probably because they could already speak Portuguese. Astonishingly, there was no reference to purchasing mosquito repellent, even under the section at the back of the book entitled, 'Phrases especially useful in Brazil'.

I painstakingly went through the vocabulary to construct my own phrase. The chemist observed my mutterings. He came over to offer his assistance.

I repeated the phrase I had written in the book: *'Estou pocurando um certo tipo de pooteccao, para poevenir o aparecimento desses pequinos empecilhos.'*

Roughly translated this means; *'I want some protection to stop the little bastards from getting through.'*

The chemist shrugged and returned with a box of condoms. He had probably interpreted my practising the phrase as English embarrassment before plucking up the courage to ask.

'No, No! I want mosquito repellent!' I shouted irritably.

The chemist looked at me blankly.

I pointed to my ravaged skin, 'A mosquito, shoo! Shoo!'

I gesticulated wildly as if brushing off a mosquito the size of a canary: 'A bloody mosquito!' I tried again, mimicking the sound of a mosquito and prodding my arm, 'EEEEEEEEEE! Go away! Go away!' I shouted and swatted away at imaginary insects.

The chemist regarded me warily. He probably thought that I had been attacked by a maniac with a dentist's drill. He started to edge away, back behind the counter. I lunged forward and grabbed a pen from his white dustcoat pocket. I drew a picture of a big, mean mosquito on a piece of paper. I showed it to him and then deliberately crossed it out saying, 'No! Nao!' several times. I put the paper on the counter and slammed my hand down hard on the drawing.

'Dead! Muerto! Mort! Kaput! Finis! Fin-it-o! Comprende?'

At this point, his assistant, a timid, lovely young girl with wide brown eyes, approached nervously. She held a small plastic bottle that she gave to the chemist. He took it from her and held it out towards my face, like a crucifix might be used to ward off Count Dracula.

'Creme insecticida?'

'Insect repellent? For Mosquito? Yes? Yes! Thank you, Obrigado, er, very much indeed.' I paid for the cream with my rapidly dwindling Cruzeiros and headed for a siesta in the hotel.

My hotel room was crummy, even by third world standards. The tired paint was peeling from the rodent-gnawed wood. The wood was flaking away from the crumbling masonry. In this state of sad decay, only the cockroaches looked fit and agile. I guess they had to be, to escape from the rats and withstand the chunks of falling plaster. The ceiling-mounted propeller fan cranked around slowly, only the squeaking noise noticeably disturbed the heavy humid air. The mosquito netting was also woefully inadequate. There were torn holes large enough for a hummingbird to enter, if it had been prepared to wait behind the hordes of mosquitoes queuing to dine on the room's occupant.

The room was so depressing I decided to go to lobby for a drink to replenish some lost body fluid.

'Uno Coca-Cola por favour,' I said using approximately fifty percent of my Portuguese. The waitresses' uncomprehending eyes stared at my sweaty, mosquito-customised face. I pointed a matching insect-ravaged arm at the bright red and white drinks refrigerator standing behind the counter.

'Yes,' I said as she turned and open the cabinet. She opened a bottle of orange juice and pushed it across the counter.

'Coca-cola?' I queried, pointing at the bottle. She smiled and passed me a plastic bucket containing ice.

I avoided Brazilian ice cubes like the plague. They are usually made from the local tap water. Their pristine appearance belies their lethal nature. Like the Brazilian emeralds, you can't actually see the flaws, with each cloudy ice cube probably containing millions of bacteria that make 'Montezuma's Revenge' seem like a laxative controlled weight loss programme. And of course, all these bacteria are deeply frozen and perfectly preserved for longer shelf life.

In a way, the threat of the ice cubes represented a microcosm of the land of hidden menace that is the Amazon Basin. The mustard coloured waters of the Rio Solimoes hide the deadly piranha. The aptly named Rio Negro conceals the alligator in its tar-black waters. Near the confluence of these two enormous river systems, where they form the Amazon proper, lies the capital of the region, Manaus. Invisible in its sultry night air are the mosquitoes. Hidden in its murky side streets are shadowy muggers. Concealed in leather boots are wicked-looking stiletto blades. And hidden in a small hotel room is a money, emerald and blood-drained businessman. I am he. Trapped by a clause in the airline ticket that states "El Presidente permitting".

The good thing about international air travel, as someone once said; is not that it makes exotic, remote places more accessible, it is that home is more accessible from exotic, remote places.

I must have dozed off under the hypnotic creaking of the ceiling fan. The sky was already a deep orange colour when I awoke. The twilight would be brief in these latitudes and it would be dark within minutes. The invisible crickets were tuning up for their performance, one that had been conducted every night for millions of years, and was as old as the jungle itself. Not being overly fond of music that predates Rock and Roll, I decided to go out in search of something to eat.

Apart from the spectacular meeting of the rivers, Manaus is famous for its 19th Century opera house. Its marble flooring and columns, the wrought ironwork, woodcarvings and upholstery were all imported from Europe. Ocean-going ships transported material into the heart of the jungle, when Manaus was in its rubber boom heydays. It has been said that an opera house in the middle of the jungle is one of the most incongruous sights in the world. Who ever said that has never been to Manaus, and probably has a potted Amazonian Philodendron sitting on top of their sideboard.

I, on the other hand, was headed for genuinely the most astonishing place in the Amazon Basin: a Chinese restaurant. It was a wonderful place. They spoke passable American, exchanged money at the black market rate, and served good, cheap food. The decor wasn't imported from Europe or Asia, and it was mercifully short on singing Spanish barbers, but it beat a visit to the opera any time. Thinking of the time, I gazed down at a strip of un-tanned flesh on my wrist where my watch used to be. If I wanted to know the time now I would have to ask a pre-mugging victim or a post-mugging mugger. I finished my meal amongst depictions of golden fish and hideous red dragons. I was painfully aware that monsters far more terrifying lurked beyond the air-conditioned sanctuary of the restaurant. I wasn't so bothered at the thought of being mugged again, I didn't have two Cruzeiros to rub together, let alone emeralds. No, my fear was the dreaded invisible Amazonian mosquitoes.

I walked quickly back to my hotel and headed for my room. I scanned the walls of the room for any particularly inexperienced mosquitoes that had failed to pull off the invisibility trick. There were none to be seen, so it was safe to assume that I was dealing with the professionals.

Let me tell you a little about these mosquitoes. The tourist guide would have you believe that they do not exist. The water of the Amazon is unsuitable for breeding mosquitoes, they state boldly. What they omit to mention is that there are millions of tributaries to the Amazon containing billions of gallons of virtually stagnant water that is absolutely ideal for breeding trillions of the little sods. I wouldn't be surprised if mosquitoes came from all over the world to spend their honeymoon here. But it is the local insects that bothered me. They are mean, cunning, and impervious to insecticide. They make a high pitched whining noise like a debutant being driven to a summer ball on the back of an over-revved 50cc scooter. Worse still; you never see them. They are completely invisible. I've never even seen a dead one. I suspect that they may be immortal.

I undressed, smeared myself with insect cream, lay on the bed, and switched off the light. This is like sounding the dinner gong to a hungry mosquito. Within seconds the tropical terrors began to assemble.

'NeeeeeGNEEE!'

I lay in the dark, perspiring as much from the fear as the debilitating humidity. The sound stopped. Somewhere, a tiny proboscis was being plunged into my poisoned flesh. I felt the itch and slapped hard at the spot. I switched on the light and looked at a lump ballooning near my elbow. No sign of a squashed mosquito.

I prowled around the room, eyes keened for a blood-gorged mosquito. Nothing, not a one. I climbed back into bed and waited to hear that mosquito hum. Not a sound. I switched off the light.

'Eeeeuumm. EEEEEUUUMMMM!'

I switched the light back on. The mosquito's whining had sounded distinctly more laboured, probably due the weight of my blood it had ingested. There was still no sign of them. I buried myself under the sheet. I couldn't breathe in the stifling heat. I sat up in bed.

'All right! Just try and get me now, you little bastards!' I shouted. As I heard the totally invisible mosquitoes drone towards me, the telephone rang. The manager had heard shouting from my room; was everything all right?

'Yes,' I replied through gritted teeth as several more festering lumps appeared on my body. I stalked around the room again, disturbing the nocturnal migrations of the cockroaches. I glanced over at the dressing table. The lumpy, anaemic face that peered back at me from the ancient mirror seemed to be flawed, even missing a few pieces. Whether this was from the mosquitoes or from the blistered holes in the mirror's silvering, I did not know. The expression on what remained of the face was beyond doubt. Utter despair.

I was totally defenceless. By dawn the invisible mosquitoes would have carried off enough fluid to make a small blood donor unit proud. I couldn't wait that long and I had used up nearly all the so-called insect repellent. I had an idea.

I dragged my almost bloodless limbs to the bathroom. I turned on the taps and cloudy, tepid water spluttered out. There was a 'not drinking water' sign above the taps; as if anyone needed telling. The taps heaved and coughed water that looked as if it had been piped directly from the Rio Solimoes. The greeny-yellow water was opaque, the chipped enamel of the tub could not be seen below the cloudy surface. I thought briefly of the emeralds I had lost. Their murky quality had hid their imperfections, but the flaws were still there. Perhaps I should have tried Colombia after all. Frankly though, I was too tired to care.

The warm bath water, disgusting as it was, was like balm to my puffy skin. Just my heavily creamed nose, eyelids and forehead protruded above the surface. I understood what the river alligators saw in this sort of life style. I wondered why I hadn't thought of this before. With ears below the water, even the sound of the mosquitoes had disappeared. Nearly overcome with exhaustion, I started to doze.

A searing pain in my leg jolted me back to consciousness. A second shock felt as if my flesh was being gouged out by vice grips. I leapt out of the bath clutching my leg. The blood seeped out between my fingers and as I grabbed for a towel, some spots fell into the bath. I saw a movement at the edge of my tear-blurred vision. The darkened bath water rippled briefly, as if something unseen had stirred in its turbid depth. I looked with horror at the raw wound and ripped flesh.

There could be no doubt: I had been attacked by an invisible piranha.

CHALK

Chalk and Cheats

The ride south along the M1 motorway in his new Jaguar XJ had been an easy journey. The trip from his hometown of Barnsley, via the gritty tors of Yorkshire, to the gently rolling chalk fields of a leafy Hertfordshire town, had gone as smoothly and as inevitably as his rise from butcher's apprentice to sports millionaire. Billy 'the Butcher' Boyd had come a long way since leaving school at the age of sixteen.

The TV commentators and master of ceremonies had loved the fact he came from a working class background and that he had briefly been a butcher's boy before becoming a professional snooker player. The alliteration of; 'Here's Billy, 'the Butcher' Boyd from Barnsley' was too good to miss; along with the oft repeated pun about him clearing the snooker table, 'chop-chop'.

He acknowledged he'd had his share of good luck: and even when Lady Luck hadn't smiled at him – the head of a large gambling syndicate had made up for it with a pretty convincing grin.

His charmed life continued away from the snooker halls. If there was a problem; something that might affect his concentration and his game, others were there for him to make it disappear, clean and clinical: 'chop-chop'. So he'd gone on and made his fortune when he'd won his trophies and then made another supplementary fortune when, against the odds, he'd unexpectedly lost the occasional big match.

Ironically, it was to be back in Yorkshire that his crooked luck ran out. It was during last weekends' snooker championships final in the Crucible Theatre in Sheffield; the game plan had come undone almost with the last stroke of the match. It was an unlucky break – that's what he would tell the big man - just one of those things.

He was paid to put up a great performance and then with the odds climbing during live betting; he was paid to lose and blow the match big time. There had been an international betting scam a few years before with top players throwing matches; but hustle had always been part of this game. The secret was to make it look good and he'd managed it for years. Still, he was in his mid-forties now and although many might laugh at the idea that a certain amount of athleticism was required for snooker; it was easy to underestimate the amount of stretching, balance, and concentration that went into the perfectly poised shot.

He turned off the motorway at Junction 10 and turned off the music station. It wasn't really his kind of music, but his new wife, Jeannie, was about 15 years younger than him and for her sake it paid to be interested in the kind of modern crap they played on the radio nowadays. He decided to use the time to rehearse his defence speech to his paymaster.

'It was like this,' he said aloud. 'It could have happened at any time, really. I was getting down low, lined up to have a pot at the pink – and it was too easy. No pro could have missed that shot. You don't want people getting suspicious do you? Not with these stakes. So I decided to give it a crack and rattle it in the jaws so it wouldn't drop – close as you like – but no cigar.'

Boyd paused his monologue and wiped a little sweat from his brow and continued for the sake of his imaginary audience.

'So, right enough, I'm lined up just a couple of millimetres off and then it happens! I play the stroke, but my back – I told you about my back didn't I? Remember, when we met up on the QT in your fancy place in Barbados – that's why I couldn't do the windsurfing with Jeannie. Anyway, my back goes into spasm. Right then, just as I played the bloody stoke. And bugger me! The pink ball flew into the pocket! I couldn't believe it. The white ball, of course, spins back and lines up perfectly for the final pot on the black so Xiang couldn't miss what was supposed to be the final shot. And then, Xiang, the honourable Asiatic gentleman he is, stood up and shook my hand to concede! He didn't even give me a chance to rectify it with a foul on the black. Anyway that would have been seriously untoward of course - and the bloody crowd went mad. I mean, what could I do?'

'Butcher' Boyd knew what he could do – he'd have to hand over the quarter of a million pound sterling prize money for a start as part of the compensation for what the betting ring had lost. It would have run into millions of dollars, laid off in Australia and all the way around the Pacific Rim gambling circles. Shit!

Okay – he would owe the big man – but it could be sorted; surely? As of a couple of days ago – he was now three times world champion – they'd get even better odds on his opponent next time.

-

He turned the Jaguar into the private road alongside the village common and steered again to drive down the secluded gravelled driveway to his house. He saw the Subaru sports car parked to the side.

Bugger! Bluey was here already! The Big Man must have sent his even bigger Aussie henchman around to have a word with him. Boyd felt nervous; Bluey wasn't the kind of man with the patience to listen to a well-crafted explanation. He was tall, muscular, sandy-haired; Boyd thought he was probably ex–forces. Despite being in his late twenties, Bluey still had something of the old fashioned thug about him. He had shown no interest in the vagaries of the movement of ball on baize, or interest in anything else outside of his minder's job so far as Boyd had been able to discern.

Boyd pulled the car to stop outside the front door and stepped out. There was no sign of Jeannie's car and the Audi was unoccupied. He left his suitcases in the Jaguar and opened the wide oak door to the large gabled house and walked into the hallway.

'Hello?' he called.

Bluey appeared in the vestibule.

'Jeannie let me in,' he said.

'Where's Jeannie?'

'Out.'

Bluey was a man of very few words. He picked the mobile phone out of his jacket pocket and hit the speed dial button. He waited a few seconds before the call was answered. Bluey said: 'He's here now.' He handed the phone over to Boyd.

It was the Big Man calling. He never called Boyd directly and Boyd never called him. Win or lose, the instructions and transactions always came through an intermediary. Boyd listened apprehensively to the voice on the other end of the phone. He walked through the house to the games room where he had installed his bespoke handcrafted Riley snooker table. The taciturn Bluey followed behind, silent as a shadow.

The Big Man's call was brief and menacing: 'You screw up – you pay up' was the message. He wasn't interested in Boyd's explanation. He laid out what he wanted; the prize money and another quarter of a million. He magnanimously reassured Boyd he would be able to pay off the rest of his debt with a few fixes here and there during the forthcoming Asian world snooker tour. He would send Bluey to watch over him as he went to his bank to make a sizeable withdrawal. Then the minder would relieve him of the cash shortly afterwards.

'It's just business. Nothing personal, Billy Boy, but we have to balance the books,' the Big Man concluded. 'We can still do business together, but now we have to re-establish the trust, right?'

Boyd tried a half-hearted protest it would take time to organise a cash withdrawal of that size, but the Big Man wasn't sympathetic. Seeing the bored expression on Bluey's face, Boyd sensed he wasn't interested in his plight either.

'I'll be outside,' Bluey said and left Boyd with the phone.

Boyd tried to wheedle a little more time from his boss, but he wasn't getting anywhere.

'You're starting to irritate me, Billy. You don't want that, do you? Remember when Doreen was irritating you, Billy? You came to me and complained the late Mrs Boyd was being unreasonable? In fact, the exact phrase you used was that: "she was being a royal pain in the arse"; threatening to go to the papers, messy divorce, and of course, the inevitably big alimony settlement. The stress was putting you off your game; you said. Remind me, Billy, this was all just a few months after you'd met the lovely Jeannie at my club, wasn't it?'

Boyd turned pale and lowered his voice: 'What? What are you saying? Doreen was killed in an accident! It was a hit-and-run, that's what the police said. I wasn't even in the country at the time.'

'An accident? Wake up, Billy! Don't tell me you never thought about it? Everyone knew Doreen always went for her morning run at the same time. Always down the same quiet lane at the back of the Common. Lucky for you, it happened just before she went to the papers with the details of your affair with a long-legged, Aussie cocktail waitress. They would have lapped it up mate, especially with our Jeannie being so photogenic – even with her clothes on – am I right?' There was a brief pause. 'The driver was never caught was he? So you get the picture, Billy? I've relieved you of your little irritations; it's only fair you relieve me and mutual friends of ours.'

Shocked, Boyd muttered he would see what he could do. The call ended and he put Bluey's mobile phone down on the edge of the table. His hands trembled as he headed for the drink cabinet to pour a large whiskey.

Could it be true? Doreen's death wasn't merely a freak of fate as he had always believed - but was actually a coldblooded hit? Christ! He'd never asked for her to be killed – he'd not even joked about such a thing to the Big Man, even when he 'were reet dowly'. Sure, he'd bemoaned his luck over a couple of drinks; that was only natural. He told the Big Man they'd married when they were too young, for more than fifteen years; but they'd grown apart, what with all the travelling he had done. Still, he'd looked after her; she'd wanted for nothing. She was a sight better off with him than if she'd stayed with the useless lump with the calloused hands who worked night shifts in the glass factory.

He thought back over those events. Doreen was mad as hell when she found out about Jeannie; a woman scorned an all that; but murdered, surely not? For someone to deliberately to lay in wait and drive into her when she was out on her morning run..! Boyd shuddered. He remembered when he'd heard about Doreen's death, he'd been in a tournament in Singapore. He'd been hot favourite to win, even without the fix in place, but when he'd been told the news, he'd immediately withdrawn from the competition and flown back home. The Big Man had told him not to worry about it – they'd sort it all out.

Another dark and deeply troubling thought occurred to him. The Big Man's syndicate would have planned to finish off Doreen; knowing all the while he'd have to pull out the tournament. The syndicate would have already bet against him as the eventual winner, all without him knowing the plan. Or - the whole story was a big con trick; it was only a freak accident after all. Perhaps the Big Man was playing mind games; threats and blackmail to keep him in line.

He sat down in the leather-padded chair and looked at the luxurious surroundings of the panelled games room with the solid snooker table sitting in the middle. He'd been in tight spots before, both in life and on the snooker circuits. But things had worked out, either through his skill or cheating, he'd come out well. After a respectful period of mourning for Doreen, albeit interrupted by discrete and comforting hotel trysts with Jeannie; his exuberant mistress had moved into the Hertfordshire home as his second wife. And it had been damn good; Jeannie continued to be easy going, game for a laugh and enthusiastic in the sack.

Boyd wasn't completely besotted though; he knew Jeannie expected the good life in return. He suspected that she regarded the clothes, the jewellery and the parties, along with a spot of recreational cocaine use, as being the main benefits of being seen on the arm of a successful sporting personality. As much as they both enjoyed these things together, Boyd was sure she wouldn't hang around if she found out he'd lost the lot; or even the half a million in cash that he'd be forced to pay back now.

Bluey walked back into the room. 'The money?'

'Look, I've got a bit of cash here, but I don't keep that kind of money lying around. I'll have to 'phone ahead to arrange a withdrawal from the bank. I'll need to go to the local branch and pick it up from the Bank Manager in person.'

'Phone him now.'

'Yes, okay. I'll make a call. The bank won't be happy about the short notice.'

'Tough,' said Bluey.

Boyd noticed the man subconsciously licked his lips. He'd seen his snooker opponents do the same when they were apprehensive about a difficult shot and trying to remain calm. He wondered briefly what Bluey had to be nervous about – after all, he was the one who was being threatened.

'Need to use the dunny,' Bluey declared abruptly and headed out the room for the downstairs guest toilet.

Boyd stood up, stretched his stiff back and groaned aloud. There was nothing else for it. He went over to the house telephone and rang his local bank. He spoke to the manager about his urgent need to withdraw a very large amount in cash and he would pick it up in person from the branch.

The bank manager was taken by surprise and protested that it was too short notice for such a large sum. However, as they were occasional golfing partners and he enjoyed rubbing shoulders with Billy and other celebrities at one of 'Butcher' Boyd's famous 'hog roast' barbeque and garden parties, he reluctantly relented. The manager consoled himself with the thought that the world champion could earn the money back quickly enough to top up his account.

As Boyd ended the call, he heard a vibrating sound on the side table. He noticed that the hired hand had not picked up his mobile phone again after he had used it to talk to the Big Man. He looked at the handset, curious to see the message. He was shocked to see Jeannie's easily recognisable number lit up on the screen. He prodded the button to open the message.

'AV U GOT $ YET?' it read.

Boyd puzzled over the unfamiliar text-speak. What did she mean: 'Have you got the dollars yet?' Why was Jeannie texting Bluey to ask if he'd collected the Big Man's extortion money? In fact; how did she even get to hear about it?

Boyd quickly clicked the screen to 'mark unread' and carefully put it back down on the table.

That was it then. He'd been stitched up, snookered even. He snorted at the irony of it. He'd consider himself the master stroke player, but it was he who had been hustled by the Big Man. The pay offs, the lifestyle, the TV endorsements, all supplemented by snorts of the white stuff at private parties. Then, what he had thought was his luckiest break; the introduction to flirtatious Jeannie in the Big Man's club. Boyd guessed now that luck had nothing to do with it. They'd lined him up and fired him off in Jeannie's direction. The result was inevitable. As he went around the tournaments, pocketing the balls and clearing the tables; she was set to screw him right down deep into the Big Man's pocket. The only remaining block to their plans was Doreen, who had been uncerimoniously bumped off the table and out of the game.

Boyd groaned softly and held his head in his hands. Even if he paid up now, the celebrity TV shows would come to an end without the Big Man's support. His name would disappear from endorsements and advertising. The nice little earners from 'Butcher's Boyd' merchandise, the range of cue sticks and chalks would be taken off the shelves. His name would be replaced by another snooker star with an equally ridiculous nickname. And the Big Man would find a new star for Jeannie to wrap her long legs around. God, that really hurt.

He thought about Jeannie's role further. He became convinced that she had to be in on it. What had she been promised? They'd only been married a short while, but she'd still walk away with a handsome slice of his wealth in the inevitable divorce. He might even suffer the same fate as Doreen; Jeannie would inherit the lot after his sudden demise. It was obvious; he'd been framed and set up from the start. The syndicate was set to clear the table, take the money and dump him out; chop-chop.

Boyd knew he'd have to think fast. He was in a very tight spot; and he had to play his way out. It required skill and finesse. Just getting out of a tricky situation didn't win you anything; but putting your opponent in to an impossible position, did.

He walked around the snooker table, making as if he were practicing some shots. He heard the downstairs toilet flush and a few moments later Bluey lumbered back into the games room.

Bluey picked up his phone and read the message that Jeannie had left without betraying any emotion. 'Time to go,' he said, indicating the door with a nod of his head.

'The manager said it would take at least an hour to get the money ready. There's no point in going early and then be left hanging around in the bank. You don't want to cause any suspicions, do you?' Boyd said reasonably, potting another shot and watching as the cue ball rolled back towards the top cushion at the end of the table where Bluey was standing. He walked round the table: 'Take it easy. Here, while we wait; have a look at this.'

Boyd lifted a small bowl of white powder to show the minder.

'What is it?'

'Well, it's not coke! You couldn't leave it around near Jeannie!' Boyd joked. 'Nah, it's some perfumed hand chalk that they've asked me to endorse. What do you think?'

Boyd lifted the bowl towards Bluey's face; as if inviting him to smell it.

As Bluey lowered his head to sniff the chalk, Boyd blew into the bowl, sending a thick cloud of dust into the man's face.

The henchman staggered back in surprise, raising his hands to wipe the dust from his eyes. He didn't see Boyd snatch the cue ball from the table.

Boyd smash the resin ball down on Bluey's temple with all the strength he could manage. He landed several rapid blows on Bluey's head. As the minder slumped under the assault, Boyd grabbed his handcrafted cue and swung it down hard. The vicious blow from the heavy ebony handle split the man's scalp and cracked his skull.

The henchman lay still on the floor. Boyd leant back against the snooker table panting with exertion. He dropped the shattered remains of the snooker cue. It had taken him more effort than he'd thought. In the films, the hero walloped someone hard over the head, and that was it, game over. Bluey was obviously made of tougher stuff.

Boyd watched as the blood oozed from his victim's head and percolated through the fine white chalk dust. He carefully wiped the blood from the cue ball with a sweat towel and put the ball back on the table. He placed the towel under the dead man's head to prevent the blood contaminating his polished wood floor.

'One down,' he thought grimly and after getting his breath back, he set about lining up his next move.

—

Jeannie was having a coffee in a bistro a few miles away in St Albans when she received a text message on her phone.

'CUM BK NOW.

She looked at the message and then tried to ring Bluey's number, but the phone had been switched off. She tossed the mobile phone back into her bag in frustration.

After Billy had stuffed up everything by winning the championship, she knew full well the game was up. The last few years had had their good moments; but she wasn't going to stay around to see if Billy could repair the lucrative relationship with the Big Man; it was time to move on. All Bluey had to do was make sure Billy drew the money from the bank and stand over him while he emptied the safe; it was that simple. Then they would meet up and be on their way. But Jeanie knew Bluey's attractive qualities of being fit and physically appealing had to be balanced out by the fact that he wasn't exactly the sharpest knife in the box. She wondered what the dumb galah had screwed up this time.

—

Fifteen minutes later she pulled the car into her home's driveway and saw both her husband's and Bluey's cars still parked there. She'd hoped to avoid any unpleasant 'domestic' arguments. Still, Bluey was there to sort it out, if Billy should be unwise enough become unreasonable. She heard Billy calling out to her.

'Christ! What now?' she said aloud and went into the house.

Boyd rushed through the hallway to meet her.

'Jeannie! Thank God, you're here! There's been an accident. It's Bluey, I think he had a heart attack. He collapsed and hit his head!' He tugged at her at her arm, ushering her to the games room.

In her confusion, Jeannie didn't question the matter that people having heart attacks rarely had the ability or inclination to send text messages.

'Where is he?'

'He's on the patio outside. Quick, go through the French windows.'

"That's right," thought Boyd grimly: "Nudge her in to position. Line her up for the next shot." He'd no intention of repeating the crude bludgeoning he had needed to finish off Bluey.

Jeanie hurried through the games room and out through the doors. She didn't notice the drag marks through the chalk dust, or of Boyd's movement as he followed a few paces behind. She saw Bluey's prone body and almost threw herself down on the patio paving beside him. She was too distraught to recognise that the injuries could not have been caused by a simple fall. Alternatively swearing and crying, she called Bluey's name and patted his face repeatedly in a futile attempt to get a response.

Boyd quickly took up his stance behind her and raised his prized Number 3 wood above his head. He reasoned the sweet spot on Jeannie's neck would be about the same size as a golf ball. There was the slightest swishing sound as the club swung through its arc, smashing into her spine, shattering the vulnerable neck vertebrae. His cheating wife collapsed forward over his earlier victim, never knowing what had hit her.

-

It was two days before he received the telephone call he had been expecting. For the first time, the Big Man had called him directly. He was angry and wanted to know what he was fucking about at; where was his money?

Billy Boyd had practiced his tone of righteous anger. He bravely told the Big Man to stop pissing him about: he knew what had happened. Bluey had come round, waited to collect the cash he'd brought back from the bank and then cleaned out the money from the safe he had on the premises – every penny of it, nearly half a million quid. Then, Boyd added in his bitterest tone; his wife had told him she was leaving and left with Bluey, taking her jewellery, her clothes and a small stash of powdered candy. He paused in his invective and then resumed in a despairing tone. He told the Big Man he was shocked and heartbroken that she could dump him, after all they had done together. He carried on with his rehearsed lines, crying about how much he loved and missed Jeannie, but his whining was cut short.

The Big Man was apoplectic – he was in no mood to hear Boyd blubbering about his Aussie tart doing a runner. As far as he was concerned, Jeannie had served her purpose. Still, he could barely believe what he was hearing; the ever-loyal Bluey had done a runner with his money, let alone left with a woman. The Big Man reiterated in strident tones that he still wanted the money, but Boyd was ready with his reply.

'You've had your money! I drew it out and I handed it all to Bluey, just as you told me; every last fucking penny! If he's gone, then he's done a runner with your money - and my wife! The bastard's obviously planned it out!'

The Big Man snorted: 'Bluey? He couldn't plan his way out of a piss-soaked paper bag! And you reckon he was screwing your missus?' He paused for reflection. 'No, it can't have been Bluey; it must have been Jeannie's idea. She could be quite smart when she wasn't replacing most of her brains cells with Colombian candy.'

The big man swore and ranted on what he was going to do to the pair of them when he tracked them down. He came back to the issue of the money. Trying to regain the upper hand, he sneeringly told Billy that he hadn't any proof he'd handed over the money to Bluey.

Boyd was ready with his follow up shot; 'Oh, but I have. The bank manager is my witness, as is the receipt for the withdrawal. I've had time to think things over. If anything unusual should happen to me, I've placed letters at several solicitors to be opened after my death. They give details of every game we've manipulated and each contains a copy of a photograph of us all together at the party in Barbados when we met up a couple of years back.'

'Rot in hell!'

'Yes, maybe I will: but I'll drag you and your syndicate down with me. We'll all end up losers. But it doesn't have to be that way, does it? I'm still game to try and win a few dollars back, like we did before; but I've paid all my debts. If you want the other money – then find where Bluey and Jeannie are shacked up.' To reinforce his aggrieved act, Boyd added; 'And let me know, too!'

The call ended with more belligerent words on both sides, but Boyd was convinced he'd done enough. He looked over to where a second safe was hidden behind the panelling, the smaller safe even Jeannie didn't know about. He smiled to himself, satisfied in the knowledge it was now crammed with half a million pounds in cash. He walked through the open French windows and out in to the evening twilight. It was nice to have a pleasant evening again after what had seemed like weeks of rain.

He strolled down the long garden path to the barbeque pit area. It was built a few years back, large enough to cater for the 'hog roast' get-togethers for which he was famed. However this evening, there were no guests or a succulent Saddleback pig on a spit, no appetising aroma of roasting pork. He poked at the glowing coals in the fire pit. He noted with satisfaction that the putrid smell of burning human entrails had passed, the remains all consumed by fire.

His old craft as a butcher's apprentice had served him well. The tools of his former trade were as sharp as ever, his hands were steady and his aim was straight. It was physically no more difficult than dealing with a large saddleback porker; chop-chop, and it was done. He had felt a moment's squeamishness about removing the human heads and innards, but it was the best way. He wasn't going to risk putting his back out again by dragging two whole corpses around; Bluey alone weighed over a hundred kilos. He reached into his trouser pocket and threw a couple of paper tickets into the flickering coals. They were from the long-term parking lot at Gatwick Airport where he had left Bluey's Subaru and from the train journey he had taken to travel incognito to get back home.

He waited until it was nearly dark and headed to the potting shed where he collected the first of several thick plastic bags containing an assortment of severed limbs. It would take too long to burn the whole bodies and he didn't want to risk any neighbours popping around to see what might be cooking on his barbeque. He'd tried to bury the bags in his garden, but the soil was too thin. He dug down a spade length only to find the crumbling chalk bedrock was only a few inches below the turf. Looking for an alternative spot, he noticed that the field at the bottom of his garden rolled down a short slope. He reasoned the soil might be thicker at the bottom of the hill. An earlier exploratory visit had shown there was a slight depression in the lower corner of the field. Although still muddy with the recent rain, the ground was easily dug, even being careful with his back.

He carried two bags down to the bottom of the field, uncovered his spade from the hedgerow and finished deepening the hole. He unceremoniously dropped the bags in the hole and trudged back to fetch another gruesome load.

-

It was midnight when Boyd retuned to the hole with the final bag. He could make out enough in the moonlight to see the hole looked as if it had been widened, but partially filled in. Even the spade that he had left there had become part submerged in the soil. Boyd wondered if foxes had disturbed the partially buried limbs, or perhaps the soil had just slumped back into the hole. Either way; he would have to dig further down again or the grave would be too shallow.

He looked around and listened, but there was no sound of traffic on the lane that was a further field away. He would not be disturbed. He put the last bag on the side of the hole and stepped down in the pit. Annoyed at having to do more work; he retrieved the spade and started to lash the dirt out again.

He felt something give and he sank a little in the soil. He shuddered as he thought he might have stepped on one of the bags and punctured it, sending his foot down on the body parts of his victims.

He dug down further and shifted the earth to point where he partially uncovered the black plastic bags he'd thrown in earlier. Strange, he hadn't thought he had dug the hole so deep. He was reaching to climb out of the hole when he felt a jolt and more dirt settled down into the pit. He tried to free himself but his legs were buried to his knees in the muddy soil. He tried to wriggle free but this only caused him sink further as if he were in quicksand. Irritated and cursing, he grasped the spade and tried to jam it into the side of the hole so that he could use it to lever himself out. The spade pulled loose as soon as he tried to haul himself out and he tried again, driving down harder. The effort caused his back muscles to spasm. With horror, he realised he was now sunk to his waist in the field's soil. He was being dragged down; his eyes almost level with the rim of the pit. He laid the spade handle flat on the soil in front of him to spread the load. He tried again to hoist his weight on the spade handle, but it was hopeless. His muscles refused to take the load and the pain in his back was unbearable. He could feel the pressure on the lower half of his body as he was slowly being sucked down into the earth.

The ground juddered slightly and he was encased up to his chest, more soil slid in from the sides; a small avalanche slowly burying him in his own pit. Too late, he realised what was happening. He'd dug the grave into the mouth of a small sinkhole. That's why there was a depression in the field. Over the years some of the underlying chalk had dissolved, leaving a void. The recent rains had washed away some of the infill and now the sinkhole had started to collapse again, pulling in the soil and everything around it.

He vividly remembered from the news that a street in a nearby village had been evacuated as the road had collapsed in to a gaping maw. He'd heard other cases of people, cars, whole buildings that had been devoured; never to be seen again. No, he mustn't think like that! Sinkholes weren't that common around here, this must be a small one. He had to stay calm: take the pressure off his back and then he could carefully crawl his way out once the subsidence stopped. The small sinkhole might prove to be a blessing; it would ensure that the corpses would stay buried forever.

He had been dozing from exhaustion when the ground shook again. The bag containing Jeannie's head teetered on the edge of rim. It slipped, sending her decapitated head rolling into the pit besides his face. Screaming in panic, he tried to knock the head away, twisting, trying to avoid the dead gaze of his victim. The movement only pulled him down deeper, drawing Jeannie's face down on top him, the rancid smell of death filling his nostrils.

-

Light rain started to fall again on the chalky fields as dawn broke. Boyd did not register the drops of rain or the light on his face. His breathing laboured as the earth packed tighter around his rib cage. Barely conscious, his nightmare continued. His body was being sucked down into hell, but in his delirium, his mind had arrived there several hours earlier.

The remnants of the thin chalk ledge finally gave way, sending Boyd, the cadavers and more mud into the void. Billy Boyd had a fleeting view of a circle of light above him as he tumbled down into the empty pocket.

QUARTZ

The Mote in God's Navel

Numwort the monk dropped his tools and sat in the shade of his menhir. He was tired, his arms ached and worse still, his navel (unworthy likeness of the eternal Navel of Tumg!) itched maddeningly. He resisted the temptation to scratch. In this, he did as all good monks should. It was probably the only rule the others still kept. He rested his back against the large lump of quartz and gazed out across the plain. His hands were blistered from wielding the hammer and chisel. Progress was painstakingly slow. For a moment he envied the scientists their comfortable life.

Numwort turned and studied the menhir that he had been bludgeoning down to size. After days of work, the hard quartz was little altered in appearance. It was still angular with many remaining sharp edges. The stone had barely settled into the earth and could not have lain long before it was found. (All praise to Tumg in whose Navel we live!) The inhabitants, their faith once more renewed by the sudden appearance of the foreign object, rushed to tell the priests of Tumg science. An inspection was followed by the ceremonies of condemning the stone. Numwort recalled the words, 'Stone, though you appear to us as monstrous, you are nothing but a mote, a speck of dirt in the Navel of Tumg. We who are but puny, will diminish you. We will destroy your blasphemous shape even as Tumg will destroy those who serve him not. We will not falter in our task, for by cleaning the Navel of God we cleanse ourselves. For Stone, in your destruction lies our salvation. Let us be pure, even as we purify the great Navel of Tumg. For we are one with the Navel. and the Navel is the centre of Tumg. May this sacred task be to the eternal glory of Tumg.'

Numwort massaged his cramped hand and grimaced. For 'We' substitute 'Numwort the Monk' he thought bitterly. For it was actually he who had been given the task to destroy the monstrous orthostat. Was he chosen for this task because he was the best? Was he the most pure? No. He was chosen because (Forgive, oh Tumg!) the Arch-priest disliked him above all others.

Numwort felt that the ancient brotherhood had become distanced from their original calling. The old monasteries had been the only places of learning in the dark times. It was natural that they would attract the finest intellects and enquiring minds. Then they had become involved in secular issues and their power grew. Science was the new master. The priesthood was now a cabal of monks and scientists and the monasteries were now laboratories.

He sighed as he remembered the high priests in their glorious robes and the ritual around the stones. The exalted Prophetess had only a simple garment and a hammer and chisel. The Texts said she worked day and night, chipping at those huge stones until her hands bled. She was mocked for her belief she was serving only the one God, Tumg, (in whose Navel we shall live forever). She preached and worked with a few followers, and when the great day of destruction arrived, she and her followers alone were spared. So now generations later, he too had been spared. Perhaps 'spared' wasn't the right word, it was as if he had been left to one side. Numwort felt he had never really fitted in anywhere. His physical appearance discouraged any close friendships. His small, but portly frame with an almost semi-spherical belly made him the subject of cruel jokes. Even his admission into the priesthood had not been without embarrassment. He had only been accepted when a kindly Elder pointed out that; despite his odd appearance, he did in fact have a navel, the mark of Tumg. Things had not gone well, however. There seemed to be a new movement in the religious order. He was regarded as a rustic fundamentalist. They eyed his ungainly physique and thought he was a buffoon by association. Despite this, Numwort had studied hard and passed his religious and obligatory scientific schooling. He was not ungrateful for the opportunity he had been given.

Now he had been posted to the Navel plains where most of these peculiar objects appeared. Great, jagged blocks of quartz, two or three times his height. In accordance with the religious rites, these blocks would have to be rendered down into rounded, smoothed menhirs. Only then would they not penetrate the surface of the earth. He shifted his position against the megalith and felt the jab of a sharp corner. He wondered again about the origin of the evil stones. They were made of a substance totally alien to everything in his world. They were called quartz or stone, because of its toughness. And yet the stone on their world, was but a thin crust of petrified skin on the surface of the Navel of God. Tumg in his wisdom had provided such for them for protection and shelter, once they had been expelled from the warm recesses in the folds of His Navel. But the alien stone was more resilient. The metals that could be extracted in small quantities from the surface, such as calcium, sodium, and potassium, were all far softer than this infernal stone. Only iron; so rare the priesthood was its sole custodian; could make any impression on the megaliths.

The Texts said Tumg took pity on the few survivors from the Day of Destruction. He scratched his skin and his blood, the very essence of Tumg himself, welled into the cut and solidified. Only in this one place was iron found. The scientists had also shown that miniscule amounts of iron were to be found in man's own blood. More proof (if it were needed) that man and the Earth and the Navel of Tumg were indivisibly linked.

As Numwort daydreamed in the shade of the menhir, he failed to notice a small party making their way to his position. Unfortunately for Numwort, they noticed him first. 'Taking a rest, with so much still to do, Brother?'

Numwort groaned inwardly and came to his feet, 'Your Eminence, the stone is hard and my hands are callused in the service of Tumg. May I be blown like dust from the periphery, if I lie!'

'Ah yes, the Navel periphery; the limit to our universe!' The cardinal raised a mocking eyebrow and smiled at the others.

'We all serve Tumg as we are able,' said Numwort, ignoring the cardinal's sarcasm. 'Indeed, so I need not remind you that it is your duty to smooth this megalith...'

'...as it is your task to flake the first chip of quartz with your ceremonial chisel, your Eminence. An exhausting task; I'm sure.'

The cardinal reddened. 'Your impudence will be punished! Prepare yourself for an appearance before the high counsel!'

'I have served Tumg for a lifetime, I will need no further preparation.' Numwort turned back to the stone and continued with his work.

-

Numwort sat on a small uncomfortable chair and looked at the twelve high priests who were enthroned before him. The cardinal had already given his account of Numwort's laziness and disrespect. Others had attacked his fundamentalist views as archaic and regressive. His lack of interest in furthering the understanding of Tumg, or 'science' as it was being called, was held against him. His general fitness for life in the order had been question again.

'Numwort, what say you in your defence?'

'I serve Tumg as stated in the Texts. Nowhere do I read that it is the duty of followers to understand the workings of Tumg; only to do his will and cleanse the eternal Navel. That surely is our sacred purpose,' Numwort paused: 'Our brotherhood has changed the humble places of worship into laboratories for dubious studies. The Texts state we live in the Navel of God. To serve Him, we carry out the only task for which we are fit, we clean his Navel which is our earth. Thus as we depend on God, He in His glory, depends on us. It is a trust, a sacred bond that ties us in the trinity of God, the earth and ourselves. What else is there to know, what else to believe?'

The high priests stirred uncomfortably in their ornate chairs. They whispered amongst themselves for several minutes before turning once again to Numwort.

'None of us here doubt the sincerity of your beliefs, Numwort. But, as a follower of our order, it is your duty to follow where the Elders are leading the movement. The greatest minds of our time are working together to unravel the workings of Tumg. They reveal more intricacies of our world daily, we marvel at the ingeniousness of His grand plan. A deeper understanding, not just a blind obedience, brings us closer to Him,' the Elder explained gently, like a patient teacher.

Numwort felt more encouraged: 'But your worship, the Texts, handed down from the Prophetess herself, say how we must serve Tumg to save ourselves, the account of the stones, the day of destruction! Her prophesies were true, there was no place for science then ....'

'We do not dispute these facts, Numwort. Would you say the revered Prophetess was a special person?'

'Well of course!'

'She was especially gifted? Wiser? And yet, compassionate?'

Numwort nodded, unsure of where the questioning was leading.

'Imagine then, she was intuitively aware of some of the science that we are now discovering. She knew of the great threat these alien stones could cause if the quartz were allowed to penetrate the epidermis of our world. How could she explain to the others, who were but simple peasant folk for the most part?'

'She had a vision from the Eternal Tumg!' Numwort blurted out, 'The texts tell us!'

'Quite! Certainly she was inspired. However, somehow knowing of the great danger, she explained to the people in terms that they could understand. As you are aware, the idea of the earth being the Navel of God predates the Prophetess by many centuries. We now believe that the Prophetess emphasised this so any matter foreign to the Navel was by definition, evil. To prevent these objects from penetrating the surface of the earth, they were made smaller and smoothed.'

'Those that ignored her warning were destroyed!' asserted Numwort.

'We do not dispute this, but seek to understand it! The Prophetess knew instinctively that these mysterious stones would bring disaster, so she set about ensuring none would penetrate the substratum, or as she symbolically illustrated the point, the skin on the Navel of Tumg,' said the Elder. He looked at his fellow high priests, who were showing signs of impatience with the debate.

Numwort was not to be cowed: 'But you, the scientist-priests; you admit this stone is unique? It is an element that is not to be found anywhere in the natural and eternal Navel of Tumg!'

'Yes the xenoliths are unique to our world! We call this quartz in common language, or silica as its preferred scientific name....'

'I call it by its true name: Evil!' interjected Numwort.

'.. and we believe that once it penetrates the surface of our earth, it brings about a complex reaction within the subterranean flux, with catastrophic results for those nearby. We call this process silicosis.'

Numwort felt unable to restrain his anger any longer: 'These words are heresy! The Texts state those who ignored the stones, were destroyed by the finger of Tumg! He was so angry and pained by the disobedience of His own people that He scraped this pestilence from His Navel and expelled them for ever!'

The Elder turned aside to his peers and talked in hushed tones before turning back to address Numwort.

'We feel his Eminence was a little over-zealous in bring you before this session. Perhaps he was tired after his long journey. You faith does our order credit, even if a little old fashioned. Come with me, I have things to show you and ideas to discuss. Science increases our sense of wonder and reinforces our faith. Science is not a Demon come to destroy it!'

Numwort could only obey and followed the Elder reluctantly to the holy laboratories.

'How do you see our world?' The Elder asked along the way.

'We live in the eternal Navel of God,' said Numwort. 'It is known fact that if one were to walk for a great distance, one would complete a circumnavigation of the Navel of Tumg and end up in the same place, exactly as one would expect.'

'I see, a rather literal and anthropomorphic view, but the point is taken. Similarly, one could draw a line around the inside of a bowl until it joined with its start, perhaps?'

Numwort agreed. 'How else could one come back to the same place?'

The Elder took a deep breath: 'This may come as a bit of a shock. Sit down, brother monk. There is another way by which we could travel and arrive at our start. That is if we were to journey around the outside of a spherical object, like this ball.' His fingers traced a circle.

Numwort looked at the ball dubiously: 'I see. And this ball, is it somehow suspended inside the Navel of Tumg?'

'No, that is not necessary. You see, when the texts talk of the Navel of God, it is an apocryphal way of explaining to – shall we say – unsophisticated people, that we are at the centre of Tumg's world. He surrounds us as if we were ensconced in His own navel. Try to see this as a spiritual concept, rather than as a literal statement of fact.'

Numwort began to understand the expression on the cardinal's face when he mentioned the eternal Navel. These scientists thought it was quaint he still clung to his pantheism in the face of their science.

'I cannot believe this; but still, Tumg forgive! Let us continue. Where then is this ball Earth of ours?'

'It is in a space, isolated from contact from other bodies.'

'So then, what gives this Earth its warmth, if not the sacred body heat of Tumg?' said Numwort feeling he had scored a point for the fundamentalists.

'We believe there is another ball, but very different from our earth. It is huge in size, and scientist believe it may be composed of burning sodium....'

'What? Burning sodium? Ridiculous! We should all be incinerated in a flash!'

'It is a great distance away. And it would also explain how the navel receives light...'

'The light is the flickering aura of Tumg! Burning sodium would blind us!'

'True; but what then of the water vapour that is present in the air? It would act as a very effective screen against the fierce heat of the flaming earth.'

'But sodium! Just how many earths are there in this, this fantasy space?'

'Well, there must be at least two, but of course there could be more, even a few dozen or so, we are still investigating the possibilities. Incidentally, the flaming earth could be made of any of the light metals. Even hydrogen gas has been suggested!'

Numwort snorted in ridicule. This science; this utter rubbish, was supposed to replace his faith?

'Very well, the periphery of the Navel, the bad lands. We can go no further. We cannot after all, walk on the belly of God. How does that fit the scientists deluded imaginings of a ball Earth?'

'The periphery is not the actual edge of the world in our model; it is what we call the equator. It is closest to the flaming earth and is therefore hotter and unbearably dry. But it is not the physical end of our Earth, it is in fact the half way mark. Perhaps there are beings on the other side of our equator holding exactly the same discussion!'

'There can not be an antipode to a navel, even the Navel of God, this is a ridiculous argument,' spluttered Numwort. 'Is this supposed to convince me to worship science and abandon Tumg?'

'No one has abandoned Tumg! Can't you see the wonder of His plan in all this? Are we not destined to discover the miracles He has performed? Could it really be Tumg's plan for us; is to be forever confined to his navel; crawling microbes, mere parasites feeding on his dead skin? No! We are not linked physically with Tumg, but in a spiritual trinity in which we can grow. Not with grovelling subservience, but through science and understanding.'

'You seek equality with God Himself through your puny science of guesses and fantasies? What of the terrible stones? And what if we should fail to purify the eternal Navel of this evil?'

'The quartz stones are an enigma, Numwort. Let us say we do reside in the actual Navel of Tumg. Where do these stones come from? It hardly makes sense that Tumg would create an element to which he himself is so adverse, and then somehow contrive to push pieces of it into his own navel! Then Tumg creates us in his likeness so we can neutralize it for him. Such a scenario makes no real sense, it is truly beyond belief!'

The Elder sat down and looked at Numwort intently. After a moment of thoughtful silence he resumed. 'In the space I mentioned earlier, we believe there is other matter floating around between the earths. This new compound; the Silica that forms these stones; may be drifting around out there, ready to crash down upon our Earth. It may be they exist in layers in the space and as our earth moves, we collide with them. It would explain why the stones arrive at certain intervals and there are periods when there are none to cause us to toil.' The Elder sighed, 'There is still much to learn.'

'We agree on one thing at least, that these xenoliths, what ever their origin, are evil.'

The Elder did not reply but walked over to a cabinet and unlocked the door. He took from the cabinet the most beautiful object Numwort had ever seen. Numwort was speechless as he gazed upon a symmetrical cube that was perfectly transparent. It was highly polished and when held to the eye, it was as if there was almost nothing there at all.

'A crystal, so pure! More transparent than salt and yet, twice as heavy! What is it?' He asked in wonder.

The Elder took the cube from him. 'Actually, it is neither a true crystal, nor strictly pure. We call it a glass. It is the silica from the stones fused with small amounts of oxides of sodium and calcium. Can something so beautiful be evil? Look at this also.' This time he produced a disc of the same material and handed it to Numwort. Once again, Numwort held it to his eye to marvel at its transparency. He dropped it as if it were hot. 'It distorts things! It destroys their balance, their size!' He was gasping with shock, 'This thing disfigures the images of all creation! It is truly evil!'

'Please, Numwort, be calm! It is but a lens, like our own eyes! Used properly it can make small things look larger and we are able to view them more clearly. I suggest to you these stones may cause a terrible destruction, but handled in the right way by learned scientists, they may bring great benefit to us all. Perhaps Tumg has spread these stones before us, not to test our faith in destroying them, but to use them for a higher purpose.'

'How? To search the skies, looking for a ball of flaming hydrogen? To look at the Earth and declare this is not the Navel of God? To look at ourselves and marvel at how great we have all become?' Numwort felt weary. 'I do not need this glass to see the truth. Our Order has all but ignored Tumg for the new science. The Navel of God is not home enough, so you must seek new worlds. In the worse heresy you say; 'what is evil can be good and what was good are now but myths.' You no longer seek to purify yourselves, or our earth, the Navel of Tumg.'

'You need time to adjust, Numwort, it has taken us years to accept these new wonders. Remember, if we dedicated ourselves to purity, we would never have discovered that impurities in iron make it harder still. Or that glass could be made from the stones. Come, join us in the search for knowledge and Tumg's plan.'

Numwort sat in silence for a while and looked around the opulent laboratories. He could never belong here.

'Holy Elder, forgive me, but I cannot. I need time to think. Dispatch me to the periphery where more stones have been sighted. Let me carve them to the smooth boulders again; this is the work I understand, not this new religion. Do you still believe the sharp stones must not penetrate the earth?'

'We do! And we seek to find out why!'

'The Prophetess has given us the answer. It is the will of Tumg that we serve him and clean the eternal Navel.'

'Go then my son, and find your solitude. You are a faithful man. And there are many stones to render down; what ever the reasons may be.'

The Elder watched sadly as Numwort took his leave. Perhaps if the revered Prophetess had not illustrated her message so obscurely, if the parables had been less abstruse, Numwort could have seen. Would they ever eradicate the ignorance and superstitions of the past?

-

The Peripheral Zone was hot and arid. Only scouts sent to search out the foreign stones ventured into these regions. Scouts and monks; the zone was a haven for outcasts and hermits alike.

Numwort started his task immediately. It was hard work but he needed this duty, this catharsis, to purify his thoughts. He set about the hacking at the stones with vigour, each blow was dedicated to Tumg, for his Earth, and ultimately, for himself. He muttered and shouted out, the words lost in the desert wind. Clear discs of stone! Equators and antipodes! Complex reactions in space, New worlds dangling in space! Orbs of flaming Hydrogen, Ha!'

After several days, the heat, the physical strain and anguish, had driven him into delirium. Numwort began to hallucinate. He had visions of seeing himself chipping at the stone. And then, even more curiously, of seeing himself, watching himself, chipping at the stone. He regarded the unfinished and resistant menhir balefully.

'You are a mote in the Navel of God!' He yelled. The words came back to him in an echo, again and again, countless times. He felt afraid. He picked up the iron hammer and struck at the stone. Sparks from the repeated blows rained around him. He stopped as suddenly as he had begun. The fat sparks fell to the ground and extinguished. A spark; a light, falling through space. Not a flare of burning hydrogen, but of oxidising iron. Close to, each spark seemed impossibly bright, but from a distance, they were only glowing embers.

Numwort threw back his head to look at the sky. That glow, the pulsating light, could it be merely a brief spark on another scale? A vision of seeing himself reflected countless times in a hall of polished iron mirrors surged upon him. He collapsed to the ground in fear. He called out his creed: 'The eternal Navel of Tumg, our earth, and ourselves are indivisible! We are one!' His words echoed and re echoed, across the desert plain and seemingly within himself. They diminished to a faint but persistent whisper. 'We are one. We are one!' He curled up at the base of the stone and slept.

-

When he awoke, the nightmare of heretical science and failing faith was behind him. He was alone on the edge of the plain with the gigantic stone before him. They were old enemies. He removed his robe and his navel cloth, and stood naked before the object. Hardly daring to breathe, Numwort raised the hammer and smashed it against the quartz. Showers of sparks illuminated him and tiny shards of the stone flew from the impact and fell upon him. The fragments were minute and yet at the same time they were monstrous boulders crashing around him. They were smaller still and then unimaginably large. They thundered around and within, reverberating as if whole worlds had trembled. He looked down at his navel. A tiny speck of blood had bloomed where he had been pierced by a sharp fragment of stone. He looked across the plain to see the earth erupting and pushing aside the enormous stones that had plunged down from the sky, piercing the surface. He struck the stone again. As tiny fragments spattered him, his earth reeled as more boulders smashed down on the plain all around him.

An awful awareness dawned on him. As he destroyed the stone on his Earth, some tiny splinters, mere motes of dust would land his navel. To any microscopic being living in his navel, these stones would appear as huge boulders, hurtling down from the sky. Then perhaps some faithful monk would carve that stone and the tiny fragments would land in his navel, and so on, slipping downwards for ever, from one dimension to the next. In the dimension beyond him, the monk in whose navel he lived, had also struck a stone, and been pelted by boulders from the dimension beyond him!

The scientists had been partially right. A universe existed beyond the periphery of the Navel. This was no expansion reaching ever outward into space, but an endless succession of interconnected dimensions. At last, he came to understand his vision. There was a reflection of his being in every dimension. He was like a doll who could be broken to reveal another doll inside, and another inside that and another. He was Numwort, he was Tumg, he was the earth, the earth was his Navel, and he lived within it. All of him was the centre, the locus point of the universe. Only the stone was foreign. The more it was destroyed in one dimension, the more it could destroy him in the next. If the stones were not rounded in the smaller dimension, they would work their way beneath the skin and poison his system. He would die and could not prevent the stones on his world from piercing the navel of himself in the dimension above. He would die again and again in each dimension.

The Numworts, in an infinite range of dimensions and time, sat down on the edge of their respective navels. The cosmos of Numwort/Tumg teetered on the edge of irreversible chaos. The concentric dimensions of Navels would become an endless dead void. There could be no light from the sparking of iron and silica, the Navel plains would fall dark and barren. No stone shards would fall through the space between one world to the next. The energy of the system would completely dissipate through all the dimensions. Only the cold, sterile mass would remain. The increase in entropy would result in an eternal stagnation.

The pandemonium the falling stones must surely be causing through the cities did not concern the Numwort-Tumg. The scientists had believed that knowledge; their science, could spare them the fate of every conceivable universe. It could not.

It was a time for decision, a time for his judgement. Somewhere the echo: 'We are one' persisted as a creed, as an instruction. The Numwort/Tumg knew that all worlds, all dimensions must be reduced to unity. The mass must be converted back to a vital energy.

Numwort/Tumg regarded their navels in a billion billion dimensions. He had accidentally scratched his navel once before and nearly caused a catastrophe. Now he did so deliberately. He picked up a shard of stone, and inserted it in his navel. The skies darkened as the fingers of Tumg descended and probed into the dimension below. The sharp stone cut into the centre of each navel and then withdrew.

The Tumgs paused, each on the edge of their respective abyss. They saw, and faith was theirs. The Tumg in the highest dimension was involuted in the navel of Tumg in the lowest dimension. The concentric dimensions were infinite, and yet with boundary. All was one.

With a sardonic cry, they leapt into their respective voids. There was a roaring of wind. The plains began to buckle and tear. The fabric of the Tumg cosmos poured into the gashes, one dimension collapsing in upon another at an ever-increasing rate. The force was irresistible as the void fed upon itself. Even the spreading shards of light from the last sparks were snared and dragged into the black maw. The matter swirled around the abyss at an increasing rate, the friction of the colliding particles generating incredible temperatures and radiation before finally being consumed.

Every last particle, every last photon was re united with the One. Infinitely dense and dark, size zero, mass at unity. We are one. Time stopped. At the node between universes, all entity, an entire universe was compressed into an infinitesimal speck. A grain. A solitary mote. Forever. The laws of science ceased.

As the Numwort/Tumg had known, Faith alone persisted. It was the sum of the cryptic dimensions. Highly curved, minuscule and obscure, they had been dominated by Space and Time in the natural universe. Subordinated for countless aeons, they had survived all for this, the recreation. Liberated, they unfurled and intertwined in pure pattern. Faith, the tool of God, was now the ultimate determinate. Its essence was a template for the new universe in the first nanosecond of its birth, before the laws and major dimensions were re-established.

Faith, whole and pure, is literal. Faith can admit no doubt, it can conceive of no irony. The template of Faith formed along the last thoughts of Numwort-Tumg;

'Orbs of flaming hydrogen! Ha!'

Acknowledgements

I would like to offer my sincere appreciation to those that have helped, contributed, and supported me along the way in writing the stories in this book and in my other writing efforts over the years. There is a certain madness of the imagination involved in writing weird tales and I thank those close to me for putting up with my odd ideas, non sequiturs and my avoiding household chores by sneaking of to the study to write. Some have gone beyond the call of duty by typing manuscripts, proof reading, drawing illustrations, setting up a Facebook page, guiding me through the Kindle electronic publishing system, making suggestions and of course, making tea. To my family and friends: Nicolene, Julie, Sarah, Adele, Jerome, Frank, Alar, and Malcolm, my grateful thanks.

Like many authors, I started by submitting short stories to magazines, newspapers and entering competitions. I was encouraged by positive comments from editors and competition judges and their willingness to publish some of my stories. Looking back to those days, I acknowledge the folk who gave me a break and the confidence (whether they knew it or not at the time) to develop my writing. These are; Christopher Backeberg, former editor of Scope magazine, Niel van Niekerk and Derek Hols editors of PROBE SFSA magazine, and Jennifer Crwys-Williams, founding editor of the Sunday Star Magazine. Also a special mention to the team at Penguin Books and Southern Sun Hotels who sponsored the national awards for South African Short Fiction that really started the ball rolling.

Thank you one and all.

Jon Ardeman

NOTES

Four of the tales in this collection have been published or received awards in short story competitions under the author's own name. The remainder are published for the first time in this: 'Tales from the Supernatural Rockery' collection.

Restless Mbuzo: *Winner of the 1988 South African Short Fiction Award, sponsored by Penguin Books and Southern Sun Hotels*

Past Tense: *Published in Scope Magazine*

Tenant Trouble: *Prize winner, Nova Short Story competition, published by SFSA* PROBE magazine No. 84 (1991)*

The Mote in God's Navel: *Editor's choice, Nova Short Story Competition, Published SFSA* PROBE Magazine No. 91 (1993)*

* Now SFFSA, Science Fiction & Fantasy South Africa

"CROSS CUT" by Jon T Ardeman.

The discovery of another woman's mutilated body strikes fear in to Lashford's community. The serial killer boasts of further victims, piling the pressure on Detective Superintendent Hislop and his team. Yet, it is not only the police who are desperate to end the maniac's reign of terror. Convinced that the murder is the embodiment of an ancient evil; a small group of locals turn to the "old ways" to put an end to the horror. Their occult efforts cannot come quickly enough for loner Simeon Gray, who is convinced he knows the identity of the killer's next victim. Haunted by the fears and guilt from his past, his nightmares are only just beginning.

A gripping read! 5 stars
A real page-turner! I've read many crime thrillers and police procedurals, but this ranks with the best. The book focuses on a horrific sadistic serial killer, seen from three perspectives - the police, an "Everyman" blessed/cursed with clairvoyance and the local coven. The plot is plausible, the characters are believable and the pace is gripping even though it's a longish read. The final twist at the end is fantastic, and a real bonus on top of a great story.

Crime, thriller, supernatural. What more could you want?
Wow - Loved reading the view of each of the different groups involved in the investigations throughout the story. Especially loved Simeon and Lauren's characters (no spoilers!). The mix of detective crime novel, thriller novel and supernatural novel is perfect mix for the start of this trilogy of books. I was kept guessing on the ending all the way through the book with some fantastic surprises which kept me up reading to the end of the story at 2am!

An innovative crime story 5 Stars
Cross Cut is crime story which follows three groups as they try to bring an end to a serial killer's rampage. The police rely on traditional detective work, a criminal psychologist, and forensic techniques; a local coven uses astrology to predict the killer's next move, and finally, Simeon Gray, tormented by his premonitions, is compelled to join in the hunt. I enjoyed the cultural and paranormal clues as the individuals puzzled over the evidence to find the 'Lashford Slasher'. Parts of the book were a bit creepy, but the ending was ingenious and an interesting conclusion!

"MINER INDISCRETIONS"

A humorous novel by Jon Ardeman; also available from Amazon Kindle or in paperback

A hilarious, action-packed story following Timothy, who sets out to explore for gold on the remote and dilapidated 'Yellow Snake Mine' in rural KwaZulu-Natal. All is not as it seems and faced with closure of the rundown gold mine, he joins with the eccentric locals in a series of desperate scams and highly illegal schemes to try to reprieve the old mine.

Timothy struggles through encounters with the African wildlife, consultants, riots, ghosts, floods, government officials, explosions and a very frustrating sex life in an attempt to find some actual gold in time to save the unique, tight-knit community.

Excepts from reviews posted on Amazon from readers around the world:

B. Simmons, Canada: *****   I thoroughly recommend this book,
As a retired mining/exploration geologist, I thoroughly recommend this book. Hell, I recommend to anyone, a mining guy/girl or not! I read this book on a plane and people thought I was weird for laughing out loud continuously and having tears running down my cheeks. I couldn't help it. I've been in many of the same incidents described in the book. Enjoy!

Alan Day, Australia: *****   A romping good read through the African bush
Set amongst the South African mining industry, it details an outsider's view ... of his new and very unusual working environment. It perfectly captures the idiosyncrasy's of the larger than life characters Timothy encounters on the mines. The pace is fast as Timothy lurches from one crisis to another in his quest for a new gold strike, but I also laughed hard and often.

JB, United Kingdom: ***** Marvellous!

I'm no book critic and actually rarely read. But after starting to read this I simply couldn't stop, on the tube; during coffee breaks and lunches and well into the night. Several bursts of laughter in the tube had raised many an eyebrow at me. One particular chapter had me laughing in such a fit; I had to stop reading. The content is well written, with lots of mining and typically South African innuendos. Certain particular comments made me reminisce of my own time in the bush.

C J Van Treeck, United States: **** A quick fun read!

An entertaining read filled with tongue in cheek character names. The main "crew" and its comedy of errors filled adventure exude the appropriate levels of self depreciation and raucous egotisticalism to give the feel of a small remote community. Love the Baboon!

TSB, South Africa: **** Surprisingly Good Read

The characters are colourful and original and in many cases downright hilarious. The humour is fantastic and varies from oh-so subtle to sometimes in your face, I actually found myself laughing out loud at times. The story flows well and just as it starts flirting with becoming ordinary, it takes an interesting, unexpected or even super-natural twist. I would definitely recommend this book

Jenny ***** Five Stars,

Hilarious!

Dom Smith, United Kingdom ***** Miner Indiscretions - a major laugh!

Miner Indiscretions ... made me laugh out loud on numerous occasions. Our hero is led on a hilarious and often painfully embarrassing quest for the illusive metal by Lazyboy Malinga, a local Zulu miscreant (deceased) and is alternately scuppered and aided by the misfit mine collective. The baboon's laconic appearances and gold smelting episode are without a doubt the funniest I have read in years.

A Mulligan, Australia: ***** Great read "Jon Earthman",
Great read "Jon Earthman". Well written expose on social distinction in the resources industry of the late 20th century. Funny as well.

S.Dawson ***** Quirky gold mine characters
I really enjoyed this book. The gold mine characters were quirky and their chaotic attempts to keep the mine going despite every thing; it reminds me of the humour of a Tom Sharpe novel. I have been to a game reserve in South Africa and the part when the (accidentally drugged) hero gets lost in the African bush is hilarious, yet somehow believable.

Wilf, United Kingdom ***** Not just for geologists - will have wide appeal
The story bowls along at a fair old pace, and many of the 'characters' encountered must have drawn on real life experience. The more racy scenes are well written and important to the narrative and the whole book is basically a lot of fun. I read this book on the train and nearly missed my stop more than once during the week.

Bill J, Australia **** Bears a more humorous resemblance to reality than many would care to admit.
A well-constructed plot that pulls together an intricate web of circumstances that individually are familiar to all who have worked in the mining industry or Africa, but in combination make a very amusing read.

Ben R **** Very entertaining and funny adventure of mining in Southern Africa,
If you have any experience of South African backwaters, mining or geology you'll enjoy Jon Ardeman's book, Miner Indiscretions - even better if you've experienced all three. It mixes observations of the various South African tribes and how they get along together, with a technical insight into gold mining, a bit of adventure, wildlife

and a hint of the supernatural. This is all accompanied by a good few laughs and plenty of raunchy humour along the way.